Asaf Ashery

SIMANTOV

TRANSLATED BY
MARGANIT WEINBERGER-ROTMAN

ANGRY
ROBOT

ANGRY ROBOT
An imprint of Watkins Media Ltd

Unit 11, Shepperton House
89 Shepperton Road
London N1 3DF
UK

angryrobotbooks.com
twitter.com/angryrobotbooks
Where angels fear to tread...

An Angry Robot paperback original, 2020

Cover by Francesca Corsini
Edited by Christopher Slaney and Rose Green
Set in Meridien

ISBN 978 0 85766 838 7
Ebook ISBN 978 0 85766 850 9

Printed and bound in the United Kingdom by TJ International.

9 8 7 6 5 4 3 2 1

To Yael, my everything, I will always love you.
To Mazzy, my beloved & loyal friend, I will always miss you.

THE FIRST DAY
OF THE COUNTING OF THE OMER*

"And it came to pass, when men began to multiply on the face of the earth, and daughters were born unto them, that the sons of God saw the daughters of men that they were fair; and they took them wives of all which they chose. And the Lord said, My Spirit shall not always strive with man, for that he also is flesh: yet his days shall be a hundred and twenty years. There were Nephilim in the earth in those days; and also after that, when the sons of God came in unto the daughters of men, and they bore children to them, the same became mighty men which were of old, men of renown."

(GENESIS 6:1-4)

According to the Torah (Lev. 23:15), Jews are obligated to count the days from Passover to Pentecost. This counting is a reminder of the link between the Exodus and harvest season.

PROLOGUE

It was the seventh raven to swoop down since his shift began.

Several were perched on the high fence or hopping on the grass in odd bounding motions between warming themselves in the outward-bound beams of the searchlights.

Jacob would have been OK with this if relieving Yaniv five minutes earlier hadn't meant stepping into the shift from hell.

Never mind that he was assigned to serve with Borislav Sverenko, the most intimidating security guard on the detail; but to be the only religious guard in the unit on the first night of Passover seemed to him more than bad luck or lack of consideration.

He had an uneasy feeling about it.

Noises validated his premonition: the Rottweilers, usually quiet as they patrolled the space between the two fences, were barking loudly; the ravens kept returning in large black flocks and couldn't stop cawing. He was beyond thinking it was all just a coincidence.

It was also the time of year – Passover and the Counting of the Omer.

His father, Shlomo Rosenkrantz, was found on the floor

by the entrance to the synagogue, on the eve of the "Great Sabbath," the Sabbath immediately before Passover. His chest was wide open and charred. His heart missing. The pathologist said it was the first time he had ever seen spontaneous combustion, and that the heart must have exploded from all the pressure.

Jacob's terror was threefold. First was a feeling, an instinct. It was in the air, you could almost smell it. You know it's there, but you don't know where it's coming from. No specific details. Nothing to latch onto, and then deny, to calm yourself down.

The second thing was the ridiculous security surrounding the house. He wondered from whom the owner was protecting himself. To reach the mansion at the top of the driveway, you had to pass an exterior fence, two Humvees patrolling it, a strip dotted with incendiary flare mines, an electrified barbed wire fence, jumpy guard dogs, and watchtowers manned by people with above average sniper skills.

The lord of the manor did not like visitors.

Jacob and Borislav sat a few yards from the gate, at the end of the access road to the manor, in a booth of bulletproof glass dubbed "The Aquarium." In front of them was a vehicle barrier.

The third thing was that Jacob suspected Borislav was anxious.

Standing nearly seven feet tall, Borislav weighed 220 proportionately distributed pounds. Jacob estimated that the thickest part of his thigh was thinner than Borislav's neck.

The Russian giant always looked like a bull in the ring: restrained, a bit apathetic, but liable to charge at any moment. Borislav was from the Ukraine, but everyone called him "The Russian". He had seen action as a commando in Afghanistan and Chechnya. Two weeks earlier, on a shift, Borislav told Jacob in a rare moment of candor that once, in Afghanistan, he had lain for several days in the snow, at the foot of a mountain, his cheek pressed into his rifle butt, until he found the perfect moment to fire at someone's head. It was the only time he had killed a man without looking him in the eye.

Tonight, for the first time since Jacob had met the giant, Borislav appeared worried, possibly even frightened.

When scary things get scared, it's never a good sign.

Jacob assumed that tonight, too, the conversation would be wanting, so he had brought along a book. Taking it out of his backpack, he let his wandering eyes rest for two seconds on the face of his Aquarium buddy.

Apparently, Borislav was not picked for the job for his physical frame alone but also for his facility with language. Nobody could better imply the subtext, "Any particular reason you're gawking at me like this?" by asking the question, "What's that book about?"

"It's by S. Yizhar. About his experience in the Yom Kippur War."

"Isn't that a Jewish holiday?"

"Yes, but there was also a war in 1973."

As often, when talking to new immigrants, he found himself simplifying phrases, as if talking to a child, not sure if he was doing his interlocutor a favor by dumbing things down.

"How many died in it?"

"Twenty-five hundred, maybe more."

His companion's nostrils flared disdainfully, but he kept quiet. Jacob felt a little resentful that the national trauma did not even register with Borislav.

"What?"

"It's no big deal, really."

"What are you talking about?"

"Look, you think on a small scale. You're spoiled. In Russia, in Stalingrad, how many died? A hundred thousand people. It didn't stop Russia from electing Khrushchev."

"What's Khrushchev got to do with it?"

"He was, what d'you call it, political commissar there."

Jacob resorted to pathos to explain the impact of the '73 war.

"We're a small country, not many people. We thought it was the destruction of the Third Temple…"

"I'm going to see why the dogs are barking." Borislav cut him short.

He extricated himself from the glass booth, bending his big frame to pass under the barrier.

His powerful Maglite shone a white beam into the night, exposing the flock of ravens crowding the fences and the lawn. As Borislav made his way to the exterior fence, the birds took to the air, but, after a short whirl, returned to the same spot.

Jacob had read five pages of his book when the cabin door opened and the Ukrainian giant was back inside, a worried expression on his face. From somewhere else on the perimeter, searchlights were probing the sky.

Jacob thought he heard horses neighing and hooves galloping, but he was embarrassed to ask Borislav if he had too. In between the beams crisscrossing the starlit sky, a bright, gleaming rectangle suddenly appeared, descending to earth.

"Want to make a wish?" Jacob joked nervously.

"A million year-old star falls, and all you can think of is what's in it for you."

The rectangle slowed its descent and touched down lightly, then scooted toward the fences. Tiny dark crescents dropped from the sky, pounding on the roof and sides of the cabin. A horrible stench filled the air. Hundreds of ravens rose at once, flapping their wings noisily.

They rushed to get their weapons. Borislav clicked off the safety; Jacob did the same and followed him outside.

The ground was covered with crushed carob, which seemed to be the source of the terrible stench.

The fiery rectangle continued its progress on the ground, coming to a halt a few yards from the exterior fence. In the distance, Jacob could see a chariot of fire led by four horses.

The chariot was burning but was not consumed. Sparks flew, the sound of crackling wood came from its spokes, but they did not crumble.

Its chassis was enveloped in smoke, streams of electric energy and blazing, bluish light. The horses looked like nothing on earth. Red flashes lit up their eyes; they whinnied and stomped, crushing embers that dropped from their hooves. A dark human figure with long hair stepped down from the chariot, patted the first horse pleasantly and made his way to the fence using a long wooden staff.

Jacob was conflicted: he wanted to flee; adrenaline

flooded his veins, but apparently his blood, which was supposed to set his muscles into motion, had turned viscous. He froze in his tracks and watched in horror the scene unfolding before his eyes.

Weapons rattled all around them, but the figure just kept plodding ahead.

A shot rang out, and the figure raised his walking stick.

The two Humvees were thrown in the air by a huge explosion, landing on their sides in flames. One of the drivers, set alight, crawled out of the wreckage and tried to roll in the dust. His screams were drowned out by the noise of shattered glass as the watchtowers collapsed, the guards tossed out like popcorn from a lidless pan. Having slipped their leashes and fled yelping into the night, the dogs triggered the mines and incendiary flares shot into the air with such intensity that Jacob and Borislav had to squeeze their eyes shut. Silence descended on the compound.

The figure in the black robe, with flowing hair and holding a gnarled, wooden staff cut from an almond tree was climbing the slope toward them.

As it grew closer, they could make out, by the light of the flares, the tangled hair and unshaven face of an old man. His robe was in tatters and had seen better days. A ram's horn and a slaughterer's blade were stuck in the broad sash around his waist.

His eyes gleamed and he hummed a marching song in a deep and sonorous tone.

For a split second, through the horror that gripped him, Jacob thought he recognized the tune.

Borislav was the first to recover. He screamed a loud,

guttural battle cry and opened fire. The old man, however, did not even flinch. He closed the distance, and with a dexterous motion whipped out his slaughterer's knife slicing Borislav in two at the waist. The Ukrainian looked surprised but didn't utter a sound as his two halves crumpled to the ground. Only a few yards separated the mysterious figure from the main gate. A few yards and Jacob.

Time stood still. He heard the carobs squishing under the soles of the old man's leather sandals. A smile appeared on the man's face, the kind reserved for long-awaited encounters.

Jacob feared his heart would explode; his hands trembled, and he dropped his weapon.

The traffic barrier rose, its hinges groaning in protest. The old man advanced toward Jacob, whose pants now bore a big, dark stain, as a puddle of urine gathered at his feet. His face was ashen, and he started as the old man stopped in front of him and rummaged through a pocket in his cloak. The man's face lit up when, after a few eternal seconds, he found what he was looking for: a small parcel wrapped in a gray rag. He held the cloth by its edges and motioned to Jacob to stretch out his hands. Jacob obeyed, and the old man placed the clammy bundle in them like an offering.

Animatedly, his thick crow-like voice began to recite a verse.

"Behold, I will send you Elijah the prophet before the coming of the great and dreadful day of the Lord. And he shall turn the heart of the fathers to the children, and the heart of the children to their fathers, lest I come and smite the earth with utter destruction."

Jacob opened the package, which, to his utter astonishment, contained a bleeding, beating human heart.

A second before Elijah's hand had ripped open his ribcage to tear out his heart, Jacob recognized the melody that heralded his death.

The lord of the manor, sitting in his parlor in the big house, looked out of the window and smiled disdainfully at the spectacle of blazing flames, explosions, and screams, like a child curiously watching ants fight a flood threatening to destroy their nest.

Throughout the long years he spent on earth, Shamhazai knew that one day the silence would be broken. Elijah now reached the top of the hill and knocked on the door with his almond-tree staff.

CHAPTER ONE

When Shamhazai saw God's servant climbing up the hill, the dark prophet looked, indeed, like the shadow of a doubt.

Shamhazai was reminded of his celestial love.

Love between God and His servants. Servants who were always ready to be called by name. But the love of Shamhazai and his brothers was not enough for God. He always wanted more. More lovers, more love.

Then God created man in His image. Male and female he created them. Adam and Lilith. The first woman and her man.

She even dared to call him by name from time to time. Shamhazai did not take offense, not really.

At first, Shamhazai did not pay her any mind. An archangel, a servant of the Almighty, can dispense with poor imitation. Until one day she pronounced his name in a new way. Sham-Ha-zai. Lips pursed, jaw trembling, teeth sibilating. A mating call. Instead of extolling and praising God, he found himself composing poems to her.

She was dark and comely, her eyelashes fluttered like turtledoves, her perky breasts like two erect towers.

Lilith, fairest among women.

Until one night she fled the garden.

Another woman was created, this time tailor-made to fit Adam, crafted from his own rib. Shamhazai continued to write to the goddess, to the woman who refused to be the mother of all the living, the one who fled from heaven, beyond the gate.

The others started referring to him derisively as *Naphil* – the fallen one – he who fell under the spell of Lilith. He bore the nickname with pride. His day of victory was not long in coming. The other woman was expelled from the Garden of Eden.

Opening the gate, he descended, together with all the other secret lovers of Lilith, all those whose Eden-like slumbers had been disturbed by persistent nocturnal visions. They numbered two hundred.

Lilith welcomed them with open arms, and a covenant was struck between them, a contract that fused flesh with flesh, a pact of fugitives from Heaven. Enraged at his wayward servants who had conspired against him, God tried to annihilate Lilith and her daughters by bringing a flood upon His creation to destroy all flesh, all spirit from the face of the earth, but Lilith and her daughters survived; Shamhazai and the other Nephilim carried them over the water on their wings.

The Nephilim told Lilith their names, thus enabling her to rule over them, to deprive them of their God-given eternal life.

They crowned her queen, supreme goddess.

A divine voice decreed their banishment; the Gates of Heaven were forever closed to them. But Shamhazai and the other Nephilim did not care. They were still in possession of their old-new love, Lilith.

Years passed, hundreds and thousands. Shamhazai and the order of the Nephilim were still on earth, but Lilith disappeared, leaving behind her daughters. Generations come and go; the blood is diluted. Future generations failed to resemble Lilith the goddess.

Once more, Shamhazai found himself serving a substitute.

And as in the days of yore, a fervor gradually awoke in him, until he was consumed by the knowledge that those women who knew his name were not worthy of pronouncing even one of its letters.

Shamhazai looked at the brothers standing around him. In them, he saw his reflection.

All the figures peering through the windows were identical, so perfectly replicated that even Mother Earth herself would not be able to tell them apart. Their faces were like Noh masks of supreme beauty, glowing in majestic splendor.

They all had blond hair, pale, barely discernible eyebrows, blue eyes, cheekbones that plastic surgeons might post in their "after" photos, and thin, pink lips – the chiseled faces of Michelangelo's angels, without a hint of the childlike plumpness of Raphael's cherubs. Shamhazai made his way to the long table, warming a glass of Armagnac in his perfect hand; brandy that was poured into oak barrels when the First World War was still called the The Great War.

Armaros was next in line to leave his post by the window.

Removing a silver pocket-guillotine from his suit, he snipped the tip off a Cuban cigar.

"Why does he have to make such a grand entrance?"

Azazel's voice reverberated around the room. "Shall we go out to greet him, Shamhazai?"

"No, he comes to talk."

"How do you know?" asked Barakiel, who had been made uneasy by the scene at the foot of the hill.

"He left his fiery chariot outside. He doesn't want to ruin the lawn, as he did last time."

They made their way to the lobby, where they formed a semicircle, and trained their eyes on the entrance. Soon a cane was heard tapping at the door. Evidently, Elijah had not lost his manners.

"I'll talk to him," said Shamhazai.

The Nephilim turned to the door. Another knock was heard, and he ordered the others to respond in a loud voice:

"Pour out thy wrath upon the heathens that have not known thee and upon the kingdoms that have not called upon thy name," they recited monotonously. At once the door opened, revealing Elijah.

"Do me a favor, Eli, wipe your feet before you enter," Shamhazai said.

Elijah scanned the assembled group, a raggedy old man in the presence of gorgeous glorious youth.

"To what do we owe this honor?" asked Shamhazai when they had all repaired to the parlor.

"He has a message for you."

Whenever Elijah mentioned Him, silence would descend on the room.

"What is it?"

"Angels don't belong on this earth. It's time to restore the order of creation."

Shamhazai picked up his Armagnac and swirled the drink around the glass.

"That might have been a possibile, had she not given her daughters the key to the chain that shackles us."

"And no man saw it, nor knew it, nor awakened, for they were all asleep. And the vision of all is to become unto you as the words of a book that is sealed, which men deliver to one that is learned saying, read this, I pray thee: and he saith, I cannot; for it is sealed."

"Elijah, what is the message you were sent to deliver?"

"The Power of the Names was taken from them seventy years ago."

Shock waves shot through the room. Azazel was the first to recover.

"And nobody bothered to tell us?" he bellowed.

"The secret of the Lord is with them that fear Him, and He will show them His covenant. We'll take sweet counsel together."

They looked at each other, stirred by thoughts of freedom.

"There are five words I learned to dread in all this time we've been here," Shamhazai said, looking warily at the Lord's servant.

"What are they?" asked Elijah.

"I am the Lord's emissary."

"I have five new ones for you."

"What are they?"

"Turn back, O backsliding sons."

CHAPTER TWO

This night was different from any other night; it was "night that is neither day nor night," a night of deep silence and earsplitting noise.

Across the table sat mother and daughter, with candles burning in their holders – patches of flickering light, kindled and extinguished in a complete cycle of life. The guests sometimes eat and sometimes are eaten, in some ancient ritual of creation and destruction, as they sit around the round wooden table at Rachel's Seder.

Rachel had few weaknesses, and at the moment she was busy hoisting one of them above her head, catching her midair as she emitted her resounding laughter that was part hysteria, part pure pleasure.

Noga, the only daughter of Mazzy and Gaby, was two-and-a-half years-old, a scion in a long line of Simantov girls.

Mazzy felt an irritating twitch of jealousy. She looked across the table at her little daughter, now affectionately perched on her grandmother's knee, and tried to remember the last time Rachel had shown her such affection. Rachel was not in the habit of hugging people for no reason; there was always an ulterior motive to her displays of affection.

She passed the torch to Noga, whispering instructions as sweet as honey in her ear. Judging by the girl's wide eyes, it was clear that Rachel's storytelling skills had not dulled over the years.

On the other hand, the fact that Noga was not speaking yet had led Mazzy to always focus on her eyes. Entire conversations between mother and daughter were conducted by exchanging looks.

It was not easy to watch Noga spellbound, soaking in the thick honeyed words, because Mazzy already knew the story being narrated; she had heard it hundreds of times.

"When the world was first created, there were no names because there was no need for names. There were no things that needed names, and there was no one to give them names. There was only earth and sky. Human beings had not been created yet, and the only names were those of angels. Their names glowed above their heads. Then God created man in His image, male and female. Adam and Lilith, the first woman and her man. They saw the angels' names and realized that objects needed names to tell them apart. Then Adam tried to give her a name, to call her by a name he had chosen.

"Lilith decided to change things, to take matters into her own hands, to find a kingdom of her own. She came down to earth, east of Eden, to Kedem.

"Adam, who was afraid of change, stayed behind, and God decided that it was not good for him to be alone, so he created helpmates to keep him company. He made the beasts of the field and the birds in the sky, and Adam gave names to each living thing. When he was done giving names and being the boss, he was ready to receive a new woman…"

That was enough. Mazzy resolved that this night would be different, that she would change it. Mothers don't like people interfering with how they bring up their kids. Mazzy was grudgingly tolerant toward Gaby's mother when she sang to Noga in Yiddish. She figured this was her mother-in-law's way of coping with her successful son's marriage to the daughter of a Sephardi witch. Perhaps a little *Yiddishkeit* would counteract the bad luck, and her granddaughter would finally start talking.

But there is a fundamental difference between a sentimental song about a lonely tree at the roadside and indoctrinating a two-and-a-half year-old with the battle of the sexes.

This night will be different. Tonight she will restrain herself and not let herself be sucked into Rachel's mind games. As a child, her questions had always received the same answer.

Why? Because! You are a Simantov.

At her mother's insistence, Mazzy addressed her as Rachel, not Mom, a practice that elicited whispers on the rare occasions Rachel came to parent-teacher conferences. Only once did Mazzy ask her mother to explain why their family unit was so small; she wanted people to understand where she came from. Rachel told her she had been born out of wedlock to an illegitimate mother.

Even though this was her childhood home, Mazzy felt like a guest in it. This was the home of the Great Mother; it was her domain, and when Mazzy tried to summon up memories of her childhood bedroom, she failed.

Several days after Mazzy had moved into a new apartment with roommates, she came back to collect a few items, and was shocked to find them packed in plastic bags, ready to go. Renovations were already underway to restore the house to its previous state. Every sign of life from the previous twenty years had been erased. Rachel's kingdom returned to its natural dimensions, stretching east, west, south, and north. Mazzy had been swept out like dust.

Now that Noga had been transferred from Rachel's lap to her mother's, Mazzy could feel her mother's gaze on her from across the candlelit table. She tried to ignore it.

When some women enter a room, all eyes turn on them; when Rachel enters a room, people feel like they are being watched.

Her green eyes, two smoldering embers that had seen too much, peered through a frame of black tresses and caught Mazzy's cheerful face framed by a garland of brown curls. When a wind blew through them, you could hear peals of laughter rolling in the distance.

If such a thing were possible, Rachel's look at once conveyed expectation, disappointment, satisfaction and resentment.

Many people feared Rachel; some hated her. That was OK with her; like all truly powerful rulers, she preferred being feared to loved.

Rachel was endowed with a rare gift for interpreting coffee grounds, and this was just one of her talents of divination. All noted soothsayers and clairvoyants had consulted her at least once. Rachel was the sun around which all heathens and idolaters revolved.

After coffee cups were emptied into saucers, Rachel would examine the dregs. At that moment all people became equal, regardless of whatever special gifts they might possess. Rachel would stare at the sediments that foretold the future and everyone held their breath. She revealed the future to the clueless, leading them by the hand, one overturned cup after another, to the point where they dared not look ahead.

Rachel did not read the future to simple folk; she read to readers.

All the guests at Rachel's Seder table were readers and seers. Mazzy realized she and Gaby had been invited only as Noga's chaperones.

"Let her taste something," Rachel said.

There was nothing inherently offensive in this, but Mazzy sensed some slight in the words which sent spasms of anger through her veins. It was an instinctive, conditioned response.

She took a deep breath, and once more resolved not to pick a fight with her mother, nor to dwell on the past. Tonight she would change; tonight she would lead herself out of slavery and into freedom. She wouldn't give Rachel an excuse to make a big row; she'd ignore the comments that were bound to drive her crazy, and exercise restraint. And if she succeeded tonight, for the next five minutes, just for now – *Dayenu*, it would be enough!

She dipped a spoon into the honey, and secretly thanked Noga for pushing it away. Surrounded by so many strangers and an abundance of colorful distractions, Noga could hardly be bothered with food. Her beautiful eyes eagerly drank in the scene.

Rachel's Seder table was conspicuously not kosher for Passover. It was all unabashedly laid out: bourekas, Laffa bread, Yemenite pitas, all flanking the *Haggadas* and causing Gaby to assume an expression that said, "This would never happen in my mother's house." Like most strictly secular people, he was extremely serious about the few commandments that he did observe.

"Why does she insist on serving non-kosher food? You call this Passover?" Gaby grumbled.

"This is how it's done by the aristocracy. If there's no bread, let them eat cake," his wife responded.

Though he had been Mazzy's partner for several years, Gaby made it a point to take no interest in the family business or the running of Rachel's court. The couple had a tacit agreement, a deal aimed at avoiding fights over mysticism.

There were clashes over ancient and modern beliefs, deep rifts and contradictions reflecting the differences between a Sephardi policewoman and a Western surgeon, between a progressive woman and a conservative man.

Gaby was skeptical when it came to un-provable phenomena. Mazzy explained that it was a matter of cumulative experience, that proof could not be found in the places he was looking. For his part, Gaby invoked the theory of probability, cited statistics and mentioned self-fulfilling prophecies. Loudly, they engaged in a dialogue of the deaf.

Eventually, Mazzy decided to spare him the details, and Gaby refrained from asking questions. As a new dad as well as a surgeon in training, he had little time for sleep, and the few spare hours he did have he preferred to spend unconscious, rather than worrying about the kind of home his wife had grown up in.

For Mazzy, this was an easy task. She kept Rachel out of her life as much as she could.

Rachel noticed Gaby's distress. From her seat at the head of the table she managed to solve the problem, but immediately planted the seed of another one.

"Don't worry, we have matzo, too," she told him, then switched to Gaelic with a short guttural phrase.

Ashling, a blind Irishwoman who, despite her age, retained the translucent skin of a gecko, rose from her seat. Gaby felt uncomfortable that she of all people had been entrusted with bringing the matzo, which he hadn't wanted in the first place, but Ashling gracefully made her way to the kitchen without a cane.

Mazzy knew what talents had earned Ashling her seat at the table. She was a seer with quite a few tricks from her Druid ancestors under her belt. Not many women were in possession of such lore, and Ashling must have been gifted from an early age in mind reading and fortune telling.

There was no room in Rachel's entourage for new-age gurus in need of recognition and adulation. It was all about work, not idolatry. They had been there from time immemorial, spinning spells, conjuring and auguring, long before those skills were discovered by the seekers of self-realization.

Next to Mazzy sat Nikko, an old Macedonian, sporting a purple French beret. Nikko had always been old, and had always worn a purple beret since the first time Mazzy saw him as a child.

Nikko practiced gut feeling, literally: he could tell your future by rubbing your tummy. When Mazzy was eight years old, she cried bitterly when the stranger tried to examine her. Fourteen years later, she allowed Nikko to prod her pregnant belly, despite Gaby's protests; his fierce objection was no match for Mazzy's superstition.

At that time she had a feeling that something was wrong with the baby she was carrying. All the medical experts summoned by Gaby and his mother could not allay her fears. She knew as only a mother knows. For the sake of her baby girl, she was willing to listen to Rachel and her cabal, to mumbo-jumbo and then to Nikko. The Macedonian explained that pregnant women are difficult customers, especially when carrying a female, because two stomachs are involved, making the findings inconclusive. Still, he was intimidated by the Simantov women and agreed to examine her.

Nikko put on latex gloves and, with rhythmic, circular motions, applied olive oil to her belly. Then he took off the gloves and laid his fingers on her protruding bellybutton. At this contact with her skin, he recoiled, flapped his hands as if scorched, and tried to shake off static electricity. Mazzy demanded an answer, and Nikko took a long time before pronouncing that she and the baby would be fine; it was the others who should worry. One of those others was Gaby, her significant other.

A moment before the hiding of the Afikoman, all the dishes were brought out at once and in no special order. The plates were passed from one side of the table to the other, pounds of grub to be sampled, savored; each guest had brought an offering to Rachel. Trout from Lake Ohrid, compliments of Macedonian Nikko, stood next to an Irish beef stew that had simmered the whole night. Herring and eel salad – a traditional Estonian dish – was courtesy of Kaya, who was now consuming most of it. Everyone seemed to enjoy Aelina's dishes – fava beans and hummus served in deep bowls next to flakey baklava and sugary kanafeh arranged neatly on shiny copper platters. The plump Egyptian with the swollen ankles stared indignantly at the East European food while chomping on greasy, blood-dripping kebob.

Blood and droppings were part of her trade. Aelina also worked with the stomach, but from the inside. There were not too many women around who still practiced hepatoscopy, divination using the entrails of slaughtered animals.

Potatoes with rosemary garnish landed on Mazzy's plate with a thud.

Mazzy hated potatoes and had managed to dodge them until now; but Kaya, whose job it was to dish them out, took advantage of Mazzy during a moment of daydreaming, and ambushed her.

Kaya was about sixty years old and had a talent for finding treasures on a map, with the help of a stick and pendulum.

From her seat at the head of the table, Rachel gestured to Gaby to start reading from the Haggadah. The clatter of utensils and plates ceased at once. Gaby seemed pleased that at least part of the holiday ritual was being preserved.

"This is the bread of affliction which our fathers ate in the land of Egypt. Let all who are hungry enter and eat, and all who are needy come and celebrate the Passover. This year we are here, next year in the Land of Israel. This year we are slaves, next year free men!"

Mazzy gulped down the second glass of wine that Aelina had poured, but Rachel had forbidden her to fill the ceremonial cup for the prophet Elijah.

The guests waited for Rachel to continue reading, but she ignored them. She motioned to Mazzy to hand over her grandchild, and Gaby hastened to comply.

"Do you want to sing 'Why is This Night Different from All Other Nights?'"

For Mazzy, this was too much.

Noga had passed all the developmental tests with flying colors, placing in the ninetieth percentile in every category. Mazzy was familiar with the entire terminology of speech therapy. When it came to Noga's communication difficulties, she and Gaby spared no efforts.

Mazzy could identify all the blockages in the mouth that can impede airflow: lips; teeth; palate; uvula. She knew the mechanics of word formation, the different functions of the tongue, velum and pharynx in the production of consonants and vowels. She knew Noga was capable of canonical vocalization and marginal syllables, and possessed permanent phonetic patterns.

But all this professional jargon didn't change the facts. The smartest, most beautiful girl in the world, her daughter, did not speak. At least, not in a manner the outside world could make sense of. She was silent, serene, and wonderful. With her parents she communicated via looks, pantomime, and peals of laughter. But a verbal conversation was yet to be had.

Rachel's question still hung in the air, and Mazzy began to wonder if it was her own paranoia vis-à-vis her mother – often supported by facts – or just an innocent, crooning question a grandma would address to a child. Mazzy felt she had once again come unhinged by Rachel's mind games.

It was another simple, effective trap. And she lost because she played along. You can't play against someone who keeps changing the rules and win. Rachel managed to make her feel like a little girl even when the question had to do with Noga.

With Rachel conducting from the head of the table, the guests sang the traditional song in a way that, to Mazzy, sounded like a monotonous and soulless children's song. She noticed that Gaby had joined in, apparently thinking that singing would defuse the tension. His inability to grasp the situation annoyed her. Rachel stayed silent; she hugged Noga tightly, pressing the girl's cheek against hers.

The girl's smooth pink skin accentuated the few wrinkles on Rachel's face. Although Rachel was twice Mazzy's age, people often took her for thirty. At this moment, Mazzy was ready to gift her an extra twenty years; she was that upset.

If there was one trait she hoped she had inherited from her mother, it was her ability to appear ageless, and to face history with a strained but triumphant smile.

Rachel shot her an inquiring look through the candles, and Mazzy, who had anticipated it, responded with defiance. From an early age she had gotten used to her mother reading her thoughts. This power of

Rachel's helped her cultivate a remarkable honesty. What point was there in lying? Now, the mere thought of heading toward the door was enough for Rachel to cast a menacing glance at her daughter. But Mazzy was not impressed.

When her beeper started chirping, she welcomed it like the bell for end of school and sent a silent prayer of thanks to Gaby. Since both of them had to carry beepers as part of their jobs, they made a pact that if one of them wanted to leave a social gathering, he or she would send the other an urgent message. Mazzy got up, apologized to the guests and reclaimed from Rachel's hands the little girl who had become a battleground in the generational war.

Gaby reacted with surprise, and began collecting his daughter's toys. Mazzy glanced at her beeper and realized that the call hadn't been a ruse. It was work.

Rachel saw them to the door. The attendees, including Ashling, rose to their feet as soon as their queen left her throne. The Simantov women stood facing each other in the hallway. They knew that everyone in the next room was listening.

"What do you think you're doing?" Rachel hissed in a loud whisper.

"Leaving."

"The one time when I host a Seder..."

"It's not always about you. I need to get back to work."

Mazzy was mad at herself. Rachel was trying to end the evening respectfully, in front of her guests. But the stories she had whispered to Noga had led Mazzy to lose her cool. Nothing good could come of her behavior now.

Gaby appeared with the bundled girl on one arm and a bag slung over his shoulder.

"Good night, Rachel," she wished her mother.

Gaby muttered, "Happy Passover," as they left his mother-in-law's kingdom. Unfolding the stroller, Mazzy rushed down the stoop, and glanced at her beeper again. It was a precinct's number, probably Sima.

"You're improving. Arranging for someone else to call you. Not bad."

"What are you talking about?" she said gruffly; her anger hadn't dissipated.

"Nothing. I didn't think we were so sophisticated. We'll be home before ten. I never dreamed we'd get out so soon. I may be able to watch the end of the game."

"Honey, I didn't arrange this with anyone. I'm driving to the precinct; you drive home from there. Forget about ten o'clock. I can't plan when a person goes missing."

"What happened?"

"Never mind. Get in the car."

His chronic exhaustion and Mazzy's fondness for driving confined Gaby to the passenger seat, as usual. When she was edgy, she needed to be in control. He had learned to accept this. They drove in silence for a few minutes, while Mazzy checked the messages on her cellphone.

Gaby broke the silence. "Everything okay?"

"It's nothing."

"I know that it's tough."

He knew nothing and they both knew it. Often, when he tried to make her feel better, he only made things worse. They were out of Rachel's house, but Rachel was not out of them; her spirit hovered over the night.

"A new patient?"

Not a patient, an investigation, a *case*. His ignorance angered her. Whatever he said now would sound like the screeching of a first violin lesson.

"Mandelbrot's daughter."

"What about her?"

"What about her? They found her!" She barked at him.

Silence until the precinct.

Gaby had no energy for another fight in which he would be defeated before the battle had even begun. Mazzy won every time, fair and square. But every time she felt she had lost.

THE FIRST GATE
GLORY

THE SEVENTH DAY
OF THE COUNTING OF THE OMER

"It is the glory of God to conceal things, but the glory of kings is to search things out."

Proverbs 25:2

Chief Inspector Yariv Biton's Passover Seder had been ruined. Again.

Precisely at the moment when his unit was handed a case that could make or break a career, he was ordered to set up a Special Investigations Team; and in his old division to boot – the Missing Persons Division.

His original mandate had been to figure out how the charred bodies of nine security guards – one with his heart ripped out – had ended up in black body bags and hauled to the "dump." But now, he would have to play babysitter to an adolescent girl acting out her rebel-without-a-cause routine.

He tried to protest, to foist the case on the Youth Division, then to palm it off on the social workers.

To no avail.

He tried to call in his markers, anyone who owed him

a favor, either small or large, but everyone had the same answer:

"Biton, grow up. You're stuck with the case. It's his own daughter, and Hizzonor wants you."

And Hizzonor got what he wanted. Yariv rushed to the elite club in the south of town, the last place where Justice Shalvi's daughter had been seen, and where Moscovitch now stood with a worried expression on his face.

A veteran detective, Moscovitch had been around the block a couple of times. If an original thought ever crossed his mind, he did his best to ignore it. Moscovitch's assets were five years to retirement, encyclopedic knowledge of rules and regulations, and a remarkable talent for ass-covering from all directions. If he was worried, there must be a good reason.

"You finally showed up."

"You can't wait to pass the buck to someone else."

"It's the Judge's daughter. Nothing good can come of it."

"Spill it."

"Estie Shalvi, fourteen years old. Went out clubbing at two in the morning with her girlfriends. Two hours later, they say she disappeared with some guy. She texted her friends that the two of them were taking off, or something to that effect. After that, she never answered her cellphone, never called or texted, left no message, and none of them has heard from her since."

"She's only fourteen. How did she get into the club?"

"When did you last look at a fourteen year-old girl?"

"Who questioned them?"

"The new cop, Libby. She said they looked OK. Said they didn't do drugs or drink, and went back home only in the morning because the fog last night was so heavy you couldn't see the road. They weren't too worried about Estie. According to them, the guy she left with was a real looker.

"She danced with him most of the time. He was blond, wore a million-dollar suit. A bit too old for their taste, but then, to them, anyone older than twenty is a senior citizen. Libby must have come across as a grandma, and she's fresh out of the police academy."

"Find anything?"

"It was foggy yesterday, both outside and in. Outside, you couldn't see anything, and inside, you had those smoke machines. There's a ton of stuff. They combed the scene with tweezers and found the usual: cloth fibers, tin foil, cellophane, two cellphones, sequins, makeup, hair pieces, some drugs. One of the bouncers turned out to have a record."

"I'll talk to the crime lab later. Has she done this before?"

"Once. Went to Eilat with some boyfriend. She called home a day later, cried and said she was sorry. According to the Judge, she's a good kid. But what father wants to think otherwise? How else will he get through the night?"

"Why are we even here? It hasn't been forty-eight hours yet."

"It was designated an 'Immediate Investigation'."

"Who designated it?"

"The mother, then Judge Shalvi, then the boss."

"On what grounds?"

"The mother says the kid has asthma, carries an inhaler, probably not full."

Yariv tried to figure out the pecking order. It was clear

he was pretty low on it. The Judge and Department Chief obviously outranked him. He tried to place the mother in the chain of command.

"Where is she?"

"She's waiting to talk to the Special Investigations Team."

"How does she know about the team?"

"Biton, she created it. She's the reason there is a Special Investigations Team."

Yariv followed the direction of Moscovitch's nod.

The Judge's wife was about thirty-eight years old, and must have been a stunning beauty in her youth. Some women improve with the years; to Leah Shalvi-Aiello, the years had been extremely kind. She had a pair of sparkling but worried green eyes, and straight fair hair meticulously styled. Yariv was reminded of someone but couldn't pin it down. Good memories, some painful, yet completely incongruous with the situation at hand. He roused himself from his thoughts. Mrs Shalvi-Aiello gave him a delicate hand in greeting.

"Chief Inspector Yariv Biton, I hope I'm not wrong?"

"Yes."

She inspected him from head to toe and it didn't take long. Some men seem taller than they really are. Yariv Biton was not one of them.

The silence was uncomfortable until Yariv realized he was expected to break it.

"You know Estie. I don't know her yet. Your husband told my officer she's well behaved. What else can you tell us about your daughter?"

"Estie is a good kid. But her father doesn't know everything about her."

Over the years he spent in the Missing Persons Division, Yariv had seen many mothers of missing children; this one didn't behave like any of them.

She hid her feelings surprisingly well. Some mothers kept their cool despite the hysteria that threatened to overcome them at any minute, but nothing like this, not this expertly. Even though Judge Shalvi had the reputation of someone who stood his ground, his wife was clearly the one in control. Yariv made a mental note to tread warily.

"She's a straight A student. Lots of friends. A very responsible kid."

"Look, Mrs Shalvi, we don't know each other, and I understand this may be awkward, but…"

"Shalvi-Aiello, and I do know you. You served several years in Missing Persons, two in narcotics, and the last three in major crime. My husband says you bring solid cases; you have a keen eye, and a good head on your shoulders. Yours was the first name that came up when I asked him who should head the investigation team. You have your own methods, you earned several citations, shook some important hands at Independence Day celebrations. But right now, the only thing in your career that matters is finding my daughter."

There was a threat in there somewhere but Yariv set it aside and threw away the key.

"OK, let's start from the beginning. How is your relationship with Estie?"

"We are quite close. She knows I'm there for her, but she's also very independent. She knows how to take care of herself."

"Do you talk often?"

"Every day. Sometimes two, three times. She always answers my calls, tells me what's going on. We are not best friends, but I think I'm on her top ten list."

A broad, proud smile, perhaps too broad, was intended to bolster that last assertion. She knows they are not good friends. She also knows that, at this age, no mother and daughter are best friends. She knows, too, that she is trying to keep her daughter on a tight leash, but it's not working. At least it didn't work last night.

"So, she also calls you quite often?"

"Not all our conversations are on the phone. Once a week we go to the Country Club, we swim, we sunbathe, we play tennis. She's pretty good at tennis..."

She stopped to catch her breath, sniffled, and then resumed her posture, like a gymnast resolved to finish her routine after an unsuccessful landing. He allowed her a moment to swallow, then tried to steer her in the right direction, because from his point of view, she was going in the wrong one.

"So she tells you about the people she goes out with?"

"I am quite sure she doesn't tell me everything, but she tells me enough to give me an idea."

"Look, I'm no great expert on kids, but if I remember correctly, she is at an age when she hates you, and she'd probably puke if she heard you call her a responsible person."

"I trust her, but this doesn't mean she doesn't act foolishly sometimes. She goes out with older boys. She comes home long after her father thinks she's back, and she did drugs at least once that I know of."

For a judge's daughter, this was a pretty good record,

and Leah reeled off most of it with a studied nonchalance that highlighted the last item.

"What kind of drugs?"

"Weed."

"How do you know?"

"We smoked together. She caught me with a joint, and I thought it was okay for her to try it once: a) to dispel the mystery and b) if your mom does it, it's probably not that cool."

Yariv's brain began working in all possible directions, creating flow charts.

The answer had a certain logic and an impressive honesty to it, but it was also worrying. If everything was out in the open, it meant she was desperate. But if she was desperate, it meant that not everything was out in the open, and what she was hiding might be crucial. Nobody tells the police everything. They're conditioned to distrust strangers, and even though she knew his CV off by heart, they were still strangers. He decided, for now, not to press her.

Not because she was Shalvi's wife, but because she was liable to break down. All mothers of missing girls eventually broke down. It was normal. It was human. It was expected. When it didn't happen, you should worry. Most times, this happened several hours after the spouse has crumpled. Who knew, maybe Judge Shalvi was holed up in his office crying like a baby? Maybe that's why he wasn't here.

"Isn't it dangerous to let a teenager with asthma smoke?"

"She doesn't have asthma. She's allergic to pine blossoms, and this isn't the season."

"So you lied?"

"She's a judge's daughter and all that. But even my husband wouldn't have been able to designate it an 'Immediate Investigation' without the asthma that she doesn't have."

Yariv snapped his fingers in the direction of Moscovitch's new assistant, a motion usually reserved for a slow waitress or a valet who neglected to tag your key at the parking lot.

Libby came over quickly, eager to please. Yariv turned his head aside and said quietly, "See if Mrs Shalvi-Aiello needs a ride home. We don't need her at the station."

"Have you found anything yet?" Leah asked. For the first time since they had met, her voice betrayed concern. It must have been his mumbled instructions. Good news is usually announced out loud.

"Nothing. We'll let you know. Right now we must make sure everyone is doing their job, so that your daughter will be home as soon as possible."

Yariv and Moscovitch made their way to the Crime Lab vehicles, parked outside the club, which was cordoned off with crime scene tape and cones.

"You used to work with Rosolio, didn't you? What was his first rule for leaving the scene?"

Moscovitch worked hard to keep the look of resentment off his face.

He had graduated the same year as the legendary retired detective, and was getting tired of the cult of personality that surrounded Rosolio.

"Go to the crime lab and ask to see the oddest thing they found at the scene."

At the mobile crime lab, they were already packing up.

All their containers, bags, and tags had been carefully stored for future cataloguing. Some of the processing was conducted on the scene, to minimize the paperwork to be done later in the air-conditioned lab. Yariv was not envious of the "plastic people."

He caught up with Doron, who he knew was in charge of all this rustling mess. Doron was leaning on the car door, trying to keep his balance as he shed his disposable plastic overshoes.

As soon as he noticed Biton, his expression soured.

"Be careful, Doron, don't fall into the plastic."

"Nonsense, it's okay."

"Seriously, you could end up buried in polyethylene."

"Biton, what do you want from me?"

"What's the weirdest thing you found?"

"You'll have to gain forty pounds to impersonate Rosolio."

"Tell me anyway."

"When we have something, we'll tell you."

Moscovitch shrugged. "The club is sealed up. We spoke to all her friends, and the mobile lab is going off duty."

"So?"

"According to the new regulations for immediate processing, the head of the Investigation Team has to report to the 'Soothsayer'."

The prospect of reporting to Mazzy Simantov's unit on a night that was already shaping up to be particularly nasty was not something to look forward to. Mazzy was the last woman he wanted to see. Ever. That is, he wanted to see her, just not now.

"Do me a favor; forget it."

"Biton, this is the Judge's daughter. You can't just ignore the procedure."

"His wife brought me in for results, not procedure."

"The 'Soothsayer' closes cases, often ones that would never be solved otherwise. As far as I'm concerned, New Age, old age, it's all the same to me. I don't care what you call it, as long as it works. What, this is all about the Simantov girl?"

"Give me a break, Moscovitch. Simantov doesn't bother me; it's all those cards, crystals, chakras, and shanti…"

"Watch your mouth. She also has that guy, Itzkovitch. He helped me crack a case once. What, you don't like Kabbalah either?"

"It's not Kabbalah, it's those who make money from it. It's all bullshit that allows people to charge four hundred shekels for the privilege of sitting around and breathing in the stench of Indian incense."

Yariv was not objective about anything Mazzy Simantov did, but this time even he had to admit that it was personal.

Since he had left her division, Yariv found ways to update himself, by checking in with Hedgehog, reading Goldfinger's reports, indirectly questioning Doron from Crime Lab. Yariv and Mazzy used different methods.

Mazzy had the right instincts and an uncanny ability to find fresh angles in data that she had examined a thousand times. He, on the other hand, would sink his teeth into a case and not quit until he solved it. They would go to stakeouts together, prepare flow charts and graphs, and dust for prints. It was all about the details. And then, after he left, she would go to work.

One time she brought in an outside consultant, a reader of some sort, and it yielded results.

And then again, and again, until eventually it looked as if she had forgotten what real police work was all about and wasted her time with her mother's mumbo-jumbo. That's when she got permission to form the new unit, the "Soothsayer."

Yariv tried to be supportive, he really tried, but she didn't make things easy for him.

In the years since their separation, Mazzy was promoted to head of the team, while he treaded water, which did not reflect well on him. But what really bothered him was not related to the professional aspect of their relationship.

Mazzy was much more than his protégée.

For a long time he told himself that it all started when he saw her outside at the shooting range and recognized her potential. But there was another moment that began inside.

The detective in him had led him to return to the scene of a crime, a place where a costume party had just ended. In the chiaroscuro lighting of the bar, he saw her in a new light, sans work gear, in a red dress that accentuated her curved neck and perfect collarbone, cascading ripples of cloth that exposed a hint of bare thigh. Her motions aroused sinful, lascivious thoughts in him.

But in spite of these feelings, there were no construction workers catcalling from the scaffolding of his inner world. The building was closed for repairs.

He didn't notice the dress (yes he did – confusing) and the imminent seduction. Another song, fast-paced to match the beating of his heart, was playing in his mind; drumbeats heralding a war in which, as they say, all is fair.

In this self-conscious state, he could barely utter a coherent sentence the entire night. She didn't even notice, or if she did, she hid it well.

Tonight, Yariv had enough on his plate without having to confront Mazzy. But apparently there was no way to avoid a confrontation. His life was about to get complicated. Again.

If someone had told Mazzy a few years ago that she would be sitting on the roof of the precinct, smoking a chillum with a subordinate, she would have laughed at the idea. Mazzy was not the kind of person to break the law in front of her assistants.

But the precinct did not exactly embrace the Soothsayer unit, and did its best to marginalize its members. At first, there were the childish pranks, such as sprinkling pepper on Izzy's herbal infusions, or sending one of the secretaries to Itzkovitch with with her blouse nearly unbuttoned, just to watch him blush and squirm under his black fedora; or telling tasteless jokes about Russian immigrants whenever Larissa walked into the room. Later, looks and whispers whenever the unit assembled, along with unconcealed disdain during departmental briefings. The last straw was a petition to evict the unit from their newly allocated workspace, which had once been a club and recreation room for policemen and office workers. This open animosity had the effect of turning the Soothsayer unit into a close-knit family that drew sustenance and encouragement from every attempt to discredit it or disprove its findings.

At first Mazzy balked at the gradual deterioration of commander-subordinate relations, until she realized there was more than one way to run a unit: if it's obvious to everyone involved that you're in control, there's no need to insist on ritual and formality. Except for the little, shared rituals that united them.

Mazzy made a point of spending time with Larissa, her 'cartomancer,' trying to correct her grammatical mistakes in Hebrew. These sessions gave Larissa a chance to let off steam and make some scathing, disparaging remarks. In her perennial struggle to negotiate between the prevailing culture of "Don't worry," and "Leave it to me," and her own professional integrity, Larissa had neglected to internalize the rules and regulations of the Hebrew language, as well as the principles of what passes for conventional Israeli behavior.

As for Itzkovitch, whenever his busy schedule allowed it, the two would meet for a study session of Torah or Talmud, an activity that pleased him and intrigued her. For her part, Mazzy had her shared rituals with Izzy, who right now was passing the Italian marble cone to her, making sure the wetted Safi cloth attached to the mouthpiece didn't slip. The stuff inside Izzy's designer chillum didn't have much kick; it only offered an agreeable buzz that left her floating on a pleasant cloud.

There was something leisurely and expansive about Izzy. She did not strive to find favor; favors usually found her. She was ruddy and had beautiful eyes, with freckles covering her tanned skin. It was obvious that her weight was acquired by pleasurable means and found its way to her curved limbs, draped in an Indian sari that did not really conceal them. At this late afternoon hour, at the end of a workday, Izzy scrutinized Mazzy's face through a cloud of smoke.

"Yesterday, you were all red; today, I detect complex shades of water, aqua, a lot more blue, green, azure."

"Didn't they teach you in Poona that it's rude to read people's auras without asking them first?"

"And it's all centered in the throat chakra. So it must be someone in the family, but it's not clear who, and why you're so mad at them. Who are you thinking of? Gaby? The way you often talk to him? Because there are traces of red from yesterday, from Rachel. And it's clear that she…"

"You're a whiz at multitasking. You can read my aura and waste my time simultaneously."

The colored beads and pebbles that comprised Izzy's heavy African necklace and earrings jingled as she laughed. But underneath the usual banter and ribbing was real anxiety. Normally, one old, familiar source could account for it.

"What's she done now?" Izzy asked.

"She's driving me nuts."

"What is it this time?"

"I arrived at the precinct on Seder night only to find out that Mandelbrot's daughter had been located with the help of a 'lead' supplied by Rachel! She knew full well why I had to leave her house that night, and yet she complained that…"

"Rachel hosted a Seder?"

"I'm telling you, she now organizes special events so she can harass me before an audience."

Izzy passed her the chillum again, but no amount of inhalation could calm Mazzy down.

"Sweetheart, what really bothers her is that you dared

step out of her purple field. Rachel's purple is dark, a fusion of her fiery red, which is her constant activity, and her vast knowledge, which is dark, ice blue. Don't ask me to analyze this blue, because its darkness is so intense that I don't want to know and she doesn't want you to know."

Mazzy smiled enigmatically. She had never told Izzy the source of the black streaks in her aura. Mazzy had inherited them from her father – Israel – the black hole in her family universe. She never told Izzy about him, because they had not reached that point yet. Also because it frightened her, and because you could never mention color without Izzy turning it into an entire symposium.

"Rachel is totally purple, deep purple. She's queen of purple, empress. This is her force and her sphere of influence, it's her idealism, everything. And here you come along and, instead of continuing this purple dynasty, you run away from her and turn indigo, almost blue. Like your little Noga, you are her indigo girl. This does not sit well with her. It's too complex."

Izzy's analysis made the vein in Mazzy's forehead throb, as if she were exerting the force of an athlete pumping iron. Not because it wasn't accurate: but because it was.

"Et tu, Brute? You don't need auras to tell you that my mother is a frustrated control freak. Since you peeked into my aura, without my permission, couldn't you see something a little more serious there?"

"Something a little more serious you don't want to hear."

"I do, I do."

"You'll say that it's psychobabble and that I'd better focus on crystals."

"I promise not to."

"Has it ever occurred to you that the reason you joined the police, even before the establishment of the Soothsayer unit, was your mother?"

"What's the connection?"

"Someone who, all her life, has tried to break out of her own home, ends up stopping others from trying to break in."

"You're right, this is psychobabble. You'd better focus on crystals."

"You know what, okay, pick a stone," Izzy said enticingly, waving a canvas bag full of colorful crystals and pebbles in front of Mazzy. Mazzy stretched out her hand and selected a smooth round stone resembling a drop of mercury. For a brief moment, she savored its coolness then handed it back.

"Hematite," Mazzy declared.

"Great, you learned something!" Izzy eyed her proudly.

"Well?" urged Mazzy.

"Wait a second. Let me breathe. This is something new, spontaneous…"

"Sensitive, nature loving, who loves long walks and the beach?"

Izzy's face made clear she did not appreciate the irony.

"Maybe you shouldn't give it back to me. Hematite could bolster your femininity, renew your aura of spontaneity, and build a defense against all the negativity you've been radiating this morning. It could infuse you with energy. We're talking about someone new here, someone who's not what he seems, even though you think you know him. Hematite may look pretty and silvery and smooth, but inside it's red and rough. The "hema" in hematite means blood. And red, as you know, is connected directly to the sex chakras."

"Gaby is not someone new, and lately he has not really connected much."

"Who said it was Gaby?"

"I haven't heard the clippity-clop of the white horse and knight in shining armor coming this way."

"You can mock and dodge all you want, but this rock speaks directly to the Third Eye; it's crucial for understanding the link between the astral and the corporeal. This new guy doesn't really believe in what you're doing."

"One could say this about eighty percent of the population and ninety percent of the men, including Gaby."

"But it's not Gaby, it's someone else, someone new. There'll be a war, a battle. Bear in mind that pulverized hematite is incredibly powerful. They used to grind it and wear it as war paint. Spartan warriors used to wear a pendant with hematite under their shield. Wait and see, there will be war. At first you'll win, then he will, then you again, but in any case, both of us should want me to be right."

"May one ask why?"

"At least you'll get a good fuck out of it."

CHAPTER THREE

Yariv Biton made his way to the precinct where he had started his career.

Like the first apartment he rented with roommates, marking the departure from his parents' home fifteen years earlier, the first precinct held a special place in his heart.

For most policemen, the precinct was a stressful place peopled by work associates. Yariv experienced it differently. Work was where he felt most at peace with himself.

It was not an ideal setting, but Yariv was not a man of routine. He needed the tension and adrenaline rush of investigations and the release that came with their conclusions. The precinct was also the place where he had had his last serious relationship, with a policewoman, with Mazzy.

It was this nostalgic aspect that he tried hard to ignore now, or at least to avoid.

He entered the familiar space, which hadn't changed a bit, and was greeted by Sima, the duty officer, with her customary frostiness. Her nickname was Hedgehog. Hedgehog knew everything, but about her, only her name was known from the tag she sported on her meticulously ironed uniform. It was obvious why she was nicknamed Hedgehog. Her short spiky hairdo, generously fortified with gel, would have made Billy Idol proud.

"Did anyone ever mistake you for a man, Sima?"

"Why? Did anyone ever mistake you for one?"

Yariv smiled broadly, but Sima's poker face and her crown of thorns put an end to the inquiry.

"What brings you here? Did you miss us?"

"I wish I had time for sentiment. It's business."

Sima was always once step ahead. She knew precisely why he had come, or at least his official reason for being there.

"She's in the office. Go in now, her schedule is full. She's already had a session on the roof with Take It Izzy, and the Snobbish Russian is already on her way."

Yariv hadn't been there since Mazzy's promotion, but he wasn't shy about prodding Sima for info.

"Where did they stick her office?"

"In the old clubroom. Goldfinger's been trying to kick her out of there for two months now."

The name was actually Goldberg, but the nickname stuck from the way he beckoned people into his office.

"How is he?"

"Ask him yourself, if you can catch him around here."

"What's going on?"

"Forget it. It's too big for you."

Yariv decided not to delve into the deteriorating relations between Hedgehog and Goldfinger. He had more urgent business to attend to.

Yariv made his way to the old clubroom and to an encounter he had been dreading for several years now. On second thoughts, what was the rush? There was always time for another cigarette.

Passing desks laden with reams of paper, and screensavers that attested to the creativity of their owners, he was greeted by distantly familiar faces and either nods or a pat on the back, accompanied by "What's up, Shithead?"

Yariv made himself a cup of coffee. Not that he needed the caffeine; he was just playing for time.

The coffee corner was still in the same place, but now sported an espresso machine with a golden plaque extolling the generosity of a Jewish American donor. There was another addition; a big sign with a crossed out cigarette that seemed to rebuke him and the smoke he was blowing.

After rummaging through the cabinet, he found an inferior brand of coffee. When the dark liquid hissed at the air, he added sugar, stirred monotonously, and stared at the clubroom door. Picking up the coffee cup he had prepared for Mazzy, he gingerly made his way toward the old clubroom.

On the door, a laminated sign proclaimed, "Soothsayer. In case of an emergency, contact Mazal Simantov."

Mazzy's cellphone and pager numbers were written in curved, seductive script, as well as her home phone – the home with the husband, a function he could have filled had he not been so screwed up, and the little girl, a person he had neither the ability nor the will to compete with. Well, there was no turning back the clock.

Without announcing himself, he entered using his elbow to turn the handle, then slammed the door behind him with his heel.

He tried to spot any change in her since their last meeting, but the optical nerve refused to transmit data to his brain and, instead, sent it straight down to his heart.

He smiled at Mazzy, trying to hide his vulnerability.

"Tell me, did it hurt when you fell?"

She didn't even smile at their private joke. His attempt to break the ice must have caused her pain. It was nostalgic banter, like the clichéd "Is your dad a gardener? So how did he raise such a flower?" – even though he knew that she barely knew her father.

Mazzy's eyes contracted to a crack.

He handed her a peace offering.

"Two sugars, just the way you like it," he said softly, putting the cup on her desk.

"I don't take sugar now. But thanks anyway."

Since their break up, they met only at public ceremonies connected with police work, such as at the President's house on Independence Day, when he smiled at her and she just walked away. On those occasions, they both behaved as if nothing had happened.

But there were other occasions, unexpected, like this one, in which they both behaved as if they were suddenly allergic to the surrounding air. This happened at birthdays and retirement parties of colleagues that neither of them particularly cared for and thus assumed the other would skip.

Once they ran into each other in a shop, which Mazzy subsequently stopped patronizing. Another time, they met at the movies, which was particularly awkward because Gaby and Yariv were obliged to shake hands.

Now Mazzy hated herself for two reasons: for involuntarily pushing a framed photo of Gaby and Noga

to the center of the desk and for wearing that particular
bra this morning; it had been washed once too often and
offered no support at all.

The last time they had found themselves alone was
long before she was pregnant with Noga. Perhaps she
should have stuck with the Pilates for a few more weeks,
never mind the shrill exhortations of the overly-gorgeous
instructor, the smell of sweat, and the deafening music.
She despised those exercises, but right now she hated her
thighs even more, her flabby waist, and the slight slackness
in her upper arms, almost imperceptible to a stranger's eye,
except that Yariv wasn't a stranger. The first time he saw
her, all those parts were on youthful display.

Yariv was the first man she shared a home with, and who
walked around in his underwear. He was her mentor at work,
the first and last affair she had with a colleague. He wasn't
her first lover but he was the first to teach her the joys of sex.

Before he came along, there had been two adolescent
bedfellows, a soldier and a student, for whom foreplay
meant licking her neck and ears and twisting her nipples
in a painful attempt to arouse her.

Yariv was the first to show her how to experience sex
differently, free from the posturing and tactics inherited
from her mother, and make her come.

She was pleased that he had shown up now, when she
was strong and independent, head of a department, happily
married, mother to Noga. Mazzy was in a good place. But
the need to enumerate all her personal and professional
achievements was proof positive that he still occupied her
thoughts. You didn't have to be a detective to figure this
out; all you needed was to have a pulse.

Yariv also knew this awkwardness was nothing to do with the sugar he'd spooned into her espresso.

Something was still simmering on a slow burner, a smoldering ember that went all the way back to that lost evening when she asked him where they were heading. He knew how big the gap was between the answer she expected and the only one he could give, so he just upped and left.

Two days later, there was no sign of Mazzy or her belongings in the apartment.

The memory was a little too close for comfort. Any newly graduated psychologist would have recognized the next question as a projection. Not that Yariv put any stock in psychology.

"Did you miss me?" he asked.

Mazzy froze, not because of the past, but because of the future and the possibilities it harbored. His visit had one particular implication she dreaded.

"Are you coming back to Missing Persons?"

"No. Why?"

"Yariv, what's going on?"

"A girl went missing. Shalvi's daughter."

"When?"

"Last night. But it was designated urgent."

She gave him a doubtful look that reminded him of Moscovitch.

"There are new procedures. I've been told I have to talk to you."

"Since when do you do what you're told?"

In the absence of a reply, silence settled over the room.

"Alright, hand over the file," Mazzy said in the most businesslike tone she could muster.

"Okay."

"What did you say her name was?"

"I didn't. It's Estie Shalvi-Aiello."

Mazzy jotted the name down on a yellow pad, and underlined it twice; then she lifted her eyes to meet his questioning gaze.

"So how does this work, exactly?" he asked.

"Izzy will try her crystals or check the parents' auras, Itzkovitch will do what he always does, and Larissa, my fortuneteller, will open her cards and surprise us."

"How about your mom?"

"She's fine, thank you. I'll tell her you said hi."

The next silence between them painted him into a corner. He was not sure what to ask next but wanted to say something to prolong the meeting.

"Do you need something from the scene to get a vibe?"

"That's not how it works."

"How, then?"

"Differently."

"Is there some detective I can talk to, or will I have to deal with my ex throughout this investigation?"

"Chief Inspector Biton, 'Soothsayer' works a little differently. We have our own angles of approach. The fact that you don't know our people and are not familiar with our methods won't stop our unit from finding the facts that you and Shalvi need pronto."

Sima's spiky head appeared around the door. "You have a caller on line two."

"We're busy. Check who it is, and I'll get back to them."

"It's your daughter's daycare."

Mazzy lifted the phone and swiveled her chair away from Yariv in one fluid motion.

"Aurora? Is everything okay?"

"Noga is still here. She's playing with Rishi in the ball pit. They're so cute together, like a bride and groom. But come soon. She's getting restless, and I don't want her to fall asleep here; you know how cranky she is when she wakes up."

Mazzy exhaled, but had Gaby been within reach she would have strangled him.

It was Gaby who insisted on this fancy daycare center with kids named Rishi, where they always told you who your kid was playing with because this was an important stage in their development and they needed to go through this spiritual experience to the max.

Anthroposophy, my ass. Mazzy wasn't keen on this daycare where the teacher never stopped smiling even while making vague, guilt-inducing comments about what a lousy mom she was. But now was the time for those breathing exercises she and Gaby learned together, time to control the anger and not give Yariv the satisfaction. She managed to say, very calmly, "Gaby's on his way. He must be in traffic."

"On Wednesdays you usually pick her up."

"I know."

"Could you call him and check?"

"Don't worry. I'll call right away."

She hung up and looked at Yariv's smug face.

"If you have nothing to do, do it somewhere else."

"Like where?"

"Not here. Isn't some judge missing his daughter?"

Yariv's raised hands signaled, "As you wish," and as

soon as he left the room, Mazzy picked up the phone and called Gaby.

A woman's voice answered.

"Doctor Pur is in surgery. Would you like to leave a message?"

"Is he already in the OR?"

"He's on his way."

"Then page him. It's urgent."

Mazzy knew exactly what the nurse was thinking: about Gaby Pur's hysterical wife, how she pitied him for having to go through this impossible residency and then home to her every evening.

But when Mazzy heard the echoes of the PA announcement, she felt better.

"Sweetie, how many times have I asked you not to get them to call me on the PA? It's so embarrassing when the entire floor has to hear that my wife is looking for me."

"Do you know what's really embarrassing? When that dreadful daycare woman calls to say Noga is still there because her dad forgot to pick her up."

"Shit! It's just that you always pick her up on Wednesday…"

"And on Sunday, Monday, and every other bloody day! You have one lousy day to pick her up from that damned Aurora! I asked you this morning because I am snowed with work and they just dumped another case on me. If you had a problem with it, you should have told me. Did you even take the car seat?"

"No, I forgot." She could almost hear the wheels in his organized, Ashkenazi head turning in all the wrong directions.

"I'm sorry. We have a rare procedure here, and I was on call…"

Breathe deeply. Relax. He didn't mean it. He really didn't.

"Don't worry. I'll pick her up. I'm much closer."

"It's a life-saving procedure…"

Mistake. Big mistake. And the reaction would be correspondingly loud.

"And what the fuck do you think I'm doing here? Playing hopscotch?"

The flimsy office partitions shook. Heads turned in her direction. Gaby was right; it was embarrassing when the entire department heard you. Mazzy took another deep breath and listened to her husband's soft voice.

One of the things Gaby was not good at was wiggling out of such situations. His voice expressed genuine distress, not because he had screwed up, but because he had hurt her, caused her grief. She was always his first priority, even before Noga, who at this very moment was waiting at daycare. He never meant to screw up. He just always did.

"You're right. Sorry. I have nothing to say. My bad."

Clearly he didn't really get what had angered her.

To make a bad day worse, when Mazzy looked up, there was Larissa Sverenka in front of her.

Larissa Sverenka was not good looking, but her face was unforgettable: arrogant and cunning but with a certain restraint that stemmed from her desire not to expose her feelings to anyone she considered her inferior. Which was pretty much everyone.

Her eyes seemed too wise for her age, but today they were particularly lugubrious. Her thin lips were so tight as to almost be invisible. She threw down a tarot card with a picture of a Hermit, the bearded wanderer, holding in one hand a lantern emitting yellow light, and a staff, same yellow color, in the other.

"Where is your cartoonist?" she demanded in a guttural accent that sounded like it could dig a hole in the road.

"Larissa, I told you that even if you find something, you don't have to come here in person. Take a few days off. Nobody expects you to show up for work so soon. The *Shiva* isn't over…"

"Where is your cartoonist? This is a picture of the one that killed Borislav."

Mazzy noticed a slight tic in the corner of Larissa's eye, despite the cold resolution in her voice. Over the last week, she'd been trying in vain to comfort and support her cartomancer, eventually realizing that it was a lost cause. To Larissa, any show of feeling, given or received, was a sign of weakness.

Mazzy summoned up her softest, most sympathetic tone.

"Leave the card here and we'll see what we can do with it. I know it's painful for you, but we really can't deal with this case now."

"Everyone else yes, but my brother no? What kind of country is this? You find people in the dumpster, and you don't check what happened to them?"

"Larissa, we don't investigate murder cases; it's not our mandate. I can't change that."

"Send me your cartoonist."

"I can't summon the identikit artist for a card. It's not going to happen. It may screw up the lineup later, because they'll find some homeless person with a hood and a cane. It could send the wrong message to the people working on the case."

"What message is that?"

"That Soothsayer interferes with other departments."

"It should!"

Larissa was a practical woman and right now motivated by revenge, but Mazzy wondered if there wasn't something else, some other need. Larissa was the type that could never remain passive. Inaction drove her crazy. She couldn't even stay home to mourn her loss. What was the point of sitting in her apartment grieving for her brother? How would that help his case?

Right now, she had a big hole in her heart, and the only way she knew to fill it was through action.

But Mazzy had seen the autopsy shots of Borislav. She did not want Larissa anywhere near the monster responsible for it.

"We just got another case that we need to focus on. If you can't handle it, let me know, but I'd rather have you working with me, unless you feel that it would undermine the investigation."

This was always Mazzy's trump card. Larissa was, above all, committed to her special gift. She rarely needed reminding. Grabbing a deck of cards from her skirt pocket, she started shuffling them with dizzying dexterity.

Like people who toss a coin every time they have to make a decision, Larissa drew a card when faced with even the most trivial matter.

This time it was the Wheel of Fortune that lay upside down on the desk.

"Everything revolves. We must leave the past behind and look ahead. There is a change. There is a direction. I guess it is my destiny to be stuck here with you."

Mazzy gazed at the card. She saw the smiling Sphinx, the four winged creatures, the Tetragrammaton, Anubis rising with the wheel and the serpent Typhon. She wondered if she could be so committed if something happened to one of her loved ones.

Larissa's expression had frozen and Mazzy guessed she had not been told everything the cartomancer saw in the card, but thought it best not to ask.

CHAPTER FOUR

Panting, sweating, tingling and an accelerated heartbeat can be a good sign when you are twenty-five. When you're almost fifty, and you wake up in the middle of the night experiencing these symptoms, along with five distinct scorch marks on your left hand and pressure in your rib cage, then terror rears its head, and wormwood fills your veins.

Even if you happen to be Rachel Simantov.

Most people fear the unknown. Most people seek knowledge. But not everyone. Not Rachel. Most of the time, Rachel possessed knowledge. Ignorance was a blessed shield for her, it was her way of hiding from herself.

But now she woke up feeling as if she had been wrenched out of her home and left shivering in the cold.

She breathed slowly, inhaling and exhaling to the rhythm of her heartbeat. Her hand touched her rib cage, feeling the feeble contraction. Despite the terror that gripped her, Rachel overcame the urge to grab the phone and dial 911. Instead, she made an effort to focus on the pain. Her left hand continued to throb but did not intensify. Soon she calmed down and the pressure became bearable, even though she still felt as if someone had clamped a vise on her rib cage and squeezed.

She pulled at her nightgown sleeve and examined her biceps.

Five tiny contusions were visible across the muscle, as if it had been gripped tightly by a hand. Another bruise was found near the wrist.

It wasn't a heart attack, but it was not exactly good news either. Rachel recalled the dream she'd been having just before the anxiety attack.

She was standing on a rooftop; a broad white canopy stretched over her head and hail pelted her mercilessly. After a while, the storm subsided but the hail continued to fall on the canopy. A soothing smell of warm milk and cinnamon wafted through the air, and a predator's confident smile flashed in front of her.

A large, menacing raptor was circling overhead. Rachel tensed her muscles and dashed across the wet, slippery rooftop. The ice pellets jabbed into her, her shoulder throbbed. Something swooped from above.

The scorching sensation returned, together with the panting, tingling, and runaway pulse. Fear flowed like venom through her veins. When it subsided, all that remained was the putrid scent in her nostrils.

A miasma of milk, cinnamon and blood. A broken covenant. An abomination.

THE SECOND GATE
GRACE

THE TENTH DAY
A WEEK AND THREE DAYS OF THE COUNTING OF THE OMER

"And I will make justice the line, and righteousness the plummet; and hail will sweep away the refuge of lies, and waters will overwhelm the shelter."

Isaiah 28:17

Hagar dislodged her laptop from its base, disconnected the cellphone from its charger, and threw a few papers into her handbag. A glance at the clock elicited a sibilant racy swearword.

3:36am

Another day going to work before sunrise. It had been much easier in her previous job, both physically and mentally. But two years ago, their representative called and informed her that she was being transferred to another department. Hagar accepted the order without a fuss. She owed it to them.

She had been in thrall to those women her entire life.

They had the means and the bureaucratic positions to

make someone's life a torment or a bed of roses. True, they were not at the top of the pyramid, but they were the architects.

They were the ones who identified her from her middle school entrance exam, who moved her and her dysfunctional family to Tel Aviv. They were the only ones who knew what her mother had told her about fallen angels was true, and they explained it had nothing to do with the voices she kept hearing all the time. They were the ones who took care of her after her mother jumped off the roof, who sent her to the ranch in the North, expunged that pesky police record, and fixed her first job, at the office in Herzliya, where she became a junior partner after a very controversial election process. They steered her back to the straight and narrow when, against all odds and reason, she lost her good sense and fell in love with a dangerous ally.

To her, they were everything: the protective mother, the big sister who shielded her under her wing.

She was beholden to them, and they knew it.

Her present job involved working with lay advocates at the rabbinical courts and other female lawyers specializing in gender discrimination. These activists hunted down the derelict husbands who wouldn't grant a divorce and used every legal means to make their lives miserable. They sued employers who discriminated against women, and delved into legal and religious issues, knocking down barriers that seemed insurmountable. They examined the legal ramifications of parliamentary legislation and their impact on the status and welfare of women.

They did all this *pro bono*, competing in a man's world, against men's laws, using men's means, and step-by-step won reputation and results; but they also made enemies.

Threats that began with letters and phone calls were soon translated into action. Punctured tires, rocks thrown through windows and scorpions in the mailbox were daily hazards. All of which meant new security measures, surveillance cameras everywhere and uniformed guards throughout the building. Security was restored.

Tonight, a hailstorm was raging. It sounded like rocks hitting the building, but this time they were not thrown by humans. The wind whistled and ice balls pelted the windows.

Hagar swiped her security pass and walked along the hallway to the elevator where the pass was needed again.

She rode the elevator to the top floor, the upper parking lot.

As was her wont, she made a friendly parting gesture to the watchful eye of the CCTV, climbed the four metal steps to the roof exit, and tried to remember if she'd parked close to the door.

As soon as she opened the door, her plans blew away with the wind.

A tall, blond security guard was standing there. He looked like a poster boy for men's underwear, the kind that men wonder if they'll ever buy and women hope they will.

He was holding an extra large umbrella, which made Hagar appreciative of the care the management took to shield her from heaven's wrath. He gave off a soothing scent of warm milk and cinnamon, a familiar scent but one that she doubted she'd ever be able to recapture. It was the smell of her simple, unpretentious childhood, when her mother was still sane and used the concoction to smooth her transition into slumber and dreams. A smell that spelled tranquility and protection, and that Barak would leave with her after a night of lovemaking. Now the source of it was smiling at her, flashing pearly white teeth, the smile of a predator.

She seemed to recognize the smile, but there was no way it could belong to the original owner. Her bosses and his bosses forbade them to meet. Daughters of Lilith were not allowed to consort with Nephilim for fear of them forming private alliances and harboring unwelcome feelings toward their subordinates. There was no reciprocity between the two sides; the daughters of aristocracy were not supposed to have feelings for servants, however ancient and skillful they may be.

She seemed to recognize him, despite the camouflage, but she was not sure. "Barak?"

"No, but you're getting warm."

The menace in his voice and the swiftness with which he positioned himself between her and the door left no room for doubt. She was stuck. Deep and hard. She had no doubt about what was happening to her.

She considered her escape options; no way could she beat a Naphil in running, but if she could get to her car, maybe she could gain some time. She made a dash for it.

The hail beat down on her; the pain penetrated through the tension and anxiety that gripped her ankles and slowed her down.

She lifted her eyes, and through the grayish-white pre-dawn light she discerned a large bird of prey with a tremendous wingspan, circling above, like an airborne shark.

With the hand that was not clutching her attaché case, she fumbled in her pants pocket for the car keys. She could hear the swooshing wind around her and realized she was running out of time.

The sounds were not caused by the storm.

When she was a few feet from the car, another Naphil materialized out of nowhere and blocked her passage. She turned around, only to encounter a third. She glanced behind her shoulder and saw his twin lunge at her. There was a rustling of wings, opening like the blades of a pocketknife; Hagar hurled her keys at the first Naphil and with a sickle-like motion threw her attaché case at the second. The case opened and by a stroke of luck, she was able to grab hold of the handle of a whip she always carried just in case, and cracked it in the air.

She had wielded the whip a few times since leaving the ranch, but not as often as she was supposed to. She had been told that the whip was an amalgam of invocations, incantations, and charms that could scorch the Nephilim, repel the Sons of God, allowing you to control them. Sweet illusions. With luck, she'd be able to hold on a few more seconds, at most half a minute.

The three attackers recoiled from the circle cleared by the swirling whip. It worked like a bug spray – driving away a swarm of lethal, dexterous dragonflies. Icy pellets still hit her, but Hagar tried to focus on her assailants, ignoring the pain. Her wrist flicked the whip swiftly, hoping to gain a few more seconds, enough for someone in the building to come to her rescue. She wondered how long she'd be able to fend them off, when her train of thought was suddenly derailed. One thing was absolutely clear, and it made her muscles contract in terror. She must come out of this battle alive, to pass this information to the other Sisters of the Order.

They must be told that the covenant had been breached.

A heavy shadow crept over her, then total darkness fell.

CHAPTER FIVE

The hailstorm had damaged Yariv's windshield wipers, which now squeaked and squealed across his field of vision. According to the radio, this time the ruckus was justified. This time there was a body, not just a teenager out to have a good time. The silence that surrounded the Shalvi case was disturbing. Not just because there was a gag order being aggressively enforced, but with no sign of the girl for three days, and no ransom demand, the silence was deafening. Yariv knew that if it were a kidnapping, and not just a kid running away from home, a note would have arrived by now.

A policeman directed him through the barrier.

"What's behind all this mess?"

"Crime scene."

Yariv crossed the makeshift barrier and encountered the familiar face of a law enforcer. Libby, Moscovitch's young assistant, was waiting for him, her ponytail swaying as she glanced left and right in an attempt to get a broader sense of the situation.

Against the ominous assembly of vehicles and patrol cars, Yariv found this sight amusing. Libby only had to look down to see a body covered in thick, white plastic.

He went straight to it, knelt down, lifted the plastic sheet and recoiled at the sight. A young man whose face had been crushed either by a fall or by being pushed into the tarmac. His arms were awkwardly placed at his side, several ribs were sticking out of his chest, and his pelvis at an unnatural angle. Both shins were completely smashed.

"Where's Moscovitch?"

"He went home. Something to do with his granddaughter. But I have all his notes."

"Shoot."

Libby cleared her throat and started reciting.

"Nir Yavnieli, law student, twenty-four years old, former paratrooper, worked as security guard in the building for the last few months."

"Looks like this time his parachute didn't open. What do you think happened?"

"The way it looks at the moment, he either fell or was pushed off the roof. Maybe suicide."

It couldn't have been suicide; the guy was a security guard. There are simpler ways to put an end to things when you carry a licensed firearm. The corpse looked as if someone had tried to actually plant it in the ground.

"Who was the last person to see him?"

Libby handed him a photo of a smiling woman in a business suit.

Libby and Moscovitch had done a good job covering the scene.

"Hagar Abizu, lawyer, thirty-three years old. Works in this building but disappeared from the rooftop parking lot. According to the security system, she swiped out at three forty-five. We have CCTV of her at the entrance to the roof. We're looking for her, and an 'all points' has been issued."

Yariv took out his notebook and wrote down the name: Hagar Abizu. He underlined it twice.

"Where's her car?"

"Still on the roof. The keys were found lying in the middle of the lot."

"She used another vehicle? Did she walk?"

"Not according to the guard who works at the exit. On the video you can see her talking to someone at the entrance to the parking lot, but his image is very unclear."

"Is it this Yavnieli guy?"

"Can't tell. Crime Lab are working on it."

Yariv surveyed the building from the bottom up. There was a security camera over the entrance and another one above over the roof railing.

"Any connection between him and the lawyer?"

"We don't know, but judging by her office and picture, she's way out of his league."

"Maybe he came on too strong and she said no and oops... over the railing? Maybe someone else was there? What's happening upstairs?"

"The hail washed up the surface, but there's signs of a struggle. We found her attaché case open on the floor, but her purse is there with money and credit cards. It doesn't look like a robbery gone wrong"

"Maybe she saw something that scared her. Does Abizu show up on any other security cameras?"

"I don't know. I'll check."

"Later. Let's go to the roof first."

When they reached the roof, Yariv had to control his labored breathing. He lit a cigarette. Something didn't sound right. He took a drag and tuned out the rookie's explanations.

Sometimes work required just that; tune out, cut yourself off. Ignore the fact that people died here, and focus on what they left behind. Hints, traces, secrets, tiny details that might make a little more sense of the security guard's death. While he was ruminating about how cases forced themselves on his consciousness and awakened his drowsy brain, Libby dragged him to the railing that surrounded the roof.

Doron and his Plastic Squad were busy at work, and Crime Scene strips were stretched from the roof all the way down to where the corpse had been found. Doron, an airy plastic cap bouncing on his head, looked like a chef on the loose.

He was holding two test tubes in his gloved hands, lifting them up to the morning sun. He ignored Libby and Yariv when they positioned themselves next to him, and continued to study the tubes.

"What do the strips tell us?"

"That it's not the correct angle and that something's wrong with this picture. The pathologist says the damage indicates the fall was from far higher than the roof."

Yariv looked over the railing; it was easier to see it from above. Judging by the angle of the cascading strips, the body was too far away from the building. Even if he had been pushed, and did not jump, the guard could not have reached such a distant point from where his aerial trajectory had begun.

"Was he dragged downstairs?"

"No sign of that. He fell, just not from this roof."

Yariv looked around. "Saving Grace" was the tallest structure in the area. A fall from any other building on the block would have resulted in a few broken bones, but not more.

"What are you implying?"

"That we don't have a clue."

"Any signs of this Abizu woman being on the scene?"

"No, no trace of her after she exits the upper parking lot."

"What's your current theory?"

"A chopper. The only thing that can whisk you off a roof like this."

"Chopper? In the storm we had last night? I hope your test tubes yield something more convincing. What do you think is in them?"

"Maybe nothing. Maybe DNA."

"From where?"

"The lawyer's attaché case and the most interesting thing we found here."

Doron lifted a sealed plastic bag containing a long leather whip with a handle like the head of a serpent.

"If this was used in a struggle, there might be some DNA."

"Could it belong to the dead security guard? Something got out of control here?"

"We'll check. Maybe we'll get lucky."

Yariv didn't like it when people told him how to do his job, but he always felt obliged to tell others how to do theirs.

"Make sure we get results."

Doron, who was taller than Yariv by a head, lowered his eyes and gave him a hangdog look.

It was open, wide open. The lawyer could also be a victim; her body waiting to be found somewhere. But right now she was the only suspect. He hoped there had been somebody else on the roof last night. Especially because his only theory involved a dominatrix lawyer capable of dragging an ex-paratrooper to a helicopter and throwing him to his death. Something was decidedly wrong with this picture and a pattern was emerging. In one week, two cases with zero clues. He was missing something.

Maybe the lawyer didn't show up on the CCTV because she didn't leave the building of her own free will, or leave by land? Maybe the security guard was just a victim of circumstance? Maybe her disappearance was the real story here?

CHAPTER SIX

The Athaliah went over the notes she had written during the deposition.

The witness was precise in her testimony, as if she had been preparing for this her whole life and now that the moment had arrived, all the sluices were breached, allowing the words and data to gush forth. Her language was technical, as if she were describing a rare breed of bird discovered during migration season. She was trustworthy and apparently well rehearsed, and yet, through the cool, professional façade, terror lurked.

It was the realization that her testimony might undermine The Order and perhaps put it to the greatest test of its existence that made her avoid discussing the implications and stick to the bare, cold, measurable facts.

The witness drank the water with determination and self-confidence. She was not afraid to be caught in a lie; she knew that the dust sprinkled over the water would not hurt her.

The Athaliah shifted her gaze to the frescoes.

From the surrounding walls, seven pairs of eyes looked at her, eyes that were clever, penetrating, resolute, warm, honest and ruthless. Long hair in varying shades: braided sternly or flowing breezily according to the artist's fancy. The Seven Maidens of the Order seemed to shield her against the moment of decision. Some were like protective mothers, others like vindictive predatory sisters, flapping their wings, waiting for the right moment to sink their talons into their prey, as soon as she slipped and made a mistake.

In retrospect, the Athaliah concluded that the decision to summon The Order after the disappearance of the Judge's daughter was the right one.

A future member of The Order had vanished – always cause for concern, regardless of her age.

If she determined that the tall blond man who had danced with Estie at the club was a Naphil, there would be grave consequences. They knew the boundaries. They were allowed to trifle with women, but not to hurt them, certainly not fool around with girls, let alone future members of The Order.

Esther Aiello had not even been trained at the Ranch.

With a long supple finger, the Athaliah pressed the intercom button. The buzz warned her secretary that her mistress was about to issue an order.

"Judith, let the other one in."

Loyal Judith pressed the buzzer.

The door opened and the second witness walked in. She bowed and opened her palms, and with a faint, tremulous voice recited the customary verse.

"Then lifted I up mine eyes, and looked, and behold, there came out two women, and the wind was in their wings; for they had wings like the wings of a stork: and they lifted up the ephah between the earth and the heaven."

The Athaliah almost smiled at the terror stricken witness.

"Blessed above women shall you be, tent dweller, the watchwoman is asleep but her heart is awake."

The witness' eyes lit up and her back straightened. Her voice became stronger and deeper.

"Who is she that comes forth as the morning rising, fair as the moon, bright as the sun, terrible as an army with banners?"

"Thou that dwellest in the gardens, the companions hearken to thy voice. Cause me to hear it."

The witness curtsied again, and the Athaliah motioned her to get up.

"You may speak freely."

"I saw him. He was an angel, I mean, a Naphil. I am sure of that."

She spoke urgently and resolutely, unlike the previous witness who sounded rehearsed; she spoke like someone who knows the truth.

"Does anyone know you are here?"

"Only the daughters of The Order, the Athaliah."

The Athaliah examined her face, looking for a shadow of a doubt, a hint of a lie.

"How did you get to see him?"

"I lifted my head and there he was."

"Was it day or night?"

"Night. In spite of the hail, I saw him. The street was lighted."

"There was no hail that night. We know this for a fact."

"There was hail, very strong. He flew in between the sheets of hail."

"Where did he come from? North or South?"

"From the middle. The center of town. He dived from a relatively high building, holding a woman under him. Then he simply flew away and vanished."

"Are you sure it was a woman, not a girl?"

"A woman, dressed in a business suit. She just dangled underneath, powerless. I am not sure if she was unconscious, sleeping or dead."

"Which night are you talking about?"

"Last night, the Athaliah."

The pieces were starting to fall into place. The night of the hailstorm, the location and the description of the abduction. The Athaliah realized that she was not talking about Esther. There were others. The slight tremor she experienced lasted no more than a second. This was a different incident. A different Naphil, at a different place, on a different date. Hagar! Hagar was not kidnapped by a disgruntled client or by one of her many enemies: she was kidnapped because she belonged to The Order. Or maybe Barak was trying to get back with her? No. He wasn't one of the brave among them, and he wasn't that stupid. She had given him a very specific order.

"Can you describe him to me?"

"Over six feet tall. He kept his legs close together when he flew, as if he only had one leg, and he was very broad. His wingspan was almost nine feet. He flew through the hail, between houses and streets, flapping his wings, and when he reached above the rooftops he began to glide."

So he was an ace flyer, one who knows his way in the air. She still harbored a faint hope that the witness was wrong. The Athaliah sighed and motioned to the witness to approach her, a sign the ceremony was over. She kissed

ASAF ASHERY   85

her on the cheeks and on her eyelids, and they began reciting the ancient incantations.

"I will pay that that I have vowed. Renew our days as of old. Let Lilith reign on earth forever. Praise her name."

The Athaliah walked over to a small table and picked up an earthen jar containing holy water. She poured some into a goblet, took a pinch of dust from a small copper box and sprinkled it on the water; then she offered it to the witness.

With trembling hands, the witness brought the goblet to her lips.

"If, during this moon, you have not seen a Naphil, and you have drunk this water, the seven curses of Eve will be upon you, and you shall never be as you once were."

"Amen," said the witness.

The Athaliah fixed her gaze on the witness' eyes. The water had its effect and her pupils were dilated. The Athaliah focused on the irises, on the disk surrounding the pupils. The answer reflected in the black box of the soul was unequivocal.

She, too, was telling the truth.

The Athaliah thanked her with a nod of her head, and the witness left the room.

When the sky is about to open, you feel very small, even if you are the Athaliah. But anxiety and foreboding were luxuries she could not indulge in. She needed to find certainty and serenity. The Athaliah took a deep breath and resumed the recitation from the first verse. Every introspection had to start with the basic words known to every member of The Order. It was the familiar path she had to tread in order to overcome her anxiety. She recited the words in a whisper.

"In the days of time immemorial, when there were no names and no call for names, nothing in heaven or earth had a name except the Glorious Master of the Universe; there was no eyewitness and no one to pronounce names. Evening passed and morning came and God created man in his image, male and female He created them. And He called the woman Lilith and her man Adam. Lilith and her man observed the angels and knew their names; they could distinguish between purity and thick darkness, between God and Nothingness. Lilith had a dream and when she awoke she trembled with fear. She went down to earth and planted a garden in Eden and called it Kedem. She stayed there, forsaking Adam whom God had created for her. And God said unto her: Since you have forsaken the man I have given you, I shall seal the Gates of Heaven. A battle is pitched between Me and you."

Except that in this battle, she wouldn't be able to make use of authority, administration, officials and documents. Something older than paper, more ancient than recorded documents was needed here. The broken covenant was an oral one; it preceded the invention of writing.

The balance of powers was clear, the chances were slim, the price horrendous. It was time to act.

The Athaliah took a deep breath and pressed the button.

"Let them in."

They would have to use the RAD Belts and the rituals that had never been tested before against the biggest threat The Order had ever faced – the Nephilim.

The Athaliah assumed a royal countenance, one exuding splendor and authority as befitting a conference with the two senior members of her cabinet, Miss Adedin and Miss Adesela.

The two walked into the room side by side. They couldn't have been more unlike.

Bathsheba Adedin had a warm and sunny disposition, looking innocent and vulnerable. She was unquestionably trustworthy and frank, like a child who has just arrived in Wonderland and requires a period of adjustment.

Na'ama Adesela, on the other hand, was an arrow about to be released from a taut bowstring. She could be cruel when necessary and often knew no bounds. She was the first to talk, and as usual, went right to the heart of the matter, in her plain, blunt style.

"Is that it then?"

"The witnesses were truthful."

The two senior delegates were tense. They knew that the witnesses had been summoned because the evidence pointed in a certain direction, but they also knew that only the Athaliah could assess the veracity of their testimony.

"So the case of Leah Aiello's daughter is conclusive?"

"Yes."

"We have to respond," Na'ama said emphatically. "Give me just one of their names. We'll punish him and then all the others will fall in line. It does not have to be the name of the one who…"

"There's only one problem with this scenario," said the Athaliah.

"What?" asked Bathsheba.

"We do not have the names."

A profound silence fell on the room.

"The names were lost when Athaliah the Sixty-Second died without bequeathing them to her successor. It's been seventy years now that they are immune from extinction, and they don't even know it. Like every holder of this office since then, I have spared no effort trying to find the names, but to no avail," the Athaliah continued.

"Why wasn't the Council informed? Why weren't we told?" asked Na'ama, who was the first of the delegates to recover.

"The decision to keep this information from all but the Athaliah was taken a long time ago. The Order has to present a certain façade to maintain its prestige without resorting to force. An unloaded gun is just as effective as a deterrent, but only if both sides do not know it is empty."

"What now?" asked Bathsheba in as steady a voice as she could muster.

"*She Shall Overcome*, phase one: The Nephilim have abducted two members of The Order. At this stage, it should be on a 'need-to-know basis': everyone else must move aside, do her job, and not ask questions because there will be no answers."

The Athaliah had thrown into the air the mobilization code with the same detachment she used earlier to inform them of the witnesses' truthfulness. Noticing how ill-at-ease Bathsheba had become at her announcement, she hastened to issue a quick succession of operational orders to the Public Affairs Division. Na'ama, head of the Security and Counterintelligence Division, had to curb her enthusiasm at the soon-to-be fulfilled expectations.

"Bathsheba, I need someone to monitor the Jabbok Crossing, another one at Shinar Valley, and at least one of our agents for the Syrian mountain pass."

"Why now? Why here?" asked Na'ama, unconcerned about the implications.

"I think someone else, someone important, has made them some promises."

A quick exchange of looks made it clear that they all knew what must be avoided and, more importantly, what must be done as soon as possible.

"With or without an OK from above – the battle is joined."

CHAPTER SEVEN

Mazzy Simantov looked about her, seeing the situation as it really was, rather than the way it was presented. The place had the trappings of a party for the Diplomatic Corps; security guards scanned the area, mumbling into their cuffs as they waited for armored vehicles to arrive, and opening the heavy doors at an angle to protect against possible snipers. Smiling uniformed waitresses made their rounds with trays of appetizers and tall glasses. A quartet was playing at the other end of the hall, opposite long tables laden with refreshments. Roy Mandelbrot was the rising star of the underworld. He had begun his career as a technical adviser with extensive military experience, and he left his mark on gang warfare and contracted killings.

When his daughter Adva disappeared, some felt the police should hang back and let the windmills of poetic justice slowly grind their grist. It was Mazzy who pointed out to her superiors that a seven year-old child was involved, and that she would mobilize all the meager resources of Soothsayer in order to bring the girl back alive and well. But, in the end, it was Rachel Simantov who located Adva's whereabouts, even though that fact was omitted from the report. Or that Mandelbrot's coffee grounds had revealed an image of a winged hammer on a pile of foliage, a picture that led Rachel to determine the girl was not in imminent danger and would soon be found. Further reading led to the house where she was being held. Rachel did not elaborate on the meaning of the symbols; she just gave the address to the investigators. Rachel Simantov, it was noted, did not ask for remuneration for her services.

Mazzy, however, knew her mother's motives were not pure. Naturally, Rachel did not want the little girl to come to any harm, but bonuses in the form of Mandelbrot's gratitude and a chance to tarnish the reputation of the Soothsayer unit were obvious fringe benefits.

When the negotiating team arrived at the address Rachel had given them, they found the kidnappers gone and the frightened, dehydrated girl all by herself. Mazzy arrived only after the dust had settled.

Now, two weeks after the return of the kidnapped girl, Mandelbrot threw a "business as usual" party, and his thanks to the Soothsayer unit were spelled out on the fancy program offered to the guests as they made their way from the open bar to the dance floor.

Roy Mandelbrot was surrounded by several of his ogres, creatures about whom the less is said, the better.

There was something familiar about the way people approached and greeted him: whispering in his ear without making any physical contact, squirming uncomfortably, visibly frightened. Mazzy watched Mandelbrot and his entourage as they made their way across the hall toward his female counterpart. Rachel stood on the side exuding self-importance. Mazzy suspected that Rachel was fully aware that her seemingly passive demeanor forced other personalities to approach her: past clients, politicians, businessmen, sports stars, models, and crime reporters. She took unabashed pleasure in the attention, like a lioness presented with a lion's share on a platter. When Mandelbrot tried to kiss her on the cheek, she rebuffed him.

Mandelbrot turned away from her, and the social part of the evening was over. Rachel was left alone in her corner to disdainfully survey the dinner tables and the people who populated them. She focused on the Soothsayer party, the bizarre and colorful group gathered around Mazzy.

If any of the women had noticed Rachel, they were not going to reward her with an acknowledgement, and Itzkovitch, the only man on the team, would never make eye contact with a woman.

The Soothsayer clairvoyants were a handpicked group, selected for their professional talent, but also for their lack of any connection to Rachel, her acolytes, or her numerous devotees.

Mazzy watched Izzy as she stirred her fruit cocktail with a miniature umbrella while ogling the buffet's lavish array of cold cuts, carpaccios, and salamis. As part of her commitment to crystals and auras, Izzy had to forgo the pleasures of flesh and its products. Mazzy appreciated her self-restraint.

Away from the others in splendid isolation, sat Larissa, whose frigid personality held the nearby ice sculptures together. Under the table, Larissa's hands were busy, and Mazzy was willing to bet half her modest salary that she was shuffling cards.

Next to these ladies sat Elisha Itzkovitch, a mystic of the worst and most dangerous kind – according to Rachel – a man who worshipped God.

The moment Mazzy was able to put him on police payroll, she added him to her team.

Mazzy watched her in-house pious man as he whipped out a small leather bound volume from his pocket and buried his nose in it. He jotted down numbers and letters into a notebook, arranging them in columns and rows, changing their order like beads on a Chinese abacus, mumbling to himself all the while.

"Fifteen equals 'spring,' but what does spring have to do with Esther? She's a girl, so maybe it should be 'spring of youth' which equals 392, whose letter value equals 'a word to the wise' or, alternately, 'salvation.' Maybe this is the key, the addition of 'youth,' which equals 376, or maybe 'peace'?"

Elisha Itzkovitch was the rising star of the Kabbalistic "Lion's Whelps" sect in Jerusalem. Popularly known as Rabbi Itzkovitch, or "The Lad," he specialized in gematria and numerology. While still a teen, he was considered an authority on Kabbalah and Jewish mysticism. His congregation raised a hue and cry when he decided to move from Safed to Jerusalem, but after assuring the leaders of the communities that he had no intention of staging a putsch or moving his followers to the Holy City, the storm subsided.

"The Find!"

All eyes at the table turned to Elisha, who thought his victory cry might have been louder than he had intended. He continued in a whisper:

"I've hit on something! I started with the number fifteen, which is the numerical equivalent of 'spring,' then I added the word 'youth' thinking I had found the answer because it has the same number as 'peace.' But then it turned out that 'youth' equals 376, which is the value meaning 'wrong interpretation.'"

Izzy and Mazzy exchanged looks. They didn't need words to agree that Itzkovitch might be a genius in his area of expertise, but listening to him was rarely an enlightening experience. Izzy was not a patient person.

"Bottom line?"

"'Spring of Youth' equals 391 involving one addition. Then I got 'Salvation' and 'Word to the Wise,' and if you add one to the initial fifteen you get 151."

"Which means?"

"A lot of things, but they all revolve around the answer. This is where 'The Find!' comes in," he declared with childlike exuberance. The perplexed looks he encountered made it clear that the twisted thread he had spun in an attempt to facilitate their trek through his inner logic did not prove helpful.

"'The Find' equals 151, which also fits 'Where it Comes from' and 'I know,' as well as 'Passover is Coming,' 'Succinctly' and 'Feather.' Each one of these expressions adds up to 151!"

"And what are we supposed to do with this information?" Mazzy hastened to ask before someone insulted her Pious Man, something that, judging by Larissa's body language, was bound to happen.

"There are several possibilities, several directions. They should check connections to Passover or spring, flowers or blooming, and ask the investigating team if anything having to do with a feather was found."

Mazzy scrutinized his resolute expression, wondering how she might approach Yariv with these breakthroughs supplied by Elisha regarding the case of Estie Shalvi, without incurring scorn. She had a problem convincing other people of what she herself was not absolutely certain. Kabbalah was not an exact science and, unlike the other disciplines she was raised on, she had to rely on the abilities of "The Lad". Izzy smiled at her knowingly, perhaps sharing her doubts, perhaps amused by Itzkovitch's outlandish approach.

"You know what else equals 151?" fired Rachel, who suddenly materialized a few feet from the table. A long moment of silence ensued, proving that Itzkovitch had finally grasped the meaning of "rhetorical question," a progress duly noted.

"Obsessive," the Godmother pronounced tersely. Mazzy's name was suddenly called out by the DJ, and before she could put out the little fire that was spreading around the table, Mazzy got up and walked to the stage.

Taking out a printed page from her pocket, she delivered a succinct, official message.

"The Israeli police carried out its duty in the same manner it would have had any other citizen been involved." Her statement elicited smirks from wall to wall. "The most important point in this affair is that Adva has been returned to her mother's arms."

It was a simple sentence, but it spoke volumes.

She added a few more words, throwing in typical press conference clichés. When the sporadic applause subsided

and the DJ pumped out heavy electronic music, Mazzy
hastened back to her seat, already plotting several possible
escape routes. Something started vibrating. Her phone.

She keyed it and covered her other ear. A man's voice
on the other end filled the space inside her head.

"This is Yariv."

"Yes?"

"A new case. Hagar Abizu, lawyer, thirty-three.
Disappeared from the 'Saving Grace' building under
bizarre circumstances, and the guy who was supposed to
watch her was apparently hurled to the pavement from an
incredible height."

"We're in the middle of Mandelbrot's shindig. Can't this
wait?"

"No, Mazzy. Look, I know we started out on the wrong
foot…"

"Now? Does it have to be now?"

"They checked the security tapes. She spoke to someone
at the entrance to the parking lot. It's not the same guy
they found downstairs."

"So who is it?"

"We don't know. No one with his build or height was
seen anywhere in the building in the last 48 hours."

"Do we have a picture of him? A sketch?"

"Only estimates of his height and weight from the angles
and compared to someone who was talking to him. And
there's something else we're not sure about, but definitely
have to look into. Assuming it's not just the reflection from
the streetlights, his hair is fair, very fair."

Only now did Mazzy notice that Rachel was sitting close
to her, listening intently. Yariv continued to report, but

she was preoccupied with Rachel. Mazzy wondered why her mother bothered to eavesdrop when she was capable of obtaining the information herself. Maybe because she knew that it would drive her daughter bonkers.

"I can barely hear you here. I'll call you from the car."

"I'm forwarding everything we've got into the system, you'll see it on the terminal in the car."

"All right."

"Let me know what you make of it … and Mazzy… this case… you've got to think differently."

The disconnecting click brought her back to the reality of Rachel's intrusive presence.

"You're going there, to the place where she disappeared?"

"There's nothing to see there. Everything is already wrapped in plastic. We'll go to the precinct, check the findings."

"You're working like them now."

"I know how to do my job."

"I didn't say you don't. But you should go to the scene. Maybe you'll sense something."

"I don't sense anything. I never do. Maybe that's what bugs you. Can I go now?"

"They don't need you to do office work."

"But they're stuck with me, poor souls."

"And the other way round."

"You mean; I should go work for the other police force? The one that doesn't exist?"

"I mean; you should decide what's best for you. I don't care about them."

"Is this why you're playing devil's advocate?"

"Someone has to."

"I'll deal with Hagar Abizu, but if I want another advocate to disappear, I'll let you know."

"Mazzy, this is too big for you. You should realize it yourself."

"That's very convincing coming from you."

As she watched her daughter gather her flock and shepherd them toward the door, Rachel wondered when Mazzy had become so resentful of her. She stopped briefly by her mother before exiting.

"You're staying here?"

"Do you care?"

"I'd rather you didn't stay here alone."

"I'll manage. Don't worry about me."

"It's not you I'm worried about."

Her team members headed to their cars; only Larissa, with a diva's impatience before a premiere, waited for the Simantov women to end their chat so that Mazzy could drive her away from the boring event she had been obliged to attend.

Mazzy kissed her mother on her cheek, which left Rachel wondering: an apology? Or just a familial façade they had to assume in public?

CHAPTER EIGHT

After a twenty-minute drive and one uncalled-for use of the police siren, Mazzy got home, planning to shower, change and report to the precinct to work on the case whose preliminary details she had just read in the car. She was familiar with the non-profit organization where Hagar Abizu worked and with the repeated threats its lawyers had been receiving.

Except for the fair hair of Hagar's interlocutor, there was no evidence to support Yariv's hypothesis that the cases were linked. Mazzy hoped that it was not a poor excuse to drag her to the office. She knew Yariv was operating on a gut feeling here; she just wasn't sure *she* could feel it.

On the other hand, as Goldfinger would remind her every time she handed in the Soothsayer monthly report, she was not merely a woman in a responsible position who had to justify the trust put in her; she was also a detective working for a unit that she herself had put together and whose work methods were a mystery to everyone else. The only relevant test was the final result.

Mazzy was greeted with the pounding of a chef's knife hitting a chopping block and the aroma of fresh salad. Gaby welcomed her with a peck on the cheek, careful not to touch her with his hands. He was wearing mesh gloves that hung in the kitchen as a constant reminder of his line of work. What bugged Mazzy was not that he wore them to chop vegetables, but that he never washed them afterwards.

"Should I work faster? You're a bit early."

"I'm going out again. I just came home to change."

"But I'm fixing…" he said in a petulant, hurt voice.

"Is she sleeping?"

"Like a baby. Which is logical."

"Any report from Aurora?"

"Nothing major. She ate chocolate pudding."

She dropped her bag on the chair, pulled out her weapon and slipped it into the gun safe.

Gaby came from behind and hugged her close to his chest.

"I'm working only morning shifts this week."

"I don't know my schedule yet."

"I was hoping we could go out sometime this week. I was going to make a reservation."

"Sounds great."

"Well, I haven't been around much lately, and we haven't gone out for a long time…"

"We'll see later in the week. I need a shower."

"Salad and omelet are not the right menu for a woman who works so hard."

"Who decided this menu?"

"Me. I prepared dinner for you."

"For us, not for me."

Mazzy knew it was not easy for him, but the proud expression he wore on the rare occasions when he did the dishes, prepared a meal, or folded laundry drove her up the wall. Gaby thought he was doing her a huge, romantic favor and failed to see why this only increased her anger. Mommy's Little Prince did not excel at household chores. Several times this week alone she had to repair his gestures. But it was a good feeling, she had to admit, to come home to a meal and a bathed child. It was time somebody did something just for her.

The amorous looks he sent her were not unpleasant either. It's nice when your husband makes an effort to please you. This was how it should be; this was what she deserved. The change Gaby had undergone in the past two weeks was finally bearing fruit, but right now she could not pick it, even though his stubbly cheeks – cultivated to the right length so as not to scratch – were sweetly rubbing against hers.

"I do appreciate it, I really do, but I have no time, sweetie. I'll get something from the vending machine or we'll order from the office, but thanks anyway…"

"We could have something delivered here, open a bottle of wine, take a bath."

Mazzy had to curb the urge to indulge; a bath was certainly an excellent reason to stay home.

"I barely have time for a shower."

"Tell them there was an emergency at home. Something you had to do."

"Like what?"

"Me."

This was the closest Gaby could come to dirty talk, and Mazzy assumed the line had been rehearsed to perfection. She was sorry to disappoint him, but she had no choice.

"I'm not really here. What you see is an illusion. I'm already on my way to work."

In the shower she turned on the hot water and shut off the outside world. A cloud of steam caressed her and, as she stood there languorously, she watched her reflection in the mirror gradually disappear. Examining the misty aura that was her image, she tried to delve into the real essence of her personality, the true self underneath the defensive shell. As she soaped up, she thought she heard footsteps in the outer room.

"Gaby?"

No response came through the steam-covered walls. Mazzy concluded that she was imagining things and had probably seen too many movies. Nobody would ever pull the shower curtain and threaten to slash her throat with a carving knife. They would simply shoot her through the glass. There was something strangely calming in modern barbarity. Mazzy returned to the hot stream, setting aside her introspection to focus on the facts that lay before her, which is what her work consisted of.

The first case: a fourteen year-old girl. She was a judge's daughter, but there was neither a ransom note nor any demand regarding past or future verdicts.

She was too old to fall prey to pedophiles, and too spoiled to be deeply involved in crime.

The second case: a woman deeply involved in crime with a long list of enemies but, in her case, too, no demands from the kidnappers. It didn't stand to reason that a robber would pick a tightly secured building that would take careful planning both to enter and escape. Connected or not, there was clearly somebody serious behind these abductions. She must be missing something here.

Then again, maybe these were two separate cases of someone skilled in not leaving clues behind. Perhaps it was someone with a previous record, someone familiar with police MOs, and procedures. A less plausible but more disturbing explanation could be that the culprit was a psycho working alone. Someone hard to track because he had no record. Now that he had started the rampage, the escalation was inevitable: from girl to woman, from a nightclub to a secured building.

The time lapse between the two incidents was also a cause for concern. The critical forty-eight hours had elapsed. Presumably, Estie is no longer alive; perhaps Hagar Abizu had joined her in what might be the first case of a serial killer in Israel.

But she must not think in these terms.

She mustn't think of the girls and women at all. Not in that way. They also needed to check connections to the security guards: those from the dumpster and the one from the "Saving Grace" building. Maybe it was a coincidence, maybe it was someone who hated women AND security guards. Maybe someone who didn't like the idea that women were protected, who wanted his victims to live in fear, who preferred a personal struggle with no outside professional involvement.

What annoyed Mazzy was the fact that all those options were part of Yariv's work, and not really part of her job. Maybe Rachel was right after all. Perhaps she had adopted the mentality of the system, gotten mired in its conception. She needed to rid herself of it all, let her imagination and suspicions take over until she reached the most absurd conclusion that only the paranormal could yield.

Mazzy tried to obliterate the image of Yariv that had taken hold of her. He was invading her home, her shower, her brain.

The shower door opened behind her, and a gust of cold air brought her back to reality. A man's hand touched her shoulder, his fingers sliding down to get a better grip and triggering an order to be fired from her brain to her arm. The elbowed assailant struck the floor and she turned to face him ready for fight or flight.

"Gaby?!"

"Are you nuts? What's the matter with you?" Her husband picked up his wounded ego from the tiled floor, examining the back of his head, ribs, and collarbone to make sure nothing was broken. Mazzy hovered above him, solicitously.

"Are you all right?"

Another joint examination yielded that what was mostly hurt was Gaby's self-respect.

"I am, but I think you're a little touched in the head."

"Sorry. I was in another place, and suddenly you came and…"

"So your first thought is to whack me?"

"I wasn't thinking anything…"

"What's going on with you?"

"With me?"

"Oh, right. What was I thinking? To take a shower in my own house. With my wife. What's wrong with me?"

"But I told you I wasn't really here. That I had to leave."

"I thought you meant that while she's asleep…like the other day at lunchtime…"

"That we do it?"

That was the term they had agreed upon. His "make love" was too cloyingly romantic and juvenile to her ears, while to him her "fuck" was just plain embarrassing.

"No, then?"

Mazzy emitted a growl of frustration. She had to restrain herself from reacting more physically.

"What do you think? That picking up Noga twice and making a salad would so wow me that I'd fuck you in the shower and forget about going to work, just because you happen to have some time on your hands? I can't even…"

"Goddamnit, Mazzy. I'm really trying here. I also have people at work who don't understand my situation. OK, maybe I wasn't so great before, but even when I make an effort, you complain."

Mazzy was suddenly tired of having to explain. "This isn't a game," she said, "I need to know that you're capable of doing things for me, for us, not because you feel like it or because you want something, but because we're partners and it's important to you. Because you care about us."

Gaby looked like a hurt child.

Mazzy switched to a softer, quieter tone.

"When I go to work… I can't think of such things. Certainly not now. Right now I need to know that Noga is taken care of, that I'm not going to come home to a sink full of dishes, that you did the laundry without being told, and that for once you watered the plants. Do you understand what I'm saying?"

"Did you even look around the house, or are you on automatic pilot? The house is clean, I gave Noga a bath and put her to bed, dinner is ready. What's wrong now?"

Silence swirled in the steamy room, like the fog of war.

Mazzy finished her frantic toweling. Gaby put his hands on her shoulders and drew his face to hers in a final attempt at reconciliation. She rebuffed him.

"You are driving me crazy," he said.

She wasn't sure if this was a final advance or a statement of fact.

"Not intentional."

"I only meant…"

"Never mind. We'll talk when I get back."

She stopped to check on Noga, then gathered her gun. This time, on her way to the precinct, she did not activate the siren or drive fast. She needed a few more minutes to regroup. No way was she going to let Yariv in on any of this. She was going to work.

CHAPTER NINE

Despite the commotion surrounding him, Azazel tried to keep his eyes on the horizon.

An emissary was about to arrive, and he was a meticulous, scrupulous angel. He had spread his wings and was poised to swoop in on his prey. Kasdaya and Pnemua were busy snipping and dyeing; they complained that Barakiel was constantly moving. The latter, however, had heftier grievances.

"Why do I have to be the one?"

"Because you know the score. You know how humans move. You'll look natural," replied Armaros.

"Stuff and nonsense! We're all the same to them. They only look at the outside."

"That's precisely why we need to go through with this."

"Yes, but why ME?"

Armaros was fed up with Barakiel's peevishness. He'd had it up to the top of his fair hair. He left his position at the desk, cluttered with fashion and style magazines, and made his way to the center of the room.

The Italian marble floor was covered with a plastic sheet; in the middle sat Barakiel, who looked like an ornery pooch at the dog parlour. Pnemua was holding a small brush and, with light motions, applying dab after dab of dye from a bowl held by Kasdaya.

Armaros stepped on the rustling plastic, staring intently at Barakiel.

"You're just getting a haircut and a dye, so stop whining, or I'll inflict some real bodily harm that will make you look truly human. Hair grows back."

"You know how long it took me to grow this?"

"How long? You're a fine one to complain about time. We each do our share. I'm sure Sahariel also has more interesting things to do than study texts about Scandinavian princes."

"Sahariel already knows these texts."

"This is why we picked him. Just as we picked you because of your affair with the lawyer."

"That was years ago, and it wasn't exactly a success story. Maybe I'm not as good at it as you think."

"Relax. You're just a backup."

Sahariel, coming in from an adjacent room, threw Barakiel a censorious look. He didn't have to be present in the room to read his twin's mood.

"Barakiel, you're not going to whine about your Abizu again, are you?"

"No."

"Fine. It's not a pretty sight when you fall apart because of some daughter of Lilith."

Barakiel lowered his eyes. Kasdaya lifted his chin so he could get on with the dyeing. As far as Barakiel was concerned, his love affair with Hagar had been short and painful.

Whatever he had learned about the mating customs of humans proved irrelevant to a relationship with a daughter of Lilith. The traditional roles he had memorized were of no use when it came to Hagar. He only angered her with his antiquated manners. And the fact that the whole affair ended in a disciplinary measure did not make it any easier.

The sound of whooshing wings came from the window, cutting short the walk down memory lane. Azazel looked magnificent in his flight.

The Naphil flapped his wings, slicing through the air, diving like a harpoon thrust into water; his strong palms stretched downward, his legs stuck together to minimize friction and his eyes blazed at the target: a weary pigeon with a ring around its leg. When he caught it, he made a perfect yawing maneuver in front of the open window, executing as stunning an entrance as his departure had been.

Shamhazai was waiting for him, ignoring the flamboyant aerodynamics.

"What's in the note?"

Azazel unraveled the paper from the carrier pigeon's ring and smoothed out the tiny square.

"Cease ye from man, whose breath is in his nostrils, for wherein is he to be accounted of?"

All eyes turned to Sahariel; he did not let them down.

"What does it mean?"

"It means they are coming. The Nephilim from overseas. Adriel is summoning his crazy cohorts and is on his way."

A uniform white-toothed smile spread throughout the room, illuminating it with the glow of hope. They all glowed with it, even the shorn one.

CHAPTER TEN

Mazzy was sitting in her office, waiting for Larissa and trying to figure out what it was that had so baffled her, so gnawed at her, other than the obvious doubts. The common denominator of the cases was the lack of a ransom demand or ultimatum, and an apparently blond guy.

None of this information came from her unit, everything flowed from Yariv as head of the investigation team. Part of the problem was that the process of deduction was based on inconclusive data, so the question she was about to pose to Larissa would be vague.

Even though the art of card reading is by nature intuitive, one needs to pose a question that will direct the reader and give her a well-defined area for investigation.

The other part of the problem was the *dramatis personae*. To wit, Yariv himself. She tried to accept the forced cooperation between them as professionally as she could, but to no avail. It only made her preoccupation with him and with herself more aggravating.

Mazzy hoped that Larissa's contribution would take the investigation to a higher level, providing data and answers she could present to Yariv, and which would allow her to become a more integral part of the investigation.

But Larissa wasn't there and, in her absence, it was Yariv who preoccupied her thoughts. But she was determined to chase him from all corners of her mind.

As the daughter of Rachel, Mazzy didn't think much of women who insisted on marrying the guy they happened to be with, but that principle held only until she met Gaby and decided that he would be hers. Not because she wanted to keep him, but because she wanted him as a partner. It was then that she first asked Rachel about her brief marriage to her father, the mysterious figure whom she had never met.

Rachel dismissed the affair in her characteristic, laconic manner.

"We got married. It wasn't successful."

This statement alone could furnish enough material for a lifetime of therapy.

"Why is it so urgent to read the cards now?" Larissa cut short her musings.

"Another woman disappeared."

Larissa sat down, her face suddenly all business. While Mazzy cleared the desk, Larissa retrieved her deck and started to shuffle.

"What is the question you want to ask?"

Mazzy settled on a two-pronged approach.

"Is it connected to the case that the head of the Special Investigation Unit is trying to solve?"

This was precise, professional and relevant, and would allow her to put the doubts and misgivings behind, focusing on the investigation itself. Larissa in the meantime counted the cards and announced them in a rigid, uninflected voice as she laid them down on the desk. The first card was placed in the center.

"The two of swords."

A blindfolded woman sitting on a shore, holding two intersecting swords over her shoulders. A crescent moon is seen over her left one.

"There is a conflict. Could be a misunderstanding, lack of communication."

Mazzy wondered if this was a reference to Hagar Abizu or to herself. Larissa's next card held the answer.

"High Priestess."

The Papess sits on a simple throne, between the black and white pillars of an Egyptian temple, a crown of moonbeams on her head and a crescent moon at her feet. She is wearing a flowing blue gown.

"This is female power, wisdom, but there are also horns, which are masculine, and aggressive. They surround her but she's too sure of herself to mind."

Mazzy had the feeling that the priestess was fixing her eyes on her, but her train of thought was soon cut short as the next card was thrown down. The tempo increased.

"The two of cups."

A man and a woman holding cups underneath a caduceus and a winged lion.

"Five of Wands."

Five young men in colorful clothes fighting each another with sticks. Another card was whipped out.

"Knight of Swords," pronounced Larissa, unable to maintain her monotonous voice. A glint of a smile seemed to light up the card reader's frozen face. A knight on a white horse brandishing a sword against an azure blue sky streaked by a white cloud.

Mazzy, too, stifled a smile. The cards proclaimed unceremoniously what was usually merely implied.

The card pointed to her recent past, with the two-dimensional figure of Yariv quite pronounced.

"The Hanged Man."

The familiar figure of the upside-down man, hovering between heaven and earth on a cross, was a surprise. Mazzy was no expert on Tarot, but over time she had absorbed and memorized the figures of the Major Arcana. The Hanged Man urges you to reexamine previous decisions, to look at things in a different way. The letter Tau formed by the branches of the tree symbolizes the confusing state of the world, torn between the material and the spiritual. This was a feminine card stressing prophetic powers, and since it was placed in the future section of the spread, Mazzy interpreted it as a good omen.

The next card was less optimistic. A figure in a black cloak examining three overturned cups, their precious liquids spilled to the ground, and behind the figure two upstanding cups and a castle in the distance.

"Five of Cups."

Mazzy was running out of time, and of cards. The General Theme card had been declared.

"Ten of Pentacles. Reversed."

"What does it mean?"

Larissa looked at Mazzy as at an impatient child who doesn't yet know the proper way things are done, but the urgency in Mazzy's voice made the card reader spit out the words quickly and gruffly.

"When the card is reversed it means that the system is collapsing. This is a card of wealth, resources, and power.

The hierarchy is changing, shifting. The generations don't understand each other. What you remember is correct, what you think about isn't. This may be related to the girl and her mother, but not a one-to-one correlation. It is general. It's bigger than the girl and the Judge's wife."

The detailed reply had its effect and Mazzy kept quiet. She let Larissa finish without further comment. The next card was the Eight of Cups, picturing a pilgrim walking away from a pyramid of cups, on a mountainside with a full moon above him.

The final card was the Chariot. The reader now focused her attention on the message that the cards delivered. She sought the general picture, seeking tortuous paths between past, present, and future.

"Your cards show many things. In your head you ask about the present, but the answers are about the past. You have swords there, but the answers should not come from the head but from the gut, from the heart. Look how many cups you've got here."

Mazzy had a few questions, but this was not the time to be distracted by her own complications; it was time to act professionally.

"You also have a lot of moons. That means time, forward movement. Maybe the message is that we need to hurry. There's a lot of flow, circular movement, madness you can't stop. If you add this to the Hanged Man then you get a lot of womanpower. You must take command of this investigation. This is where it's going. You also have wings twice, once in the future card. A messenger is trying to tell you something."

"What about the last card? The result?"

Larissa tapped her finger on the Chariot card. A princely figure driving a pair of sphinxes, one black and one white. Here, too, Mazzy noticed representations of the moon: crescent moons adorning the charioteer's breastplate. There were wings, too, on the front of the warlike chariot, and on both sides, turrets of a walled city.

"We have here a struggle between spirit and matter, between man and woman. You see a lingam under the wings? It's a symbol of the unity of the male and female. Some say that the ancient Egyptians knew about the yin and yang – this is why one sphinx is white and the other is black. We have a battle, but also victory. Great force that comes from above. And then there is something that I don't get."

"What?"

"You have twice two and twice five in the reading. Two always comes before five. This may mean something, or it may mean nothing, but it is no coincidence. The cards are trying to say something, but I don't understand exactly what."

"Anything else?"

Unusually tired, the reader shook her head. Observing sweat on her brow, Mazzy leaned forward and examined her, almost putting her hand on her shoulder; but then she remembered that Larissa did not appreciate gestures of love or sympathy.

Larissa rummaged through her bag and took out a small cardboard box containing tobacco and rolling paper. She rolled herself a cigarette and lit it. Mazzy kept looking at her intently. This time the reading had been particularly hard on the reader.

"Never mind. This will pass soon."

The card reader drank from the bottle of mineral water she always carried in her bag. The water in Israel was not to her liking. You never knew who poured what into your glass. The cigarette dangling from Larissa's mouth only added to the exertion. Mourning for her brother had left black circles under her eyes. She looked as if she had just finished an obstacle course or a long night of lovemaking. Mazzy compressed all the sympathy and guilt that Larissa's appearance aroused in her into one simple question.

"Are you all right?"

"Sure. I just want to go home."

Mazzy sighed. She called a cab and, making sure Larissa took it, handed the driver a note. Then she went back to her office. Perhaps it was time to call the subject of the question she had posed to the card reader. The less important question, presumably.

"Yariv?"

"Yes?"

"Mazzy here. I had a session with Larissa. We read the Tarot cards."

"And?"

"It's not clear cut. There's a struggle between men and women, something like yin and yang. A circular motion that has to do with time. It may result in an ultimatum that could have already been issued, except we haven't been told. The hierarchy is changing, there's a shift in the balance of powers involving a generation gap. Maybe it has to do with the Judge's wife and his daughter or with the lawyer. I'd like us to examine this further."

"OK."

"Your place or mine?"

As soon as the words came out of her mouth she could seed the smirk on his face. She would have to be the responsible adult in the room.

Yariv said nothing.

"Well?"

"I'll come over."

"Where are you?"

"Here at the crime lab. They're still processing the findings. You have to be on Doron's back if you want credible results, something that will hold water."

"I know the feeling."

"Except that your experts don't testify in court."

That was true. And infuriating. Exactly the way "they" would do things.

"Fine. Let me know if there's anything new."

She waited in her office, mulling over the possible interpretations of what the cards had presented.

THE THIRD GATE
ETERNITY

THE FIFTEENTH DAY
TWO WEEKS AND A DAY OF THE COUNTING OF THE OMER

"And there came forth a spirit, and stood before the Lord and said, I will persuade him. And the Lord said unto him, Wherewith?"

1 Kings 22:21

Barakiel's scalp tingled. He thought his hair was itching, but he knew that was impossible. It had nothing to do with his shorn hair or the fact that his roots were dyed black. He itched inside and out. Even his wings, tucked inside his chest cavity, were itching. It wasn't physiological; he knew the sensation, and what it heralded. The first time he had felt it was before the gate was closed and they went down.

The second time was when he met Hagar. He tried to ignore her, but couldn't: not her, or the itch.

Barakiel tried to calm down; it was natural to feel like this when the return to Heaven was so imminent. He had a peculiar feeling, and not just because of the unpleasant itch. He was sitting in the middle of the theater, acutely aware that on this side of the stage there was not a single man or woman that resembled him.

The only one who did was Sahariel, waiting behind the scenery for the right moment.

The gala night was in homage to Milka Umm-Alzabian.

The British troupe had grown around her, and this daughter of Lilith looked like a natural for that role. They had started as a marginal troupe, a fringe theater, but a string of well-orchestrated reviews and a carefully selected repertoire brought them to the top.

The "Alternative Shakespeare Company" came on stage, with Milka as its uncontested star. In a program entitled "Evening of Tragedies," Barakiel had just watched a modern dance version of *King Lear*, a gospel adaptation of *Othello* that sorely tried his patience, and died a thousand times during *Julius Caesar*. Saharel had elected to watch *Hamlet* and *Macbeth*.

Milka Umm-Alzabian had a pivotal position in this important theatrical enterprise; Saharel paid a hefty sum for someone to give up their coveted tickets.

The audience finished clapping, and a hush descended on the theater. The empty stage suddenly filled with thick smoke. A wind blew in from the north, billowing into a big cloud that gave off sparks of electricity. Such a sound and light extravaganza was unexpected, even in an "alternative theater" performance like this.

Sporadic applause from Shakespeare aficionados was heard in the hall, but mostly the surprised audience stared expectantly at the cloud-shrouded stage. A curly haired, stern looking critic turned on a penlight and started scrawling on her pad.

"The Alternative Shakespeare Company blew us over with an innovative, pyrotechnical interpretation of the encounter between Hamlet and his father. Four figures on unicycles burst out of a cloud of smoke. After a short display of acrobatics, the actors presented a stunning and inspiring spectacle. With gigantic wings attached to their backs, the four ran around the stage filling the air with the divine text of William Shakespeare; clearly something original and pregnant with meaning was occurring. The actors wore *commedia dell'arte* masks representing a lion, bull, and eagle; only the actor portraying the ghost – as could be inferred from the sign around his neck – wore a white human mask with a long nose, in the style of the *capitano*. Excellent lighting created an aura around the actors, investing them with celestial radiance. The felicitous choice of *Hamlet*, the prototype of modern tragedy, was greatly appreciated by the audience."

Barakiel stopped reading over the critic's shoulder. He could not fathom her meaning and wondered if it was because she was a human, a woman, or a theater critic. He turned his eyes back to the stage.

"Angels and ministers of grace defend us! Be thou a spirit of health or goblin damned, bring with thee airs from heaven or blasts from hell, be thy intents wicked or charitable…"

The actor playing Marcellus wore the bull mask. The critic's pen worked furiously. Milka continued to exhibit her artistic credo.

"Why, what should be the fear? I do not set my life in a pin's fee; And for my soul, what can it do to that, being a thing immortal as itself? It waves me forth again: I'll follow it."

Only now that the words had come out of the mouth of Lilith's Daughter did he grasp the subtle irony that so delighted Saharel. He watched her arguing with her friends, insisting on following the ghost, and appreciated the irony too.

"Have after. To what issue will this come?"

"Something is rotten in the state of Denmark."

"Heaven will direct it."

Barakiel shot looks in the direction of the stage and the wings. As the fifth scene progressed, the activity and the noise intensified, with the shifting of props and the muffling of footsteps. Between the folds of the curtain he discerned a female figure dressed in gray rags, presumably one of the witches from the next play in the program. The tattered rags reminded him of another unearthly creature, the one from Seder night who turned their world into total chaos. On stage, the lines followed one another, and the *Hamlet* segment was about to end.

"O day and night, but this is wondrous strange!"

"And therefore as a stranger give it welcome. There are more things in heaven and earth, Horatio, than are dreamt of in your philosophy. But come…"

An old man next to him coughed audibly, causing the actors a momentary distraction. Four pairs of masked eyes stared at the row where he sat. Barakiel imagined it was Saharel reciting the last verse from behind the stage.

"The time is out of joint: O cursed spite, that ever I was born to set it right!"

Thunderous peals of applause unfurled. Milka hurried backstage to change. The troupe celebrated her theatrical achievement by including her in every scene, though not always in a leading role.

The clapping subsided only when the three witches came on stage. One crone asked the others to help her wreak vengeance on a sailor's wife who refused to share her chestnuts with her.

"I will drain him dry as hay: Sleep shall neither night nor day hang upon his pent-house lid; he shall live a man forbid: weary sev'nights nine times nine shall he dwindle, peak and pine: though his bark cannot be lost, yet it shall be tempest-tossed. Look what I have."

That was the cue for Barakiel to get ready. The tingling in his hair intensified. A drum roll from the edge of the stage cut short the imminent panic attack. The moment had come. There was no room for shilly-shallying.

Whatever was shall be, be it eternal life or death.

Milka uttered her last verse. The three witches murmured an incantation, lifting their eyes. Barakiel was afraid they might notice Saharel lurking between the beams and the curtain ropes.

"The weird sisters, hand in hand, posters of the sea and land, thus do go about, about: Thrice to thine and thrice to mine and thrice again, to make up nine. Peace! The charm's wound up."

Barakiel shot up from his seat, ready for action. If Saharel made a mistake, he'd have to correct it.

Saharel flew down from his perch, spreading his wings, and to Barakiel it seemed as if all eyes were focused on his comrade. In the hushed hall, all he heard was his own heartbeat. A gleaming bright light blinded the audience and thick smoke filled the air. Barakiel saw his accomplice grab Milka, then sprinkle a handful of shorn golden hair over her. Milka collapsed, but Saharel seized her by the waist before she hit the floor and carried her upward, disappearing into the forest of ropes and lighting equipment.

The star of the evening was no longer on the stage. Milka Umm-Alzabian had vanished into thin air.

CHAPTER ELEVEN

A peculiar sensation, born of a mother's instinct, again caused Rachel to wake up with a start and gasp for air. No mother is immune to anxiety, but this kind was reserved exclusively for her one and only daughter.

There were nights when she could justify the fear.

When your little girl is asleep in the adjacent room, an invisible umbilical cord winds its way from your bed, through the hallway and over the rug, straight to the center of the tiny brittle universe, which is your offspring. It was the tugging of this invisible cord that made Rachel's stomach turn and alerted her to possible danger. Rachel could not dismiss her premonition as hormonal imbalance or unfounded anxiety.

She knew; she had experience.

The invisible cord became a hissing serpent.

It was a recurring nocturnal vision, but she was not dreaming; the vision did not originate in her mind. It was transmitted by bursts and spurts, open spaces, unfamiliar scenery, being hoisted from the ground and hovering in the air. Burnt feathers drifting slowly to the ground; an acrid smell in her nostrils. Looking down she saw scorched earth and smoldering embers whose blue flames were fanned by a wind. In front of her a huge white cloud spewed tongues of fire and flashes of electricity. Four figures on unicycles emerged from the cloud, with huge wings that blocked her view. She was dragged upwards, disappearing into what looked like the masts of a galleon or a forest of ropes.

Rachel sat bolt upright in her bed. It took a long moment before she could breathe normally.

She must talk to Mazzy. She must warn her. A glance at the window confirmed it was already morning. On the nightstand she noticed a jar of night cream she had used before going to sleep. The cream smelled of nuts, milk and wild berries. But the odor of burnt feathers was overwhelming. The combined scent of cream and fear reminded her of distant nights when Mazzy would sneak into her bedroom, frightened and weeping, to complain about monsters in the closet that had invaded her dreams. Rachel was not your average mother, and her solutions were not conventional. She would open the drawer of her nightstand and take out the magic potion, a vial of anise perfume given to her, God knows why, by one of her suitors. This was the anti-monster spray. Sometimes she would pretend to be asleep when she heard the pitter-patter of Mazzy's bootie-clad feet approaching the bed. A tiny hand would open the drawer and hurry out again. The next day, when she came into her daughter's room to wake her up for school, a strong smell of licorice would greet her. On those rare mornings, she allowed Mazzy to linger in bed.

Rachel needed some fresh air, the smell of a new day, or at least a whiff of licorice in an airless room. But when she opened the window, she discovered flakes of ash descending on the city like black snow.

CHAPTER TWELVE

Outside the precinct windows, black flakes floated in the morning breeze. But as far as the pair was concerned, the world could go to hell in a handcart. After being cooped up there for two consecutive days, they ignored the ashes raining down like dark cotton candy. The air pollution monitoring stations were reporting unprecedented levels and instructing asthma sufferers and pregnant women to stay home. After several attempts to identify the source and point fingers at possible culprits, it was surmised that the cause was volcanic activity, except that no volcano in the region was smoking. Yariv, on the other hand, was averaging three packs a day.

He and Mazzy were busy looking for new clues to crack the case, something to connect the dots, or at least steer them in a new direction, away from the data and the witness reports they had gone over dozens of times.

In an attempt to relieve the tedium, Yariv took his cellphone outside and dialed the number of the crime lab. He waited a few seconds until he heard Doron's weary voice on the other end of the line.

"This is the Special Investigations Unit. Can I ask you a few questions?"

"Biton, what do you want?"

"You still owe me an answer."

"About the business with Rosolio? I left you a message this morning."

"Doron, you know I don't listen to your messages. Why do you insist on leaving them?"

"Biton, what do you want from me?"

"What's the oddest thing you found in the nightclub where the Judge's daughter was abducted?"

"A black feather. Someone on our team said it didn't belong to any known bird, but it wasn't synthetic."

This was unexpected. And inconvenient. What could he do with this finding?

"How does this person know that?"

"His hobby is ornithology."

"Tell him to stay away from my dick."

"That's urology, dickhead. Ornithology is the study of birds."

"So what d'you call the guy who straightens your teeth?"

"Give me a break, Biton. I have a whole storehouse to sort out. I don't have time for this."

"OK, hand it over."

"What will you do with it?"

"I have a gut feeling about this feather. Anyway, what do you care, you'll have one less thing to catalog."

"Fine, we'll save it for you."

Yariv hung up and returned to Mazzy's office. His face was expressionless; he had not yet decided if he should share Doron's news with her.

Mazzy lifted her head from the desk that was covered with reports, photos, and drawings. She carved out a square from the clutter and tapped on it to draw his attention.

Some of the reports had colored tags attached to them, and rubber bands collated others, but a complete picture had not emerged from the pieces of the puzzle.

"We're missing something here. It's like those pictures you see at the mall or at the Central Bus Station."

"What are you talking about?"

"You know, those 3D pictures. You have to focus on the dots, on the patterns, and then suddenly something appears. Dolphins."

"I don't think so. I've been up to my neck in these papers for two and a half days, and nothing. Not even dolphins. Maybe I'm not smoking the right stuff."

She let the air out of her lungs. He blew smoke from his.

"Let's refresh ourselves."

"Yeah, I've seen you refresh yourself."

"Come on, breathe some fresh air."

Mazzy ruffled the papers in front of her.

"Let's go over it again."

Yariv cooperated, reviewing the data in a monotonous voice, clutching at straws, hanging on for dear life.

"First abduction, nightclub, blond guy, no ransom, no body, no evidence."

Mazzy squinted, as if to sharpen her vision.

"Second abduction, rooftop, a guy with blond hair, no ransom, no body, hail, no evidence except for a partial print."

"Maybe it's weather related?"

"How come?"

"Maybe he waits for unusual weather conditions, and they enable him to carry out the abductions? A night of heavy hail, or like today, when people's windows and shutters are closed. No witnesses, no line of vision. Anything like this the night Estie was kidnapped?"

Yariv took out a notebook and leafed through its crumpled pages.

"It was foggy, and there was smoke from smoke generators. Is this what you have in mind?"

"Could be. Maybe these cinders provide an excellent opportunity for another abduction."

"Maybe we're stuck on this blond guy?"

"Meaning?"

"Maybe he's not blond. Lots of people have light hair, and anyway we don't have a real suspect that we can confidently place at both scenes. What about your guys?"

She scrutinized him, trying to gauge his readiness.

"Itzkovitch says we need to focus on a feather, spring, Passover, or even flowers."

"Feather?"

"Yep."

"Are you sure that's what he said?"

"I'm sure."

He thought it best not to say anything. It was one of those coincidences that become significant only when someone says something at the right moment. Or the wrong one. Yariv needed time to think, to be sure of himself. Over the last few days they had reverted to their old routines. He needed to be in the driving seat for now.

"You know what, maybe you're right. Perhaps it's not the same guy, but two different cases. Which one do we stick with? The Special Investigations team was set up for the Judge's daughter, but we both know that the chances are slim that she's still… you know. The second abduction could go in a dozen different ways. It could be criminal; it could be romantic. It's a bit too elaborate to be political. If we separate the two, what have we got? What can we work on separately that we didn't cover as one case?"

"Yeah, that doesn't leave us much."

"We could wait. Eighty percent of our work is waiting."

"Wait for what?"

"Another abduction. Two cases don't make a statistic. Another one will create a series. If your theory is correct, we won't have long to wait."

This made sense, warped sense, but still. It was the toehold they needed to make progress. She was tired of treading water.

"We need to get out of here. To get something done."

"Want to go to the shooting range?"

"Are you serious?"

Every couple has their own private therapy, their own method of relaxation. Some, when things don't work out and they need to take a break, go to the movies or to a good restaurant.

Others prefer to take a walk or visit friends. Some go south to the desert, or to a B&B in the Galilee.

In the old days when Yariv and Mazzy had issues, which were quite often, they went shooting. They were no longer a couple, but therapy is therapy. And they needed some fresh air.

They shouted hello to the range supervisor as they hurried in, and he bawled them out for being so cavalier about security. There were no other shooters around. Yariv took out his Jericho, then a deep breath, closed one eye and focused the other. He could almost feel the bullets spinning down the barrel as he pulled the trigger. He aimed the first round a little lower, aware of the flinching effect, then fired a cluster. The bullets hit the target a little too high. He wasn't focused.

Yariv was not thinking about his own Jericho but about the shooter next to him whose gun emitted measured, regular barks. He stopped and listened to Mazzy in the adjacent booth. When she was his subordinate, she had made a point of flaunting her Jericho, to show everyone she was using a proper gun, not just a .22.

He fired ten more bullets that tore the bullseye off its wooden frame, but he kept hearing Mazzy, firing furiously. Was she using magazines with more bullets? Even so… Son of a gun, she had switched to a Glock since they were last at the range together. It was a bit of a blow to his ego. He reckoned she had six bullets left.

Yariv knew what he had to do to restore the balance. He bent down to his holdall, drew out an ancient homemade Double-barreled Beretta, chambered two shells and let loose with both barrels at his target. Splinters shot to the ceiling; the paper target turned to confetti that swirled around the floor. Silence fell on the firing range.

Yariv took off his ear protectors. Two familiar human sounds filled the air: Mazzy's cascading laughter that stopped only when she came up for air, and the range supervisor ordering both of them to leave the premises forthwith. Even when they were out, Mazzy could not control herself. It took the entire ride back to the station for Yariv to get a straight answer out of her.

"You're completely screwed up."

"Why?"

"You destroyed the entire firing lane. What was that cannon you were using there?"

"You mean the Lupara."

"I don't care what you call it. What is it anyway?"

"Double-barreled sawn-off shotgun, the kind favored by Sicilian Mafiosi. It's homemade. I got it in Naples about two or three years ago."

"You were in Italy?" Her smiling voice was tinged with disappointment. When they were together, she had planned a trip to Italy, but Yariv called it off because Europe, he said, was for old folks, and he would go there only when he retired and needed comfy hotels; in the meantime, as long as he could stay in hostels, motels, and guesthouses, he would rather go to more exotic destinations.

"Rome, Florence, Venice, Naples, Capri. Fourteen days, including shopping. A terrific deal. I was in Rome, too…"

"You said Rome."

"That's where I had the best time. When I got to Naples, I missed my *stazione* and had to look for a modest B&B. To cut a long story short, the landlady's mom, about a hundred years old, eyed me suspiciously. One night, when I was almost asleep, there she was, standing above me, aiming this ancient firearm. I'm lying there, looking these two barrels right in the eye, when the old lady turns the gun around with the butt towards me, and hands it over, then out of her pocket she takes a coarse jute bag with squashed bullets and tosses it on the bedspread. She mutters something in Italian and leaves the room. I check the thing, and, realizing it's not loaded, put it in my suitcase.

However, in the middle of the night, I'm consumed with curiosity, so with my Leatherman I open one of the bullets, and inside, mixed with the powder, I find all kinds of ground bones, dried herbs, and pieces of what look like animal entrails. The next day, when I checked out, I asked the landlady, half in English, half in phrasebook Italian, what it was the old lady had said to me. She turned white and said her mother was very old and tended to believe in superstitions, demons, and spirits. She apologized for what had happened. But I insisted, and finally she told me that what her mother said was: This can finish off anything, angel or demon."

Mazzy pursed her lips in appreciation. They continued to drive without uttering a word.

"Tell me, you expect me to believe this nonsense?"

"Why not?"

"Where does it really come from?"

"An old woman sold it to me one Saturday at the flea market in Jaffa. At least that sentence she said is true."

"I'm happy for both of you."

"I even carried it on me for about a week, while we were together."

"Fascinating, Yariv. It really warms my heart."

It was clear from her facial expression that he should have left out the last detail, perhaps the entire story. At least he was smart enough not to tell her that the old lady sent regards to Rachel and Mazzy. Enough with all the nostalgia; it would only get him in trouble.

"But it's a nice story, isn't it?"

"Terrific."

When they got to the precinct, they found Sima waiting for them with crossed arms.

"Goldfinger wants to see you," she said to Yariv.

"Me?"

"No, the other idiot who blew up the shooting range today. When will you grow up, Biton?"

"What did he say?"

"That he's going to dock your salary and, in the disciplinary hearing, you'll probably get a fine. And that, instead of solving your personal problems, you shoot at things."

That was not the image he wanted to project to his boss right now. He was an investigator; his job was to bring things to light, either from the ground or from the air. Perhaps what he heard from Doron might yield something useful. Anything to advance the investigation.

"When Goldfinger is done razzing me, I have something to tell you," he said to Mazzy.

"About what?"

"About a black feather our plastic friends found."

CHAPTER THIRTEEN

The minutes Gaby spent meticulously scrubbing his hands were his quiet time. He held the small bar of soap between thumb and finger, rubbing the skin vigorously and shedding dead cells, making way for new ones. He always discerned shapes, patterns, and images in the frothy lather. This was his very private secret.

When you perform the same ritual more than a hundred times a month, thousands of times a year, and often for nothing because the operation has been canceled or because your role in it is inconsequential, you find special ways to renew your spirit.

Here he was, retreating back into his work and introspection. Next, he'd blame the long hours and paucity of sleep, the stress and the constant shuttling between the ER and the wards.

Today he had to talk to her. It was becoming embarrassing. He'd put it off long enough. If you can't have a conversation with the woman you're married to, then maybe you do have a problem expressing yourself. Perhaps the gibes about his strict upbringing and his demanding mother had some truth to them.

But it wasn't only about him. There were more important

things than his hang-ups and his fear of confrontation. Noga needed to learn sign language.

She was his daughter, too, and her future was at stake. It was time he became proactive, not just a passive participant in her upbringing.

He had done all the preparation: read the relevant articles, consulted colleagues, spoken on the phone with experts. Now it was time to tell her how simple and obvious the solution was. Noga was smart, this was not just a proud father's opinion. Even Aurora told him so whenever he picked Noga up from daycare. His cute little girl had no problem absorbing information. The problem was with dishing it out. He knew this trait first hand and blamed himself for having bequeathed it to her.

Gaby looked at his reflection in the mirror and saw a confident surgeon in uniform and cap. He rehearsed the prepared speech in his head, focusing on the crucial section.

"Young children who learn sign language make significant gains and show great progress; they score better on IQ tests, their verbal comprehension is broader, they enrich their vocabulary. Sign language serves also as an incentive to vocal language, encouraging the emergence of the first words. Studies show increased communication, reduction in frustration, improved self-image, a richer inner world and finer, more nuanced connection with the immediate environment."

He sounded just like the articles he had read, the explanations and testimonies he had heard. This data should suffice. It was irrefutable.

Gaby rinsed his hands, folded his elbows and spread his fingers out like a fan. The next stage in the ritual was entering the OR and having his hands dried by a nurse.

The nurse was a young one, eager to please. She had prepared the right size gloves, the right thickness and no talc, just as he liked it. It was as if he were the master of ceremonies, the chief surgeon. Except that here, too, he played second fiddle. In the background, Gaby heard *Pure Souls*, the chief surgeon's favorite CD.

At a certain point during the operation, he had to restrain an urge to pick up a scalpel and drive it hard into Professor Pomerantz's palm. If he had to hear the one about "Bertha's coffee" one more time, he might just succumb to temptation. But for now, he smiled at the professor's oft-told joke, a feigned smile that employed only his eyes above the surgical mask. Then he bent over the patient, swabbed the slight bleeding, as requested, checked vitals when needed and above all, tried to muster the courage to confront Mazzy.

CHAPTER FOURTEEN

Something was gnawing at Rachel. She was in the middle of interpreting coffee dregs and was eager to end the session. With a subtle motion, she urged the client to finish her coffee. The latter brought the cup to her lips, drank the liquid and handed it to the reader. Rachel turned the cup upside down on a china plate, and proceeded to examine the dregs.

Her thoughts, though, drifted to a man's face reflected in the shiny, dark surface of her own coffee. The stern, chiseled face was surrounded by long black tresses interspersed with a few silver strands.

Rachel fell silent for a long moment, trying to focus on the task at hand.

The client, something of a coffee reader herself, was annoyed. It shouldn't be taking such a long time. Not for someone of Rachel's stature. Rachel always knew the answer, pure and simple.

"Do you see anything?"

Rachel shook off the memory of the man's face, his burning eyes and ardent determination. The surprise visit of Mazzy's father would have to be put on hold.

"He's all right. Just overworked. That's the truth; there's nobody else. You're the only one."

"It's hard to see straight when it's so close, when it's your own family."

"That's why I'm here. If you still have doubts, we can check again. Right now, everything seems fine."

Rachel's client got to her feet, leaving some cash in the straw basket by the door. She wanted to turn around to watch Rachel drink her coffee, but something stopped her, so she made her way to the main entrance and left.

A shudder coursed through Rachel's body, followed by a sudden stinging cold. An unmistaken sensation, shattering, gut-wrenching.

The first time she had experienced this feeling was when she met Mazzy's father. This time it was a little vaguer, but still scary. She knew something was going to happen, something bigger than herself and Mazzy combined.

She grabbed the phone.

A curt, impatient voice answered.

"Yes?"

"There's another one."

"I know. Sima just told me about the actress. I'm on my way there."

"There'll be others."

"How do you know?"

"From the coffee, and that's what worrying."

"Who visited you?"

"You must let me help with this investigation."

"You're not answering my question."

"I will, but it's a bit ambiguous. Apart from the fact that this is much bigger than we thought."

"You're welcome to come to the precinct whenever you like. After the crime scene, I'll come back here."

"I'll be there."

"OK."

"And, Mazzy, double check everything."

"It's my job; I'll manage. Is there a connection to the ash that came down earlier?"

Rachel hung up without answering. She believed her daughter when she said she'd manage, but she still worried. She looked outside the window and realized that Mazzy had been right about the falling ashes. But her mother's instincts were on high alert. Something was threatening her daughter, casting a shadow over her, a large heavy shadow. Like an eclipse obscuring the sun.

Rachel walked over to the big mirror and removed the cloth that covered it. Israel's image was reflected in the shiny surface. It lingered for a long moment before evaporating, leaving behind a blazing message:

For three things the earth is disquieted, and for four which it cannot bear.

CHAPTER FIFTEEN

Almost three hundred people sat facing the stage, and not one of them could bear witness. Some thought they had seen something, but most repeated the same vague story: the swirling smoke and dry ice turned the drama on stage into an impenetrable conundrum.

Backstage too, there were no great revelations. The spotlights were positioned exactly as they had been during the abduction. Mazzy stood in the middle of the stage, and Yariv could not take his eyes off her. She was not doing anything out of the ordinary – marking various locations and trying not to disrupt Doron and his team who were staging a sound and light show of their own. Mazzy had just finished a phone call, and to Yariv, the motion of returning her phone to its case was the most charming sight he had ever seen. Then she started leafing through her notes and the magic was gone.

Yariv felt in his pocket for the black feather Doron had given him. There was something comforting in it, something novel. He wasn't sure why he found it necessary to keep it so close to him. Yariv hastened down the stairs to the stalls, skipping steps. Mazzy looked agitated, which only added to her charm.

"What happened?"

"What happened? Everybody is nuts. A theater full of people, and no one sees anything. Doron and the Plastics are already spouting conspiracy theories about an alien abduction. They found hair scattered around. Hair that does not belong to the victim and without roots, as if it had been cut. And it's not just the regular investigation. My unit's gone crazy, too. Rachel calls to offer her help; Izzy insists on checking out the witness. Larissa is nowhere to be found, and Itzkovitch, who you can normally call at four am, on his way to the *mikvah* or the synagogue, is suddenly unavailable. Have you got anything?"

"Sort of. We got lucky with the invitations. We checked the list of people who didn't show up. There's only one, a critic who scalped his ticket. He asked us not to tell his editor, but he just couldn't say no."

"Someone threatened him to get the ticket?"

"Someone offered an incredible sum. Must have wanted to see *Macbeth* really bad."

"We have a name?"

"Yes. The critic left the invitation at the box office, and the guy picked it up there."

"Should we go?"

He was eager for them to get into the police car, where just the two of them would fill the space, without the noise and commotion of the crime scene. Even though Mazzy did not spend much time in her official car, she treated herself to a superior sound system, with sub-woofers and an equilizer. This was her way of personalizing the car, after being penalized by Goldfinger for decorating the dashboard with fluffy pink fur and hanging a voodoo doll on the rearview mirror. Since then she had to make do with this funked-up sound system and a huge *Hamsa* charm glued to the dash. Let the boss try to chew her out for a *Hamsa*!

As she tapped on the steering wheel to the rhythm of some track he didn't recognize, Yariv reminisced about a trip they had taken to the desert in a rental car. When the radio died, Mazzy said that from now on, she would be their station. If only they had continued their duet, he thought.

A few turns and junctions later, they arrived in the neighborhood where the critic lived. The address was in an area that looked deliberately designed to have no distinctive character, an architectural conglomeration of cottages, terraced houses, condos, and single-family homes. None of them left any impression or possessed any individual traits. They reminded Yariv of witnesses trying to describe a totally unremarkable scene.

"I think that's the address."

"How can you tell them apart?"

"Numbers help."

Mazzy exhaled through flared nostrils, like a thoroughbred mare, and got out of the car. They were in front of a cookie cutter duplex, with a manicured lawn. A few steps later they were standing by a ceramic sign and on a squeaky clean doormat. Mazzy rang the bell. A tall, handsome man with short-cropped hair opened the door.

The moment he laid eyes on him, Yariv decided he couldn't stand him. He ascribed it to a detective's gut feeling. The fact that the stranger was taller, stronger and handsomer did not help, either. He was the type Yariv saw at the gym, admiring his own reflection in the mirror.

"I'm Chief Inspector Yariv Biton, and this is my partner. We're investigating the incident at the theater."

"I already spoke to one of your people at the theater."

"We'd like to go over a few details."

The tall man moved away from the door, letting the detectives in. As soon as she entered, Mazzy detected a whiff of anise; the strange smell afforded her a sense of security she had not felt in years. She hastened to give the man her hand.

"Mazzy Simantov."

"Pleased to meet you."

"And you are?"

The routine question made him raise his shoulders, as if someone had stuck a stave between his blades.

"You've got it written down, don't you?"

"It says Barak Almadon."

"If that's what it says, then that's what it is."

"Are you related to Almadon from Haifa?" Yariv tried smalltalk.

"I doubt it. We're a very small family."

Mazzy looked around. There was something weird about the room, as if a designer had worked hard to invest it with a "natural" look and achieved the opposite effect. And in spite of the soothing anise smell, the décor gave the impression of something strained, ominous even. She tried to be nice.

"You have a lovely house."

"Thank you, but you didn't come to look at my house, right?"

"No."

Something in the quick repartee did not sit well with Yariv. Ditto for the aroma. He smelled *shakshuka* being prepared with fresh tomatoes and herbs, except that Almadon did not look like a candidate for Master Chef. This, too, registered with Yariv.

"Sometimes people remember things after the fact, all kinds of details that didn't occur to them at the time."

"Not me."

"Have you witnessed such events before?"

"No, but I deal in details. I'm an information broker."

Mazzy and Yariv exchanged inquiring looks. This Barak was obviously a strange duck. He wanted to be questioned, but his answers were selective. He would make an excellent witness in court.

"Pardon my ignorance, but what does that mean?" Mazzy said.

"I collect information and analyze it for companies and individuals."

"Like a search engine, a sort of human Google?" Yariv suggested with a hint of mockery. Mazzy shot him a menacing look.

"Yeah, kind of."

"So there's nothing new you can tell us?"

"Not really. I've already said everything I had to say."

"Do you earn a lot of money from this job?"

"I make ends meet."

"And yet you shelled out two thousand shekels for a theater ticket."

"Is it a crime to pay for a good show?"

"Every ticket has a price, and yours was just too steep."

A flash of anger passed over Almadon's face. He quickly resumed his serene look.

"Would you mind coming to the police station with us?"

"Am I being charged with something?"

Mazzy took the reins.

"No, no. It's just that we have experts there who might be able to obtain more information from you." She hoped that her use of "obtain" would do the trick. She continued:

"These are people with good ears. It's very helpful when they hear something first hand. The more info we get and the sooner, the sooner we can make progress in the investigation and find the missing Ms Umilzaban."

"It's pronounced Umm-Alzabian. The Umm is separate, as in Umm-Kulthum."

Names were important to him, Mazzy noted. He made a point of pronouncing them correctly, insisting on every detail.

Yariv was not interested. "Umm-Shmumm. Do you know her?"

"No. But I read about her. I always read about the actors before I see a play. There was some write-up in the brochure they handed out. Didn't you read it?"

"Tell me, BA-rak," Yariv deliberately mispronounced his name. "Is there anything you don't know?"

"It's pronounced Ba-RAK," corrected the witness.

"And when you were little, what did they call you?"

"That was such a long time ago. Seems like it never happened."

Mazzy was becoming impatient. Both with this man's evasions and Yariv's time wasting.

"So, will you come with us to the station?"

"Can I drive myself?"

"Sure."

"Do I need to call a lawyer?"

"No. Why?"

"Because if I do, I need to find one."

"There is no need, really."

"When people say 'no need,' it usually means 'you'd better do it.'"

Mazzy thought of all the times that Naomi, Gaby's mother, said, 'No need to worry,' or 'you don't need to work so hard,' or 'you needn't always prove you're right.' The guy was pretty perceptive.

"Well, you can get one if you want."

He gave them a distrustful look. If they didn't leave soon, they'd need a warrant to summon him to testify a second time at the police station, after he had given a written statement at the theater.

"We'll wait for you."

Barak nodded and, without a word, showed them the door. Yariv shot out of the house, almost running to the police car, but Mazzy took her time.

"C'mon," he urged her.

"If you don't want to walk to the precinct, you'd better calm down. Someone once taught me that it's best to keep the cards close to your chest and not just throw them on the table. Do you know who it was? Yariv Biton."

"When you're holding a full house, the timing doesn't really matter. The actress's clock is ticking."

"But now, because of the pressure you put on him, he'll lawyer up. Why do you have to complicate everything?"

Yariv got in the car and didn't say a word during the

ride. He didn't share with Mazzy his gut feeling about the witness, and his pulse was racing from being cooped up with her in an enclosed space. He'd have to do something about this soon.

Mazzy wondered who the best person would be to interrogate this Barak Almadon. She knew the answer and it displeased her. Her cellphone rang.

"Well, when are you getting here?" Rachel's exhortation was just as disagreeable to her as Yariv's was earlier.

"Where are you?" Mazzy wanted to know.

"At the station. Waiting for you and Almadon. Your hippie is here too."

There was no point asking Rachel how she knew his name, nor rebuking her about Izzy.

"We're on our way."

Sima greeted Mazzy and Yariv with a sulk.

"Next time you open a Situation Room here, let me know beforehand."

Mazzy glanced at the crowd waiting in the room and, to her surprise, saw not only Rachel and Izzy, but also Ashling and Aelina. Doron from the crime lab was sitting on the edge of the bench, trying to keep his distance from the clairvoyants. When he saw Mazzy and Yariv, his face lit up.

"Which room is available?" Mazzy asked.

"Three. And Goldfinger would like you to coordinate such things with him, if possible."

Yariv entered the interrogation room and began his usual meditation. He stared at the empty chair across the table, imagining Barak Almadon sitting in it. Outside the room, pandemonium reigned, but Yariv heard nothing but his intuition. He'd only just met the witness and already couldn't stand him. But this feeling was easier to deal with than his other trouble.

CHAPTER SIXTEEN

"How did they get to me so fast?"

"Technical error. Will be corrected."

"Yes, you paid far too much for the ticket."

"Happens. That's not important right now. Calm down."

"Don't tell me to calm down!"

"How are they?"

"I don't know."

"You think you'll manage?"

"I'll manage. Do I need a lawyer?"

"It will only take longer. Just play dumb. Cooperate and they'll have to let you go. It's not a crime to see a play."

"The woman – there's something grating about her."

"Do you know who she is?"

"No, does it matter?"

He thought he felt Saharel's lips stretch into a grin on the other end of the line. Barakiel was still perturbed.

"When do we go collect the next one?"

"In a day or two."

"The professor?"

"What do you care? Right now, all you need to do is give them a few simple answers and bide your time."

"When this whole affair is over, we're going to have a long talk."

"We're not going anywhere."

Barakiel called a cab to take him to the police station.

CHAPTER SEVENTEEN

Almadon was too calm for someone who was clean. Yariv could tell the difference between a nabbed perpetrator under pressure and an innocent man in the same situation. Those who were guilty without showing any sign of stress were the toughest clients.

"So you have no objection?"

"Do what you want. I have done nothing wrong. You can bring in all the Uri Gellers in the world. It won't bother me."

Mazzy thanked Almadon for his open-mindedness and, as a gesture of good will, ordered him a cup of coffee. Surely, an innocent witness would not refuse a cup of coffee. Rachel and Doron were eagerly awaiting the findings, and when they arrived, they each hastened to apply their craft. Rachel emptied the dregs onto a saucer, and Doron took the cup straight to the lab.

Goldfinger sat in the observation room as the responsible adult, making sure that nobody overstepped their bounds.

Izzy came out of the interrogation room and entered the observation room in a state of great agitation. Yariv and Goldfinger were watching Ashling as she felt the witness's temples. Goldfinger was about to protest when Barak Almadon calmly turned his face to the camera, smiling beatifically.

Ashling left Almadon and flapped her hands, as if trying to dry them. It was now Aelina's turn to face him.

"I hope she's not trying to hypnotize him. No judge in the world will admit such evidence in court, especially if it's self-incriminating, if that's what you're looking for."

Yariv tried to allay his boss's fears, even though he himself was just as disconcerted by the scene.

"Don't worry. This may look unconventional, but it's common practice in Europe."

Mazzy approached her aura-reader, who sat in the corner looking preoccupied and conflicted.

"Well?"

"I have never seen anything like this."

"What?"

"He's perfect. Simply perfect."

Mazzy agreed that Barak Almadon was an exceptionally attractive man. His physique and posture were made for sculptures and poets. But she hoped that Izzy would approach him more professionally.

"This is all you have to say after an interview?"

"It was like examining a rainbow. His aura is the most colorful and stable I have ever seen. He could be the poster boy of auras. They should use him in aura reading classes, like a skeleton in anatomy lessons."

"And what have you deduced?"

"Well, here's the thing. There is nothing to deduce. No tremors, no changes, no defects, no energy channels. Nada. This man is a *tabula rasa*."

The woman who was always ready to take action looked perplexed. Mazzy tried to redirect her to where she wanted her to go. "What did he pick from the basket?"

Izzy sprang back to life and started rummaging in her basket of crystals. She selected a green stone with gleaming striation: dark and light green patterns of perfect circles. Triumphantly, she held it up to Mazzy's face.

"This, too, is remarkable. Nobody has ever picked this one. It took me awhile to remember where I got it."

"What is it?"

"Malachite. One of the oldest stones I have. In essence, it offers protection and draws negative energies. But this is not what fascinates me."

"What does then?"

"The fact that you can read the eyes of the stones. I mean, you're supposed to. The energy that flows through them is supposed to be expressed in the reading."

"Eyes of the stones? Izzy, are you OK?"

There were people in her unit who heard voices and had visions, but Izzy wasn't normally so confused and unfocused.

"No, that's the point."

"Do you want to drink something?"

"Mazzy!" Goldfinger thundered. "This has to stop!"

She looked at the screen. Aelina was standing in front of the witness, her hands drenched in blood up to her elbows. She must have been kneading the cow's entrails in the bowl in order to capture a picture in the mirror that Ashling was holding over her.

"I'm just telling you that if a drop of blood stains his shirt, it's not going to be just a dry-cleaning bill. You'll have to buy him a whole new wardrobe! I'll have your ass for this! I'll set the public prosecutor on you!"

"Don't worry, Goldie, these women know what they're doing." Having said this, Yariv lifted pleading eyes at Mazzy, hoping for confirmation or a glimmer of hope. His view of the goings-on in the interrogation room was not much different from his boss's, but he kept mum. Mazzy turned back to Izzy, who was obsessively fondling the stone.

"What's so strange about the stone?"

"There are circles in it. They're called eyes. Since I hardly ever deal with this stone, I don't remember what the original pattern was. It seems to have changed somehow. You understand how maddening this is?"

"I can't hear anything," Goldfinger grumbled. "I can't do my job if I don't hear what they're saying there."

Mazzy looked at the screen again. Rachel, having finished reading the coffee dregs, had come into the room and was conferring with her acolytes.

All of this was pretty unsettling. None of the investigators would later say they had any inkling of what was about to happen. A second later, they all jumped from their seats and rushed for the door. Rachel had pushed aside the table that stood between her and Barak Almadon, and was pulling him up from the chair by his shirt collar. The investigators knew it had gone too far.

CHAPTER EIGHTEEN

"Listen to me, and listen to me good, you piece of shit."

Barakiel was stunned. Nobody had ever spoken to him like that. Even back then, when the Athaliah reprimanded him, she had addressed him respectfully. But not Rachel. The woman with the fierce blazing eyes was pulling him by his collar and rasping in his ear,

"I have a message for you."

Barakiel recovered from the initial shock and tried to grab Rachel's hands, but she shook him off. Again, she said in an undertone, "I advise you to stop. Think about what you're playing with here."

Barakiel retorted in a quick, mordant hoot, like a colossal owl.

"Nobody's playing here."

Rachel did not recoil from his luminous skin, and Barakiel was surprised at the confidence she displayed. He leaned in until their cheeks touched and through his perfect lips whispered, "And in any case, there's nothing you can do about it."

Rachel whispered back, "For three things the earth is disquieted, and for four which it cannot bear."

He was visibly shaken by the resolute woman before

him. His scalp started to tingle. She knew, or whoever sent her knew. The door opened and the three detectives entered. It was best to keep quiet.

"What did she tell you?" Yariv demanded. He stood panting between Rachel and Barakiel.

"Nothing. It wasn't important."

Goldfinger was more persistent. "I'm putting an end to this interrogation. If you want to talk to this witness again, check with me first. And I suggest you keep your witches away from him."

Rachel and the other two witches looked disdainfully at the police chief. As Barakiel left the room, he threw a glance at the Simantov women. Yariv motioned to a detective to follow him, just to be on the safe side. Mazzy pounced on Rachel.

"What was that supposed to mean?"

"You have to understand, I had no choice. I wanted to shake him a little, to see what would come out."

"Rachel, only you think that there were no other choices."

Rachel did not respond. Her daughter did not understand, or perhaps was not yet ready to understand.

"Well, what came of it?"

An uninvolved bystander might think that Rachel was weighing her words, but Mazzy recognized her mother's expression. It suggested that Rachel was smiling inwardly, a superior, secret smile.

Except it was not a secret, it was information, and Rachel was not about to share it with her, at least not yet.

"Rachel, is there something you want to tell me?"

"Look, Mazzy dear, this isn't a simple matter."

Mazzy was encouraged by the term of endearment her mother had used. In Rachel's world, showing affection was the first sign of weakness.

"It is extremely simple. Few things in this world are that simple."

"But, honey…"

"I'm not done!" Mazzy raised her voice by one octave, but without changing her expression, as Rachel had taught her to do. "It is very simple; either you work with Soothsayer sharing your info with the team, or you leave right now and cease to be part of this investigation. I'm not sure how you view the situation, so I'm explaining, to prevent any future misunderstanding."

Rachel motioned to her entourage to walk away, and they obliged.

"The moment you enter this building, you become my subordinate. I cannot worry about your feelings as my mother or play your little mind games. Three women have been kidnapped; they may be somewhere safe and sound, or carved up and wrapped in plastic in some garbage dump. So you'll forgive me if I don't play your games right now."

Rachel recoiled from the blatant affront, but there were more important things than her self-respect or Mazzy's realization that her mother had only her welfare at heart. She must keep her out of harm's way.

"You should be nicer to people you need," Rachel said.

Mazzy knew where this phrase had come from, and felt slighted. Apparently, Rachel was able to roam quite freely in the recesses of her daughter's mind.

She took a deep breath.

"Simply put, either you're with us, or you step aside."

Rachel left the room, leaving behind a trail of anger and resentment. Mazzy wasn't sure if she was mad at herself for giving her mother a choice or just taken aback by the fact that Rachel, as usual, had opted for her own way.

By the time Rachel joined her disciples, she seemed to be over the hurt that leaving Mazzy had caused her.

"You have a location?"

Aelina nodded.

"Time?"

Ashling confirmed.

"Who is it?"

Ashling handed Rachel the identikit sketch she had produced. The hairline was only approximate and the restrained muscles were not reflected in the charcoal drawing. But Rachel knew that now the task had become easier. She recognized the woman's face. She was the next snatch victim in the countdown.

THE FOURTH GATE
WISDOM

THE TWENTY-FOURTH DAY
THREE WEEKS AND THREE DAYS OF THE COUNTING OF THE OMER

"And the angel of the Lord said, 'Why do you ask my name, seeing it is miraculous.'"

JUDGES 13:18

The hours ticked by and no Naphil arrived to abduct Abigail.

She was calm. At the end of the day, she would be proven right. Abigail Odem got up from her computer. It was already dark outside.

The professor kept a tight schedule, which helped her maintain her sanity; even on days when she was not teaching, she worked into the wee hours. She glanced at the four young women in the adjacent room and surmised that they, too, must have better things to do than being cooped up in her house.

The women were attuned to every little motion she made, trying to anticipate her next move.

All morning they had prowled around the house frantically, checking the cameras and the hastily installed motion detection sensors. The slightest sound sent their hands to their strange-looking belts.

Abigail got up and, with measured steps, strode out of the room.

"Where to?" asked one of the guards, whose name Abigail could not remember because of the great turnover.

"I'm going out for some fresh air," said Abigail, in as polite a tone as she could muster.

The girl whispered something into her sleeve, and her colleagues suddenly sprang to life. The professor went down the stairs, preceded and followed by footsteps. The whole idea of waiting for a Naphil who might come to abduct her sounded silly.

Abigail went to the greenhouse, her sanctuary. She opened the door and was greeted by warmth and humidity. Blue fluorescent lamps had hoodwinked the plants into believing that daylight never ended, and an elaborate system of drip irrigation and climate control pipes provided the ideal conditions for growth and development. Just like The Order, she thought, except moister.

She proceeded into the thicket of the greenhouse, inspecting the plants affectionately, stroking the feathery leaves of the sumac, the bumpy tongues of the sage, and the tomato tendrils that coiled around tight nylon wires. Tiny greenish balls, on the verge of ripeness, hung from the tomato bushes. Professor Odem opened the partition that divided the greenhouse and walked into the orchid section. She left the partition open so that her human shadows could follow, fulfilling their function.

One of them sat down on a plastic stool; it was obvious from her facial expression that she would rather be somewhere else. The stool was so low that her quaint weapons belt touched the floor, making a screeching metallic sound. Visibly upset, she got up from her seat.

"What do you call this thing you're wearing?"

"Standard RAD belt issued by *She Shall Overcome*."

"Which means?"

"It includes devices for Restraint, Assault and Destroy. Hence RAD."

"I hear that in Hagar's case it didn't really work."

The guard's inscrutable expression suddenly changed, to either confusion or contempt. Abigail wasn't sure which.

"It works."

"How do you know?"

The guard was getting impatient. It had been a long day.

"At the nuclear reactor in Dimona they don't make test blasts either."

Abigail didn't want to disabuse the girl of her innocent assumption.

"What's in the belt," she asked.

"That's classified," another guard hastened to add.

"I'm important enough to warrant protection, but not enough to know by what means?"

The first girl relented and began noisily opening fasteners and Velcro strips, revealing a long coiled whip, a rounded dagger, and an antique sawn-off gun.

"As you can see, we have answers to various situations. 'Balance of Terror' just under the belt."

Abigail decided not to delve any deeper and not to make any witty comment about the last statement.

A blue light suddenly exposed the silhouettes of the women who stood guard outside the greenhouse and now seemed to surround it like a human wall. Professor Odem sensed she was about to find out all about RAD belts when a man in a suit appeared at the door. He had blond hair and eyebrows, blue eyes and tight cheekbones, and in the palm of his perfect hand he cradled a glass of Armagnac.

The guards deployed to clear a field of fire. All belts were open and hands ready to draw. Abigail was surprised that any of them had shown up. She knew the possibility existed, but his appearance still astounded her. He gave off a distinctive yet pleasant odor of steaming tea and Madeleine cookies.

"You knew I was coming. You were expecting me."

"They are here only to enable us to talk quietly."

The "us" could be interpreted either way. She opened a door for him; he could come in if he wanted. It did not have to be personal. It was not about him or her. It was bigger than both of them, and it was important that he get this point.

"Isn't it a bit late for a 'quiet' talk?"

Abigail always thought the Nephilim's eternal youth left them with a certain juvenile quality. She decided to try another tack.

"We want to stop this before someone gets hurt."

Again, an inclusive "we" as if to say: it's us against the whole world, just as it always was. Until recently.

"So why are they here?" He made a wide gesture with his glass, nonchalantly splashing the expensive liquid. His angelic grace evidently masked great strength, now deliberately unleashed by Shamhazai.

"When you have a tear, you first use a safety pin, and later you sew it properly."

The Naphil seemed in total control, oblivious to the guards surrounding him who had enough firepower to fell him. Abigail decided to play for time, to test the ground. Perhaps there was no need for escalation; the two of them could resolve it. She needed to change the subject, to diffuse the tension.

"Are Estie, Hagar, and Milka alright?"

She made a point of mentioning them by name, to give them an identity, to stress that they were not merely bargaining chips. They were individual women, Daughters of Lilith, members of a respectable order, cherished and cared for. Besides, she knew the importance of names for the Nephilim. Names meant power.

"Yes, we will take care of them."

"This is important. Nobody should get hurt."

"No, nobody wants that to happen," Shamhazai said sardonically, emphasizing "that." Abigail knew not to let him feel too self-confident. Anyone connected to the leadership of The Order knew that this was the source of the problem: the confidence they had accrued over time.

"We want you to release Estie first. The mother wants her daughter back. Then we'll discuss how soon you return Hagar and Milka to us."

Again, precise names. Again feigned deference. Give him the impression that they will do his bidding. Appeal to the grace of his celestial personality.

"Really, you'll let us?"

"Estie is a child. She is not part of the deal."

"They are all part of the deal."

She realized that from his perspective, childhood and adolescence were incidental. When you had existed for more than five thousand years, age fourteen took on the same significance as four hundred and ninety or thereabouts. The personal angle was not going to work here.

"We want to maintain the status quo. There are two very skilled guards here who are exercising great restraint at the moment, because we'll have to live together for many more years."

"Why?"

"Because the status quo has to be maintained; you know this as well as I do. You may be much more affected. I may be terminating my forty years on this earth here and now, but you will determine what the next centuries will look like."

"Unless we don't intend to stay here."

Abigail did not quite understand his tactics; he was standing there, cocky, smug, rebuffing all her attempts to meet him half way. Obviously, they intended to stay here. They had nowhere to go. No arguments existed for or against such an eventuality because it had never been disputed. The Nephilim preferred earthly delights to celestial boredom. The ardent love they felt toward ancient Lilith was at the core of the covenant; it was the cornerstone of the elaborate structure of the order of the Nephilim, that love and the fact that there was no practical way they could return, without the consent of the Superior Power, who did not particularly care for them. Abigail glanced at the greenhouse walls and at the figures surrounding it, lit by an eerie purple-bluish light, and felt secure and confident. Still, something didn't seem quite right. Shamhazai took a few steps forward and the guards sprang to action, whipping out their daggers with sharp metallic clicks.

"It doesn't have to end like this," Abigail tried to defuse the situation.

Shamhazai continued to advance, taking small steps, like a panther about to pounce.

"One more step and I blow his head off!" cried the guard on the left.

The sawn-off gun was already taking aim. Shamhazai, however, looked frightfully calm.

"Remember what you were told! One drop of blood and everything changes! It's a point of no return!"

If the Naphil himself did not scare them as much as he scared her, at least the warning about spilling blood and the instructions of their commanders would stop them from taking any rash step.

As if on cue, Shamhazai took out a long tiepin with a pearl at its end and, grinning broadly, cocking his left thumb into a "thumbs-up" gesture, pricked himself with it.

Jaws dropped at the sight of the rounded crimson dewdrop. How much angel's blood could dance on a pinhead? Shamhazai presented the drop to the incredulous eyes of Abigail and her guards. It was in that split-second that she realized what had been wrong all along with the circle of guards. If there was blue fluorescent light inside the greenhouse, where did the bluish-purple haloes surrounding the silhouettes standing outside come from? Then, with one loud, synchronized whirr, the outer circle spread its wings and the soothing figures of the guards became looming silhouettes of Nephilim.

They had been surrounded all along.

Like an emperor in the Colosseum, Shamhazai turned his thumb down, letting the blood drip onto the greenhouse floor. Eddies of fury roiled the hitherto placid water of the covenant that existed between the Liliths and the Nephilim. The Nephilim flew through the glass walls, dragging hoses, irrigation devices and pots in their wake. They swooped down on Abigail and on the guards who had no chance to defend themselves. Seconds later, Abigail was hovering between sky and earth, captured in a net, which the Nephilim must have brought with them in order to avoid touching a contemptible daughter of Lilith with their exalted hands.

Many bizarre thoughts ran through Professor Odem's head, but two almost made her burst out into crazy laughter. One was associative: she was reminded of the cowardly lion in the Wizard of Oz, carried by the winged monkeys at the behest of the Witch of the North. Now the witch herself was lifted into the air, too scared to look down. The second thought was petty but all too human. Through this historic cataclysm she was witnessing, which could furnish her with material for many years of research into arcane Jewish lore, one uncontested fact emerged: she had been wrong.

CHAPTER NINETEEN

Mazzy locked the door behind Yariv and herself and crashed into the nearest chair, stealing a few moments of quiet without the scathing criticism she surely merited on account of the mess Rachel had left behind. Her own self-criticism was enough. She knew she had screwed up.

Following Rachel's assault, there was no sense in detaining Almadon. The evidence against him was all circumstantial. The only possible clue they had in their investigation disappeared with Rachel. But Mazzy, instead of grilling her mother, which would have benefited the case, was busy settling old accounts.

Yariv sat on a chair backwards, his arms hugging its back and his chin resting on the top. It was clear to Mazzy that he did not see the urgency; he was a conventional detective examining a clue. To him, it was only a matter of time; the hunt had just begun. Not so from her perspective. She saw how tense Rachel was. The silence was getting oppressive, so she broke it.

"Do you have any new insights?"

"Actually, I do."

"Would you care to share them?"

"Not a good idea."

She gave him her bittersweet smile, with a hint of appeasement.

"Biton, we've hit rock bottom. Couldn't be lower than that."

"You sure?"

"Dead Sea level, sweetheart, lowest place on the planet."

Her reference to the Dead Sea elicited a conciliatory smile. At the time when they had shared a police car and a bed, the two of them were unsuccessfully tailing one of Mandelbrot's rivals, another gangster by the name of Almaliach. This was Mazzy's first job undercover. When she returned from the stakeout and was asked how low her spirits had sunk, she coined the phrase Dead Sea level.

Yariv took a deep breath and placed his hand lightly on her shoulder.

"It'll be all right."

The warmth scorched Mazzy's skin. While she was waging a war against Rachel, other, distant emotions were sneaking in, and the only man who could pacify her in such situations was to blame. Mazzy refused to acknowledge those feelings; the walls of her heart had been fortified, the moat filled with water, the bridge hoisted.

"No."

Yariv disengaged and returned to the back of his chair.

"This is really out of place right now."

"Out of place?"

Footsteps fell outside the door. Someone was either listening in or making up their mind whether or not to knock.

"I don't know. Yeah, maybe so."

"Be kind, rewind and we'll both forget about the last thirty seconds, Okay?"

"I thought you were no longer my radio."

"Haven't been for a long time."

The door handle rattled, followed by a determined knocking.

"I doubt your suggestion will work," Yariv protested.

"Yours will definitely not," Mazzy said as she reached to unlock the door.

Caught off balance, Elisha hurtled forward, his fedora askew, his side locks and *tzitzit* flying in all directions. Larissa made a more dignified entrance.

"Well?" asked Mazzy.

Their task was to decode the words that Rachel had whispered to Barak Almadon. That they had found something was clear from their faces. Larissa nodded graciously at Elisha, and he launched into his explanation.

"There's more than one method of gematria," he said.

"Gematria?"

"Listen, Biton, you may even learn something," Larissa said disdainfully.

"Assigning numeric value to words. It's my method for solving problems, and a bit like math. You identify an X, graph it, and then project the result onto the partial sums of the entire series."

Not being understood had never discouraged Elisha from continuing with an explanation.

"You take the result of the gematria and compare it with a known sum and proceed slowly, from one link in the chain to the next, until you reach a solution."

"Do you have the answer to what Rachel said?"

"Only the beginning. We're looking for a seven. 'For three things the earth is disquieted and for four which it cannot bear.'"

"Seven what? Continents? Wonders of the world?" Yariv wanted to know.

"Here comes the good part. You may still not understand it, but it makes sense," said Larissa, like a mother proud of her child prodigy.

"In gematria this verse equals 4225, which has the same value as 'In the seventh month, on the first day of the month, ye shall have a holy convocation; ye shall do no servile work: it is a day of blowing the trumpets unto you.' It's as if someone is trying to call me with a ram's horn and I don't hear it. I stand in front of a door but have no key. And then it hit me. This has to do with Rosh Hashanah, and the abductions started on Passover. Except that in Biblical times, Passover was the start of the year! The verse refers to the month of Nissan that used to be the first month of the year. Thus we find the answer at the end, not at the beginning, the last, not the first! So, I proceeded in the method of numerical intensification of the Proverbs, 'There be three things which go well, yea, four are comely in going,' which when taken in a row come to 1735. A quick calculation yields that it is equal to, 'Which the clouds do drop and distill upon man abundantly.' From the Book of Job."

"Do you mind telling us what all this means, instead of spouting numbers?" Yariv was getting impatient.

Elisha ignored the lack of enthusiasm and became even more animated.

"I'm getting to the meaning in a minute. So I take the sum of the first verse, 4225, and subtract the sum of the second verse, 1735. I deduct the end from the beginning."

"2490," Yariv pronounced, surprising everyone. "Maths was kinda like a hobby when I was growing up."

"And the solution is also from the book of Job. Chapter Two, Verse One. 'Again there was a day when the sons of God came to present themselves before the Lords, and Satan came also among them to present himself before the Lord,' which, as the Chief Inspector correctly deduced, equals 2490."

Nobody was particularly pleased with the conclusion. The references to God and the Prince of Darkness did not make them feel any better about the investigation. Larissa was the first to react.

"It's just like the cards we were reading. Seven again and again. Two of Cups, Two of Wands, Five of Wands and five of Cups – seven."

"And you're excited because…"

"The word seven in Elisha's gematria is 372; this brings us to what everybody is thinking about Satan and his Boss, but nobody has the guts to say it."

The silence was deafening.

"Apocalypse!"

"So why are you so pleased?"

"Either I'm going up to meet Borislav, or I'm going down to settle the account with whoever killed him."

CHAPTER TWENTY

Rachel had expected the Athaliah's visit since the phone call. She tried to stay focused and recited verses to keep her mind from straying to forebodings about Mazzy's situation. A pewter coffee pot simmered over a small stove, heavy curtains covered the windows, and chains of silver coins hung from a copper lamp that gave off soft, oil-fragrant light. On a low, finely carved table stood a rounded mortar filled with coffee beans and a long pestle. All the chairs were facing west, except the reader's stool. A bold knock on the door heralded the visitor's arrival.

"Come in!"

An elegant, dark silhouette stood at the door exuding self-assurance. Her bodyguards hung back.

"Rachel." The Athaliah's mellifluous voice filled the room, echoing from corners and nooks. For all her apparent gentleness, the Athaliah offered no greeting, she summoned as if to a roll call.

The Athaliah was in charge of hundreds of women placed, over the centuries, in positions of power, women who had learned how to maneuver intricate bureaucracies and to control the various branches of authority. Rachel's life could be turned upside down if one day the tax authorities, Social Security, City Hall and the Land Deeds Registrar decided to take an interest in her.

By way of an answer, Rachel stood and extended her arms in greeting.

The Athaliah inspected the room at length while Rachel turned her back and attended to the coffee. She needed the Athaliah to understand this was Rachel Simantov's domain, where she felt secure and unencumbered.

She lifted the pot from the stove a second before the coffee boiled over. It was as if she had anticipated the exact moment of her guest's arrival. The Athaliah sat down on the stool facing the door. Without turning to face her, and in a tone one uses to address a clueless child, Rachel said, "You're sitting in my chair."

Wordlessly, the Athaliah moved to a worn rattan chair. Rachel poured the bitter beverage into porcelain cups, one for herself, one for the venerable Daughter of Lilith. Between them stood an empty saucer.

"So are you going to tell me, or did I just drop in for coffee?"

Rachel and her guest studied each other. The silence was becoming oppressive, like a dry desert wind. The Athaliah was getting restless.

"This is not how it works."

Rachel kept her tongue.

"I work with our Order and with people that we hire. Jobs exclusively tailored for our needs."

A strong smell of freshly ground coffee beans mixed with cardamom filled the air.

"This time it's different," said Rachel finally.

Sipping from her cup, she fixed her gaze on the Athaliah and her two smoldering charcoal eyes.

"I can spare you time, money, and hassle. You are running around like a headless chicken, spreading fear in people's hearts. But there are no bullets in your guns."

The Athaliah sat unprovoked, maintaining her composure. Her breathing was regular; she did not sweat or swallow hard. She exhibited no signs of distress, yet Rachel knew she had hit the nail on the head. So did the Athaliah. The usual control methods and power games no longer applied.

"So you are aware of our problems?"

"Oh no. The hail and ash were just a coincidence. A barometric depression caused by an accident at a power plant."

"I see; you are not as naïve as the others. At least you keep your eye on the ball."

"You wouldn't be here otherwise. Sure, I'm a good reader, but not so good that the Athaliah would drop everything and come visit me after one phone call. You also know that I am smart enough not to bother you with trivialities."

The Athaliah drank her coffee with deliberation, then handed the cup to Rachel who turned it upside down on the porcelain saucer, waited a few seconds, picked it up and examined the texture of the dregs, their thickness, roughness, the distance between the circles left by the black liquid, the patterns and the pictures that emerged. On the right side of the saucer she saw a drawn curtain, on the left a suitcase. The curtain indicated a desire to conceal, the suitcase suggested an urge to flee, disappear.

The Athaliah might be trying to hide behind threats and imperial gestures, but in the bottom of a coffee cup there are no corners.

"So you'd like to work for us again?"

"As it says in the Bible, 'man is born unto trouble...'"

The Athaliah completed the verse in her head, "as the sparks fly upward," and the association made her tense up.

"How much do you know?"

"I know who, and I know where and when."

The Athaliah scrutinized the woman before her. She was holding her cards close to her chest, and probably a few up her sleeve.

"What's your price? How much is this going to cost me?"

"My daughter Mazzy. Even if later on she becomes important to you, I want you to keep her out of it, as far as possible."

"I have someone in the police. She'll keep an eye on her, from a distance. But I need time. If something goes wrong, I have no control over her replacement."

"Fair enough. I don't want her to know. Right now, you are on a collision course. I hope you can avert it, but I don't want to find out later that she was injured because she was in the wrong place."

"I hope the whole business comes to an end soon. At any rate, she will not be part of the confrontation."

"Let's hope so."

"Just make sure you give us everything you've got."

"I know how to pick my enemies, the Athaliah. I've no intention of turning you into one."

From her pocket Rachel took out a note on which was written the name of the woman whose sketch had been earlier drawn by Ashling. She handed it to Lilith's Daughter, sealing the deal.

The Athaliah smiled without betraying any emotion, and was gone.

Rachel gave herself five minutes, then checked the cushions, the flowerpots and the herbs in the yard for charms and listening devices.

She picked up the phone and dialed only three digits. Someone answered immediately and it wasn't the emergency services operator.

"Yes?"

"I want to speak with Israel."

A long silence, followed by a deep voice that sent shivers down her spine.

"Hello, Sibylla. You got my message."

His use of her old nickname did not help steady her nerves.

"Have you lost my number? Might have been easier like this, you know."

A long silence from his end prompted her to ask the more pressing question.

"On a scale of one to ten, how much help do I need from you?"

"It's actually you who needs help. All the help you can think of, and then some."

Israel was able to evade even the simplest question. Her ex-partner's answers had always been mysterious and evasive.

"If it was so important that we talk, why didn't you come to me? How could you be so sure I'd contact you?"

"She's your daughter, and she's in the middle of all this."

"My blood has to hold on. At the end of the world, it can let go."

"When the end comes, it won't matter anymore. You know what they say about those who calculate the end of the world." As soon as she said this, she knew what his response would be.

"'For the vision is yet for an appointed time, but at the end it shall speak, and not lie: though it tarry, wait for it; because it will surely come, it will not tarry.'"

"Not exactly what I had in mind."

"This is the only version I know."

"If I come, will she be okay?"

"If you come, she may have a chance."

"And until then?"

"Until then we shall not rest."

CHAPTER TWENTY-ONE

The road zigzagged under the tires. Mazzy gripped the steering wheel, trying to tune in with the music blaring from the sound system. Like the singer, she found herself in a place she no longer wanted to be. Someone, a lover perhaps, was standing in her way. "Now who could that be?" Mazzy asked herself.

Sometimes you have to dive into the pool, even if you're not sure there's water in it. The song ended, Mazzy reached home, killed the engine and sat in the dark.

His cab arrived and Mazzy thought he looked tired, or just old, maybe both. The cab driver and Mazzy both sat and waited for something to happen, for someone to tell them where to go next. The babysitter came out of the house, fiddling with her cellphone and not noticing Gaby as he stood at the door to see her safely into the cab.

One by one the lights in the house came on, as Gaby went through his ritual of making sure everything was in order. Mazzy gathered her strength and stepped up to the front door. She felt like a mechanical doll with a tightly wound spring. This night so far had been like a whirlwind that scattered her in all directions. Steadying her breathing, she found her key and unlocked the door.

Ever-vigilant Gaby was waiting for her.

"Hey there," he whispered.

"Hey," she whispered back, although she knew Noga could sleep soundly through a heavy metal concert.

Gaby stepped forward, nuzzling up against her but getting no response.

"How was work?" he asked politely, evoking in her feelings of shame and guilt.

"Fine."

"You caught all the bad guys?"

"Not really."

"Some at least?"

"Not today."

"We had a crazy day. Massive pileup on the Ayalon freeway. I was assigned to trauma, don't ask."

She didn't ask, only wondered when she would tell him what was on her mind.

"Are you OK?"

"So-so. Not great."

He let it go at that. When he broke off the embrace, Mazzy felt as if a spotlight had been swung away from her. She watched him step toward their bedroom, shedding clothes along the way.

"I need a quick shower."

She smiled at his back but was fed up with these polite nightly routines. As he closed the bedroom door behind him, guilt and a sort of loneliness engulfed her.

Placing the Glock in the safe, she hoped that both work and Yariv were now locked away in her other world.

But there he was, his face burned into her retina, giving her no release. As she looked in on the sleeping child, she could still feel him tickling her earlobes, holding her ankles, strumming on her tendons, smelling of cigarettes, soap and sex. She moved to her own bedroom, perhaps not quite ready for what had to come next.

Gaby was naked under the ceiling fan, vigorously toweling himself, but sparks and flashes of Yariv flickered all around, as if through a spitefully constructed prism. Now dry, Gaby gathered his discarded clothes and tossed them into the laundry basket, his shoes went neatly under the bed. There was something comforting, homey, predictable and yet annoying in all this.

Mazzy clicked the door shut and walked toward him, unbuttoning the top of her uniform shirt and pulling it over her head. She knew the lacy bra she had worn for Yariv would have the same effect on her husband. She could see it in the way his eyes widened.

"Are you just going to sit there?" she asked, stepping out of her skirt.

Before he could collect his thoughts, Mazzy took the initiative. Wordlessly, she pushed him back onto the bed. He submitted with outstretched arms as she shrugged out of the bra, letting her breasts graze over his chest, belly and down to his thighs.

Mazzy knew exactly what she was doing but she had no idea why.

The desire to touch, to bond, to escape, clouded her mind. Gaby played with her panties before pulling them down, the way they both knew she enjoyed. She held his head, pulling him close so as not to have him see her face. Her face, she thought, would betray her. Her hand told her he was ready so she mounted him. The ugly thought that she was still damp and sticky from Yariv, was pushed to the farthest recesses of her mind as Gaby thrust into her, closed his eyes and surrendered to the moment.

Every motion awakened sensations that had lain dormant during their marital drought. Mazzy's body rocked and swayed, and when she heard Gaby begin to moan, she rocked faster, arching her back and lifting her misty eyes toward the ceiling.

Finally, she collapsed on top of him, panting against his heaving chest.

"Hey, what was that? I pick up the kid from daycare a couple of times and make a salad, and suddenly I collect my reward? I can't even…"

He couldn't contain a burst of lusty laughter. Mazzy joined him, greatly relieved, and they laughed until Gaby ran out of breath and gently wriggled out from under his wife.

She hushed him so as to not wake Noga, and got under the sheets.

"The sink is empty, the laundry drying, the plants watered, and all without you having to tell me. The babysitter helped with some chores. I paid her extra, don't worry."

"I'm sorry I was nasty before."

"It's all right. Just tell me what I did to deserve this."

"You didn't do anything."

"I really want to know."

"You don't want to know."

"Can we do it again?"

She smiled.

"I missed you."

"Me too."

"All this madness with your detective work and my internship…"

"Yeah."

"Is it so selfish of me to wish you'd caught the guy because I miss my wife?"

"It's excusable, but don't mention it to others."

"Now is not a good time to talk, right?"

She didn't answer. She was enjoying every second away from the office, finally not thinking about Yariv. Not turning over the details of the case. Not worrying about missing women. In the here and now she was content to be with her husband, to dive headlong into the heated pool of her marriage. Mazzy had always preferred pools to the open sea. Perhaps it was the salt water that stung your eyes, perhaps the bottomless depth.

"Turn off the light."

"You want to go to sleep?"

"Dying to."

"Like this?"

Mazzy did not like to snuggle, especially in the summer. She needed space and air, the absence of sweat. But her husband was a spooner.

"Okay, but just this once. Don't get used to it."

Gaby turned off the reading lamp and darkness pervaded the room. Serenity, peaceful breathing, finally silence. Until the phone rang and wrenched her from her slumber, sending her into the predawn mist and the start of another day.

CHAPTER TWENTY-TWO

Mazzy recognized the scene from afar: emergency crews and fire trucks with flashing lights that flickered through the morning fog. As she made her way among early risers and inquisitive neighbors, two ambulances came from opposite directions. Two Search and Rescue volunteers were dragging a sealed black bag to a police car.

Whatever awaited her there was serious enough to put her own problems on hold.

As she entered the cordoned-off area, someone with the white epaulettes of a police cadet and carrying a red StickLight demanded identification. She smiled and patted his shoulder gently. When she gave him her name, he apologized.

"They're waiting for you there," he gestured toward the greenhouse. Mazzy spotted the white tent that Doron and his team had set up, and her partner's silhouette inside. When she opened the zipper, she realized that Crime Lab had set up so many spotlights, the greenhouse was flooded with artificial daylight. Daylight and unbearable heat.

Beads of perspiration glistened on Yariv's forehead and dark circles stained his armpits. Mazzy jumped right in.

"What's going on?"

Before Yariv could answer, his phone rang.

"Constant visual contact? He was there all the time? Not even for five minutes? Okay, stay with him. Give me a buzz if he so much as takes out the garbage."

He pocketed the phone, and swung his attention to Mazzy.

"That was the officer tailing Almadon, we might not like the look of him but he wasn't anywhere near here."

Mazzy felt her shoulders drop.

"Libby," Yariv called out, "fill the inspector in."

Libby hurried to Mazzy with a pad full of notes written in a rounded curly hand. Mazzy hated frills of any kind. But she reminded herself that Libby was new to this, and still had to learn not to take things personally. Not just because scenes like this one would become routine, but because all the men around expected her to stumble, so she mustn't provide them with ammunition.

"The owner of the house, Professor Abigail Odem, is missing. We assume she was the target."

"Professor of what?"

"Jewish studies. The last phone call she made was to her research assistant. She told her that the messenger had delivered the material. The delivery service confirmed that their guy had been here at noon. He was the last person to see her. Well, of those who survived. Yesterday morning, she called in sick. We woke up her secretary, who told us the professor hadn't missed a day of work in years…"

"Hang on a sec. What do you mean 'of those who survived?'"

"Professor Odem's house was well guarded. The messenger told us he saw a whole team of female security personnel. Some were quite good looking, in his opinion. The yard was full of wires, cables, cameras, and footprints of the guards. No one survived to tell the tale. There were bodies strewn all over, but no sign of the professor. It's as if something came from the sky and whisked her away."

Mazzy nodded to indicate that she had enough information for now, and moved deeper into the greenhouse, where Yariv was leaning over Doron as he scraped something from the concrete floor and put it in a test tube.

"Anything?"

"He found some dry blood, not much though."

One drop was not indicative of an escape route, or that the attackers or abductee had been injured, but it was something. Considering the mess surrounding the scene, it might have been significant.

She came close to Yariv, and he let her into his space. This was encouraging.

"We'll give Doron's team another hour here, then pack up. There's a pile of stuff and it'll take us all day to decide what's relevant and what's not."

"Anyone else investigating the case?"

"There's a homicide team looking into who killed the guards. They were here, they saw, they photographed and then rushed to the morgue and the hospitals. There were eight bodies here when I arrived, and several ambulances with their sirens on. We'll be lucky if any of those women survive."

"Were they all women?"

"I saw only women's bodies taken out. Their uniforms were from some small security company. The same as the Seder night case. They must have an exclusive clientele."

"Why does a professor of Jewish studies need so much security?"

"These are dangerous times in academia."

"I'll hit you, you know."

"At least I'll get something from you."

"So this is how it's going to be now? First you ignore me, then you whine that I'm ignoring you."

"I don't know, Mazzy. It's weird, isn't it?"

"Yes, it is."

"I tossed and turned all night trying to decide if I should quit the investigation, give you more space. But this time I'm not going to give up so easily."

"Cut it out, Biton."

"I can't."

"You're the best detective I know, and we're going to continue as is."

"You don't know many detectives, then."

"That's my yardstick. Not too high; about your height."

"Hey, I'm trying, aren't I?"

He grinned and she grinned back. It was weird, as he had said, and a little embarrassing. Suddenly it was Yariv again. Nothing good could come of it.

"Let's return to the precinct and check what they have. You might as well call your people. Maybe Izzy or your mom had some vibes."

"Let them sleep. I can send Izzy and Rachel here later today to see if they can find a trace of energy. The professor's scent won't disappear. They're not sniffer dogs, you know."

"Can they really do that?"

"You're so gullible. I told you it doesn't work by 'vibes.'"

Yariv wasn't amused and was losing patience.

"I'm packing up here with Doron. Meet me at the precinct."

Mazzy felt like a little girl, playing with trifles, instead of dealing with the really important business. Sure he had provoked her, but she agreed to play along. Just like with Gaby.

THE FIFTH GATE
INSIGHT

THE THIRTY-FIFTH DAY
FIVE WEEKS OF THE COUNTING OF THE OMER

"The anger of the Lord shall not return, until he has executed, and until he has performed the thoughts of his heart; at the end of days ye shall see her, insight."

JEREMIAH 23:20

Libby sat in the open jeep, hidden by a thicket.

She knew the location of the watchtowers, and she was monitoring their occupants. One of the guardswomen spotted her and trained her binoculars on her. Libby watched how the youthful guard used the radio to communicate with the ranch, her hand ready to pull the rope and activate the alarm bell. But as soon as someone responded to her message, her face registered relief, her hand let go of the rope, and she even waved at Libby before resuming her watch.

Libby directed her binoculars at the ranch, over the basalt wall that surrounded the compound, the wall that rose with every new class of cadets; upon graduation, each girl would pick a stone from a nearby field and put it on top of the pile, connecting herself to the stones and to the place. After

hundreds of years and countless thousands of girls, the wall
had reached a considerable height. Libby was reminded
of her own graduation ceremony, at which they struggled
with pulleys, ropes, and climbing gear. She remembered
her classmates' jubilant cries and smiled to herself.

There was something strikingly artistic about the cadets'
maneuvers taking place in the compound; row upon row
of white-clad girls dancing like cascading waves, gracefully
brandishing their daggers and whips above their heads. Then
the wooden door of the balcony opened, and the dignified
figure of Doula Ashtribu came out to honor her cadets.

The intervening years had not left their mark on the
Doula's face. Libby did a quick calculation; at the time,
she had been fourteen, which made Chief Doula in her
forties now. Libby wondered if her youthful looks came
from the austere, rigorous, natural life of the ranch that
had preserved the woman and stopped the clock, age-wise.

Doula Anat Ashtribu was a human manifestation
of Mother Earth: suntanned and warm, soft on the
inside, rough on the outside, always ready to impart her
knowledge, yet insisting that you learn from your own
mistakes. Her lessons focused on the essence of being
Lilith's Daughters, on their appearance and behavior;
the importance of presenting oneself as other women
while projecting normal, acceptable femininity to ensure
a smooth and unencumbered existence. Classes in the
Seven Curses of Eve taught them about menstrual pain,
which would never plague them, and how to deal with the
absence of the hymen and, of course, detailed preparation
for childbirth that included proper behavior during
pregnancy and parturition.

Libby decided that she had observed long enough, and it was now time to enter the green, pastoral, serene ranch, so full of the grace and youthfulness that was planted in the basalt landscape of the Golan Heights like a lily among thorns.

An instructor greeted her, pleasantly scrutinizing, with a hint of derision, Libby's police issue belt with handcuffs and radio. The instructor's own RAD belt was burnished and ready for action.

Libby entered a wooden structure. Unlike the old days, Doula Ashtribu's door was wide open. Without a door to knock on, she just waited; there was a threshold to cross, like the cattle grids she had rattled over on the way.

"Are you waiting for an official invitation?"

Libby walked in, determined not to let the Doula's rank intimidate her. Over the years she had learned how to deal with authority, and she could put this knowledge to use in dealing with the Doula.

"Takes some getting used to," she said.

"My door is always open to graduates. I told you before."

"Right."

"I thought you'd find your own way. I didn't think you'd pick this path."

"The Order decides."

"That's true. Many tend to forget this. The Order is bigger than either of us."

"Is this why you wouldn't agree to security?"

"I am not so vain as to think the Immortals would bother with me."

"But Rachel Simantov said…"

"Rachel Simantov does not belong to The Order."

Libby was about to tell her that Rachel could still be right and that the information she supplied was accurate, but Ashtribu scrutinized her former student, trying to detect doubt, change, and the real reason for her presence there.

"You think I'm old fashioned?" asked the Doula.

"No, Doula Ashtribu."

"Anat. Graduates can address me by my name."

Libby repeated the name Anat in her head, but somehow found it inappropriate.

"After four members of The Order have disappeared, perhaps it's time…"

"To take precautions?"

"Exactly."

The Doula didn't answer; her soothing, maternal smile didn't change. Libby thought it was incongruous to the tenor of the conversation. Tiny furrows appeared on Libby's brow; the Doula really did not value herself. How Zen-like, she thought. The older woman keeps silent. Silence was the weapon she wielded to teach her charges.

"Why Hagar Abizu? Why Professor Odem? What are they looking for?"

The Doula's face registered astonishment. She didn't delve into details. It was hard to focus on details when they concerned a friend, a daughter of an ex-cadet, a woman you admired. The Doula preferred to stick to generalities, to the tried and true precepts she was familiar with. She had no answer to the disappearance of the women, and she was not about to discuss her own feelings with this eager and spirited graduate.

"The police are working on a timeline, a pattern, a modus operandi: what connects a fourteen year-old girl in a night club with a stage actress? A lawyer with a professor of Jewish Studies? What's behind the names? The professions?" said Libby.

"Don't you find these things insignificant?"

"Why, if it brings us closer to finding them?"

"Because we know where they are; we know where we are. The question is where do we go from here? What is the next stage?" said Doula Ashtribu.

"And what do you think it is?"

"Whatever was shall be. We need to restore the equilibrium, return to the status quo, to Kedem. The past is the future."

Libby remembered the lessons dealing with the Day of Equilibrium. The Final Aspiration – the return to the days before the apple was plucked from the tree. Days preceeding the Proposition. The return to Kedem, to time immemorial. She had never put any stock in this fantasy; she thought it would never happen.

But now something had happened. And refusing to believe that someone might harm The Order or oppose it, had already cost them four victims. She herself had succumbed to the general torpor that afflicted The Order as it wallowed in its past glory and yearned for a future of salvation and redemption.

Libby was about to lash out at the Doula when she was stopped by a loud peal of bells. The alarm bells on all the watchtowers were ringing, echoing around the ranch. Teachers and cadets looked surprised as they scrambled up the basalt walls to their assigned positions. They were well trained and knew this wasn't a drill, but the sight that greeted them was totally unexpected.

Libby had joined them on top of a rampart and watched the unfolding scene with disbelief. The orange hues of the evening sky were a perfect backdrop to the spectacle. She turned her face from the twilit west toward the north, whence "evil broke forth." The Nephilim were coming.

The majestic figure of Adriel emerged from a horizon that seemed to be closing in. He spread his glorious wings and each motion sent waves of fear toward the defenders. The black-winged angels flying in formation behind him swooped down in a turbulent display of primordial force.

Whips cracked and steel scraped leather as weapons were drawn from RAD belts. There was a guileless naiveté about the way the cadets and instructors urged each other to fend off the onslaught. The Nephilim attacked their targets with implacable efficiency. The girls were tossed aside, cast down on the earthworks at the base of the wall. A winged cyclone now circled the main building and, seconds later, Libby watched as Doula Ashtribu was dragged from the window and carried into the air by four Nephilim. Libby drew her service gun and ran toward them, but something strong and flexible, like the tip of a bamboo stick, hit her right shoulder and sent her hurtling to the floor. The gun flew from her hand, landing on the black dirt. A whiff of orange juice and buttered toast with jam engulfed her like an intoxicating perfume. When she managed to pick herself up, she was facing a resplendent Naphil, with shining black wings looking down at her like an aardvark surveying a nest of termites. Incredibly, it was from him that the soothing smell of juice and toast emanated. The condescending grin on Adriel's face prompted her to whip out her backup gun and empty the cartridge with maximum rapid fire.

Folding his wings, the Naphil hugged himself, displaying the beautiful feathers. The bullets seemed to be absorbed by all the blackness. Libby jammed in another clip and fired again, this time more slowly, desperately, at her target. Adriel stood firmly, unperturbed and unhurt, emitting his soothing smell. She regretted not retrieving a RAD belt from a wounded cadet or from one of the hysterical instructors who fled when the defense line collapsed. When his body was about to take the last bullet, he switched positions and spread one of his wings.

His gaze was fixed on her, and she noticed a spasm of pain go through him when the bullet struck, but it only lasted a second; then he spread his other wing and again stood imposingly before her, exposing a tiny hole under his left nipple. He leapt at her and his face bent to hers until their eyes were level. He started poking at the wound in his chest until his whole fist was submerged. A sound of tearing and crackling, like that of a dry twig, echoed in her ears. Behind his back she could see Doula Ashtribu disappear into the sky. The Naphil withdrew his fist, dipped in angel blood. The drops fell to the ground, hissing like a provoked snake ready to strike, quivering and bubbling as they mingled with the dust and basalt. A sweet smell of blossoms gushed out of the wound.

Adriel stretched out his other hand, grabbing the red-hot gun from Libby and tossing it aside. Gripping her open hand, he folded her fingers into his and looked her straight in the eye.

"I don't like being shot at, even when it's for a good cause. Next time we meet, I'll make sure you never shoot at anyone again. In the meantime, keep this."

He spread his wings and was airborne with a flourish that ruffled Libby's hair.

Whatever was in her hand felt sticky and rough. Opening her fist, she found a flattened bullet and a bone splinter covered in a greenish material that looked like coral reef. Libby was used to threats from her work as a police officer and a Daughter of Lilith, but this one evoked something new: desperation.

CHAPTER TWENTY-THREE

Doron made his way to the lab, relieved not to be part of the investigating team. Microscopes, vials, pipettes, and test tubes were his instruments, and this was fine with everyone, provided the results were delivered on time and with the correct color codes.

Libby, Moscovitz's sidekick, was waiting for him in the hallway. She looked funny, as if she had gained a whole career of experience overnight.

"What are you doing here?"

"Like everyone else, waiting to see how it ends."

Doron still remembered what it was like to be young and enthusiastic, to try to impress your veteran colleagues. He continued on his way, but Libby stopped him.

"Where's Biton?"

"Summing up the case. He and Mazzy want to make sure he has nowhere to run when they arrest him."

"What's he charged with?"

She didn't look good, as if something was haunting her from the inside, something bad.

"Do you want something to drink? I could make coffee."

"What is he charged with?"

It wasn't a question really, more like an order, one that

had to be obeyed. Doron couldn't say what it was that bothered him, but the discomfort made him blurt out the information quickly, so that she would leave him alone.

"There's a match between the DNA in Almadon's coffee and the snippets of hair found on the stage in the theater. Also between those and the drop of blood found in the professor's greenhouse. Now it's conclusive: he's a serial killer and we've nailed him."

"So why aren't we celebrating?"

"We still don't have anything to link him to the Judge's daughter. Hizzonor wants heads on a platter. And they can't find a connection between the cases. When Biton and Mazzy are done checking all the clues and angles, they'll wrap it up and get Almadon from his house. See if they can get a confession out of him this time."

Libby mulled over his last words; her hand rummaged in her bag, looking for something.

"How long will it take?"

"A day or two."

Too long. She expected an answer within hours, not days. Less than an hour ago she had been facing a Naphil and shot him. In return, he had handed her a bone, a shell, and a threat.

"Are you very busy right now?"

"As far as I'm concerned, the case is closed."

"And if I give you something that will move us forward, will you check it?"

Libby took out an evidence bag. Doron shot her a dismissive look.

"Where did this come from?"

"I don't want to look stupid, but I have something…"

"That just wound up in your bag?"

Libby knew she could not hand the bullet to forensics. She wasn't supposed to be at the ranch, and she couldn't shoot at something that didn't exist. She knew the ballistics experts wouldn't be able to track the bullet's trajectory inside the Naphil's body. And they'd laugh at her if she told them how it was retrieved. But she knew that she had to hand over the Naphil's other souvenir; she had to involve somebody else in this affair.

Even if her story was fantstical, someone would find it hard to ignore what she held in her hand. Doron looked at the contents of the bag.

"It's a bone. What's the connection to the case?"

"I have a feeling the answers you may come up with will be more intelligent than my hunch that this is somehow connected."

Doron examined the bone, its greenish spongy texture. He could not identify the substance, but the way it was spread out aroused his curiosity. Two hours and a dozen tests later, he decided that the bone was intriguing enough to interest Biton.

CHAPTER TWENTY-FOUR

It was morning. Rachel rose from her makeshift bed and started up the mountain. She knew her way along the narrow winding paths.

Members of the other order allowed her to approach and she had time along the trek to mull over the consequences of her move.

Rachel arrived at the cave, her destination. She gazed down at the hidden spring where her spouse was bathing. She had to admit the man still looked great.

But looks weren't everything.

Her fears and misgivings were rooted in the past, in memories of the man she had loved, the one who was permitted to love her. It was the only time she had allowed life to carry her away, to take control of her. The renewed contact beginning with the violent eruption of his image into her mirror and coffee cup, the phone call in which he said they would not sleep until their daughter was safe: all these had shattered her peace of mind. Rachel continued to gaze at the father of her daughter, the love of her youth, and tried to muster the courage to approach him.

It was the seventh time Israel immersed himself and the baby he was holding in the spring water. Despite being immersed, the baby, who appeared to be about two years old, was not crying. Israel continued the ritual, dunking and lifting, allowing the water to cover and then buoy the child. It was early morning; her man had always favored those hours between light and darkness, between day and night. Daybreak ushered in shadows, and Israel felt more comfortable when shadows fell across the land. But now, at the crack of dawn, with Eos's eyelids just starting to flutter, the shadows were slow to rise.

Rachel shivered. She watched his body and noticed how his skin stiffened and his hair bristled. He had apparently retained his muscular physique; the monastic life in the Galilee had curbed his natural tendency to put on weight. His long hair dripped water but even in the dim light of dawn, Rachel saw that the silver hairs outnumbered the dark ones.

Israel raised his hand to pick up a towel from a nearby rock, exposing his unique tattoo in all its glory. Written along his arm was the verse, "He that is slow to anger is better than the mighty; and he that ruleth his spirit better than he that taketh a city." The arm with these words enfolded the child's body, then made way for the white towel. After drying the child, he dressed him in a warm woolen garment and proceeded to dry himself.

When he raised his eyes to the roof of the cave where Rachel was standing, tears of joy filled his eyes. The light in the valley below was beginning to chase the shadows from the gullies and ravines.

"Homesick?" he called out to her. His voice reverberated around the depths of the cave. Rachel stayed at her post, determined not to let him trip her with his silvery tongue, not to let him throw dust in her eyes. She would promise him nothing until he had named his price. Israel's ambitions always came with a price tag, while he was an expert at evading payment.

"You can't be homesick for a place you've never been to."

"I meant did you miss me."

"I know."

He lifted the child and showed her his face.

"What do you say?"

"About what?

"About him."

The child was calm, seemingly unperturbed by the cold, the early hour and the fact that Israel did not really know how to hold an infant. The last time she had witnessed such self-assurance was when Mazzy held her daughter Noga.

"He's got your eyes and Aunt Malka's ears," Rachel said. "Is this why you summoned me?"

"We live in perilous times. Times that are a-changing."

"Interesting times. Some people make a career of uttering vague pronouncements and later claiming that they were right. Some of them even work with our daughter."

One of Israel's ambitions was to live in "interesting times," but unlike the Soothsayer team, when times were not interesting enough, he tried to change them.

Now he looked calmer. His *basso profundo* addressed her as if she were an accomplice in an as yet uncommitted crime.

"Tell me a little about our Mazal."

"I'm afraid she's going to disappoint you. She lacks the distinction you always sought."

"And how is our granddaughter?"

She kept quiet. This was Israel's way to unnerve her, by showing her how up-to-date he was: he knew about Noga and about her own vulnerability where the little girl was concerned.

"What do you want?"

"To turn back the clock."

"Meaning?"

"To make you a mother again."

Rachel immediately thought of the days and nights she'd have to spend in the role of mother and nurse. It wasn't only sleepless nights, diaper changing and the long wait to see if the investment was worth it; Rachel wasn't afraid of hard work, but she was not willing to go back to first grade in the school of life. It wasn't making space for an inquisitive toddler taking his first steps, it was the empty space when he left the house one day. The emptiness, vulnerability and helplessness that would accompany his declaration of independence. The child would grow up while the mother stayed behind. The fact that her daughter now roamed the world freely, without her supervision, made her reject the pleasure of repeating the experience. The events of Mazzy's life in the last few days had turned a mother's fear into a reality.

"You're on the wrong platform; that train left the station a few years ago," Rachel said.

"I would still like you to be a mother to Zohar, to raise him, to make sure he realizes his potential." In the meantime Zohar had succumbed to sleep, Israel gently laid him in the shade, covering him with a prayer shawl.

"Where's his mother?"

"She's not really fit for the job."

"What's the rate you're willing to pay the babysitter?"

"Our daughter will go on breathing. At least until Zohar is old enough to get to know his half-sister."

Rachel was visibly alarmed by this last pronouncement. His attitude toward his nearest and dearest always bordered on the extreme, like the way he conducted his life. He may still have had some feelings toward them, but just as he had abandoned them twenty years ago, he would surely do so again. He had become cold and calculating, as if dealing with complete strangers.

"How do you know where all this is going?"

"A little bird told me."

"A pigeon?"

"With a message. They didn't even bother to encrypt it. Just a verse from Isaiah. A message you can find in any house."

"Which verse?"

"Cease ye from man whose breath is in his nostrils, for wherein is he to be accounted for."

"What does it mean?"

"Bottom line? The Gates of Heaven are about to open."

After all these years, he was still capable of shocking her with his blunt honesty.

"This indeed sounds worrying, but why to Lilith's Daughters in particular?"

"The primordial order is restored. For women who refuse to be helpmates, this is bad news indeed."

Rachel's face reflected her calculation of the survival odds of whoever was embroiled in that conflict. For Israel, however, this offered an opportunity. Rachel knew that she had to bargain for what she wished to achieve.

"What is it you want," Israel asked, when she didn't respond.

"I want them to keep away from her. I want to cause enough damage to scare them, or to make them focus on me. Anything to keep her out of it. I want the same thing you want, but not for the same reasons."

"This means hurting one of them."

"If that's what you say," said Rachel.

"So you want what everyone in this game wants. You want the names."

Rachel knew that Lilith's Daughters were the only ones possessing this knowledge. At least, that's what she had thought until now. She had no time for shilly-shallying, for tactics.

"Do you have the names?"

"Not *the* names; I have names. Not enough to win, but it can make the difference, pave the way."

"So what do you need me for?"

"I have the perfect plan. It is not without risk, but it will satisfy everybody in the end. I need one madman to carry it out and lots of luck. I'll give the madman the names that I have, and he'll forestall the opening of Heaven's Gate. Everything will remain as before, and except for the Nephilim, everyone will be happy."

"And if you can't find a madman, a madwoman will do."

"Actually, a madwoman is preferable; it will instill in them enough doubt about fighting. Whatever you say about Lilith's Daughters, they managed to domesticate them pretty well."

"So how come everyone is satisfied at the end of the day?"

"The appropriate name will enable you to kill the appropriate Naphil. Everybody's happy. The Gate of Heaven stays closed, Lilith's Daughters calm down. You are endowed with the ability to heal all wounds. Even if something does happen to Mazzy, you can heal her and be at peace with yourself. The end of the world does not come; Zohar gets a babysitter. I am content."

"And all this happens without you risking yourself one jot. Really! At worst, something might happen to the babysitter."

"I told you my plan was perfect."

"How will I know which one? Who to pick?"

He smiled at her, impressed with her gumption, her desperation and her love.

"It's luck, but I trust you to know. You will know when you call his name, when you look him in the eye, when you get close enough."

She kept quiet. Thoughts whirled in her brain, but she tried to maintain as cool a face as she could.

"Is it your boss's idea for you to stand here in this spring?"

Israel looked down at the slumbering child, "Thy path is in the great waters, and thy footsteps are not known."

This was as close as he would get to supplying a motive, and even this offer would be for a limited time. He preferred her to be the madwoman, but if not, he had a Plan B. Israel might be insensitive on occasion, but he was never out of control.

"I must say goodbye to her."

"I'd advise you to do so also in the event that your mission fails."

Rachel mulled this over silently. It was a moment of quiet, cool morning air. Israel came closer and broke the silence, whispering in her ear the names of the Nephilim that had been captured. She etched them in her memory, then turned back and hastily ran down the mountain to change her daughter's fate.

CHAPTER TWENTY-FIVE

Gaby was unstoppable.

He was enthusiastic, energetic, dynamic, and didn't stray from his script. If Mazzy had not heard him practice his spiel a week earlier, once before bed and then while shaving, maybe the initial impression would have been different. Maybe not.

"I honestly believe that this is the breakthrough we've been waiting for. It's a win-win situation, and the investment will yield results in a fairly short time. Toddlers who learn sign language exhibit more gains the more progress they make. They score better on IQ tests and they build the foundation for a larger vocabulary. They play more sophisticatedly than their peers. Sign language can also be an incentive for the emergence of first words. Communication is accelerated, frustration is reduced, contact with parents improves, the children's inner world is richer and they show more interest in their surroundings."

Gaby's performance was spot on. He kept an even rhythm in his speech, so she could not cut him short, and he had chosen the perfect timing, at least as he saw it. But Mazzy's reaction was not what he expected.

There were moments when she was ready to strangle him. All the love in the world could not compete with such a cold, precise analysis of something that concerned their daughter. But then she realized that her reaction hadn't really much to do with him. This time it wasn't about him.

"Are you done?" she asked.

"Yes."

"No chance," she announced categorically.

"Why?"

"Maybe at Aurora's day care, it's OK for kids to speak with their hands, but in every other kindergarten and sandbox it's going to look weird."

"But this will take place at home, not at day care, and anyway she doesn't play in sandboxes."

Mazzy took a deep breath and steadied herself. The chasm between Gaby's well-planned, sterile, analytical world, where kids didn't play in sandboxes because they were dirty and full of dog poop, and her present world, where nothing was certain, had apparently reached a new peak. And it wasn't about sign language, either. She had stumbled just as clumsily as he had.

Mazzy scooped up Noga from the carpet and hugged her close, as if to distance her from Gaby's influence. Noga smiled her bewitching smile and did not complain about her game being interrupted. For a moment, her sparring partner watched in silent delight; then they resumed their argument.

"Look at her, does she look like a child who needs help?"

"Perhaps not at the moment, but she must learn to communicate, and not just with people who know how to interpret every smile and gesture she makes."

He was right, of course, but it wasn't really relevant. Yariv would have understood her, would have grasped what riled her and never tried to sell her on such an idea. Yariv wouldn't have needed her to spell it out.

"She is a very happy little girl who has a much richer inner world than all the kids in her play group put together."

Mazzy herself was surprised at how much of Izzy's vocabulary had crept into her speech.

"Why do you have to drag day care into every argument? I told you most of the project would be carried out at home."

"It's our daughter, not a project!"

"Come on! You know that I don't really view it that way. Don't hang on my phrases. You know what? Ignore the way I presented it and tell me what you think of the idea itself."

Their little girl was normal. She had a small problem with her speech development, that's all.

Gaby obsessed about her development; he checked it constantly and came to the conclusion that she was normal by all criteria, but for the unforgivable fact that Noga had not yet said her first word.

Mazzy had asked him to be patient. They bounced around between speech therapists. One by one, the list of experts shrank. They started with the best in the field, and then went down the pecking order to ones that had yet to build their reputation. They both agreed that they were not going to try any alternative therapies. Curiously, it was Mazzy who objected to alternative treatments. She wanted to keep the girl away from that cabal of soothsayers, mystics, clairvoyants, sorceresses, witch doctors, psychics and mind readers. Noga giggled happily.

"I need to think about it."

"What's there to think about?"

"There is. Plenty."

"Why is sign language different from what we've done so far?"

"It's different because it's visible. Children will see it when she plays, and their parents will jump to the wrong conclusions. We'll be fending off questions..."

"What kind of questions?"

Mazzy bit her lip. She could imagine all the smirks, teasing and name-calling. She'd had enough of that growing up, trying to invite friends home, or when Rachel attended social gatherings with her. People don't approve of things they don't understand. There are laws, there is logic, and this is how it should be. When there are deviations, problems arise. Then you need to explain, clarify, prevaricate and lie.

"Mute children are very rare. People will assume she's deaf or has special needs, some weird disease. They'll invent an explanation and give it a name."

"But it has no name. If it did, there would be a cure, a treatment. This is not a disease. She simply does not talk. There is no physiological defect."

"If there's no label, they'll come up with one, because they want to understand the phenomenon. If she were deaf, they'd know what to say and what not to say, they'd know how to act around her."

"But she's none of those things. If people ask, we'll simply tell them."

The discussion of normality and how important it was for Noga to be normal would have to wait for another time, when they were both less stressed. She had no intention of making a decision under duress.

"People see sign language and right away they think 'deaf-mute.'"

"But this is not regular sign language: it's much simpler. Some kids use these signs unconsciously; it's almost intuitive. They get it right away. Noga will acquire it in a jiffy, and then we'll be able to talk to her, to communicate with her."

"I communicate with her."

"But I don't. I can't. You have your methods, your feelings, and the looks she sends you. You know how to interpret them. I don't have it."

"So now it's about you?"

As soon as the words exited her mouth, she regretted them, but it was too late.

"That was uncalled for, Mazzy. There was no need to go there."

"You're right."

"It's not about me."

"No, it's not, but you stress me out and then I say things I don't mean."

Gaby restrained himself from saying anything that might escalate the argument into a full-blown fight. He suspected Mazzy of often saying harsh words to provoke him, reigniting the fire. She was much better at arguing, and she often won. She complained that he lacked initiative, always asked her what to do and let her make decisions, and that, he knew, drove her nuts. Here he was telling her what he thought they should do, being decisive and resolute, and still she rebuffed him.

"Since when do you care what people think? What counts is what's good for Noga."

"You just don't get it and I haven't got the time to explain."

"Try anyway."

"You're treating her as someone different, and she's not."

"All I care about is her welfare."

"You see? You don't get it. This is something I know first hand. When they stick you with a label that doesn't fit you at all, you can't ever shake it off."

Gaby sensed that this was somehow connected to growing up in Rachel's shadow, but he knew he wouldn't get a more precise explanation. Anyway, pursuing the matter wouldn't advance his cause.

"Shall we defer the discussion to the weekend?"

He saw that Mazzy was angry but wasn't sure if it was because he was too persistent or not feisty enough.

"Yeah, the weekend is fine. What's your work log?"

At once they reverted to being a regular couple trying to mesh their schedules: checking their calendars and planners, leaving each other notes on the fridge.

"I'm not sure, but if we're going to work this out, I'll make time. At least I can be home on-call."

"But they always call you on weekends when you're on-call."

"Well, that's the best I can do this week. We really need to make a decision. We've been dragging it out for too long."

Mazzy's pager beeped and she saw it was from Sima.

"I'll do my best, but this case I'm on might be coming to a close. Maybe the Judge will issue a warrant for the suspect's arrest, in which case, our weekend plans will go kablooey."

This sounded like an excuse, a copout or a retreat. Like their pagers rescuing them from family dinners. He also knew that he might as well be happy the round ended with a tie. It was the best score he could get right now at his home game.

CHAPTER TWENTY-SIX

Rachel tried to do as she was told and not think of anything, but it was a ridiculous demand, considering her situation. Ashling was feeling her brows with fingers that operated like suction cups on octopus tentacles, as she tried to pick up subcutaneous signals.

The names Israel had given her were the key, and like the sketch that they had been able to extract during the previous investigation, it was a specific name they were looking for. This was a puzzle that even Israel couldn't solve. The names themselves were an unrealized potential because she couldn't distinguish one Naphil from another. She had too few names and too many candidates.

Ashling tried to establish a connection between the names written down and the information stored in Rachel's head. She was positive that the answer was there and that they could decode it together.

Aelina's hands were smeared with blood up to her elbows. She examined the cow's entrails in the divining bowl, checking the texture of the dark liquid.

Ashling removed her fingers from Rachel's brow and shook them.

"I only have a few letters. It's in Hebrew, which makes it a bit more complicated. It's either five or six letters, with one repetition," said the blind Irishwoman.

Rachel wished her protégée had invested a little more time in studying Semitic languages.

"What are these letters?"

"Aleph, Mem, Resh and Samech. But they keep rearranging themselves all the time."

The three women looked at the names on their list. There were too many possibilities.

"Try again," Rachel commanded.

Ashling chose her words carefully. Rachel didn't know if this was a sign of trepidation, or because she was translating from her ancient mother tongue. Ashling thought in a language that few people spoke.

"You won't let me. You are shrinking the information."

"Make an effort," Rachel said.

The Irishwoman rubbed her palms and once more placed her hands on the coffee reader's temples.

"Close your eyes," Ashling said, proving that her blindness did not interfere with her vision.

Rachel obeyed reluctantly.

Aelina's divining bowl, in the meantime, began sputtering and overflowing.

"What exactly did he tell you?" asked Aelina.

"You'll know when you call his name, when you look him in the eye, when you are close enough," Rachel answered.

"The entrails tell you what's outside. There is a balance between the symbol and the answer. This doesn't happen here."

"What did you see?"

"An eye in front of a baboon watching an ibis that looks back at it. These are two symbols of Thoth facing each other."

Rachel tried to recall what she knew about the Egyptian moon god, the one that gave humanity wisdom and taught the world the skill of writing. The symbols Aelina saw in the blood and in the cow's intestines always reflected the answer sought. But a symbol identical to the answer was the equivalent of cosmic stuttering, a mere echo.

"So they see eye to eye. What is this eye, and what should we see in it?"

"It's the Udjat, the gouged eye of Horus, which Thoth restored to him. The eye is a symbol of healing, of the return to order and perfection. It suggests renewal and fulfillment or the rise of a new regime."

Rachel was familiar with the ancient Egyptian symbol: an eye with lashes resembling the crest and tail of a falcon, a shattered eye.

"So, OK, suppose this fits in with the change that's coming; what has this reflection got to do with the letters of the name?"

Ashling shushed Rachel and increased the pressure on her temples.

"Aleph, Resh, Mem, Samech. This is the order."

"Aramas?" said Rachel.

"Yes, like Hermes, in the Greek version, or Thoth. The cult center of Thoth was the city of Hermopolis. It was he that gave humans the knowledge of magic," Aelina explained.

Rachel didn't need to scan the short list of names again. She knew which Naphil it was.

"Armaros was the angel who endowed men and women with the power to control the supernatural. But how does this help me identify him? It is still only one name and two hundred identical faces," she said.

"It's the baboon staring at the ibis. Thoth's eyes always reflect his image. If you were to look into the Naphil's eyes, instead of seeing your own reflection, you would see his."

"So when you look each other in the eye, you'll be able to tell which one is Armaros," Ashling completed the thought.

Rachel took a deep breath. Now she had the missing piece of the puzzle, the information that would allow her to kill God's emissary. She had the name and the method by which to identify him in a sea of identical faces.

She no longer felt anxious. She possessed certainty; it was not one of the names on Israel's list. She had the key to obtaining change and peace of mind.

There was a certain clarity in the combination of letters in Armaros' name that kept turning in her head. She felt she had power at her disposal; it was no longer mere wishful thinking; it was the conviction of inexorable destiny.

CHAPTER TWENTY-SEVEN

The female detective led him in. Everyone saw her taking him in; it was her arrest and, apparently, it didn't bother her partner even though he had the insignia of chief inspector on his shoulders.

Barakiel had brought a hefty sheaf of documents with him; if it didn't exhaust the detectives, it would at least delay them.

The detective had only one page in front of her, face down.

Barakiel accepted the new situation calmly. He assumed he was smarter than the police officers who were about to interrogate him. The chief inspector took the initiative.

"Shall we begin?" he asked.

The detective shrugged. Barakiel wanted to end the oppressive silence.

The chief inspector read aloud what he had written.

"Name: Barak Almadon. How do you want us to address you: Barry? Ricky? Barush? Barak?"

The string of names irritated him; he cringed at the mention of each one. Trying a trick Saharel had taught him, he focused on the others' names, which he recalled were Mazzy and Yariv. This helped him regain his self-confidence, his advantage. He knew their real names and consequently was in control.

"I told you my name is Barak."

"Why do you sound so anxious?"

"I'm tired of answering the same questions."

"So I have a new one for you," said Mazzy. Barak straightened in his chair. "When did you start snatching women?"

The itch in the wings returned. Barakiel felt it under his skin, in his ribcage. It was not as pronounced as before the play, but it was still bothersome.

"What?"

"Did you know these women?" Yariv continued. Barak had no time to answer. Mazzy bombarded him with more questions.

"How long have you been following them? Did you spy on them? Did you rummage in their garbage trying to find their schedules, cultural activities, invitations to parties?"

"What is she talking about?" Barak turned to Yariv.

"I'm talking about Estie Shalvi-Aiello, a fourteen year-old girl; about Hagar Abizu, a lawyer; Milka the actress and and Abigail Odem, a university professor. Where do you keep them?"

"Just a second," he said calmly, searching through his papers and handing Mazzy a neatly collated pile. While she examined the packet, Barakiel continued his line of defense. "As you can see, I have signed affidavits, from five or six people, regarding the nights in question. In the Passover night case, I was with my friends. The same regarding the case a week ago, involving the professor, whom I've never met. Now, as for the incident in the theater, you already have my alibi and, if you examine the security cameras outside the 'Saving Grace' building, you'll conclude that I was never there on the night in question."

Mazzy ignored the papers he was waving. She leaned forward and fixed her eyes on him.

"Let me tell you something about myself. You don't have to tell me anything about yourself, just listen. When I was a little girl, we used to play 'Truth or dare.' I always chose dare, because I didn't know what they might ask me and I didn't want to lie. This is something my mother taught me."

He did not react.

"Did somebody instruct you not to say anything you're not sure of?"

"No, I figured it out myself. Just tell the truth. It's the easiest thing to repeat."

"You don't like lawyers, do you?"

"I have no problem with them. Sometimes you need them, sometimes you don't. It seems, right now, that I don't need a lawyer."

"What about Attorney Hagar Abizu?"

"What about her?"

"Did you love her?"

Barakiel burst out laughing. What could he tell her about love and Hagar? Nothing. What you didn't know, they couldn't get out of you. This woman was so careless, throwing about names as if they were worthless, spelling them out deliberately. Well, what did she know?

Mazzy returned to the form she was holding, filling out the details, trying to pigeonhole him using his answers.

"Are you married?"

"No."

"A widower?"

"No."

"Divorced?"

"No."

"Single?"

"Yes."

"Do you believe in God?"

"Yes."

"Do you know the Ten Commandments?"

"Yes."

"Thou shalt not covet, thou shalt not steal, thou shalt not kill? All of them?"

"Yes."

"What do you think God will say to you when you next meet Him?"

He knew he had to keep mum, but he couldn't help himself.

"I'll tell you when I see Him."

For whatever reason, Mazzy's questions seemed to have hit a nerve, cracking Almadon's frozen mask.

Yariv's beeper began to dance on the desk. When he ignored it, the cellphone in his pocket joined in. There, he found the sealed evidence bag containing the black feather. He had been carrying it with him all the time, not really sure why; somehow, the feather gave him confidence.

Yariv read a text from Doron, alerting him to a new finding. Perhaps it would bring the hoped-for breakthrough in the investigation. Almadon in the meantime would be lulled into a sense of security, and they could spring some airtight proof of guilt on him.

Barak Almadon's alibis were good. He was not on stage when Milka Umm-Alzabian was abducted. This had been established. On the other hand, if he were in the audience, whose hair was scattered on the stage? Who put it there? And why? There was no logical reason for planting incriminating evidence at the scene of the crime.

Yariv hoped that Doron would have at least some of the answers to these questions.

But instead of answers, Doron presented him with a piece of bone covered in some strange green material. According to the tests he had conducted, the proud owner of the bone had lived five thousand years ago.

"I don't have carbon dating; for this I need confirmation by archeologists. But this is a very ancient bone, absurdly old," said Doron.

"And you got it from Libby? Where is she?"

Doron shrugged. Yariv got impatient. "Sima!" he called.

"What? Why are you shouting?"

"I want Libby here ASAP. Not today, not in an hour, NOW. She can't just drop forensic evidence on us and vanish, without reporting, without explaining the circumstances."

Sima went back to her cubicle. Yariv knew she'd locate the policewoman wherever she was hiding.

"She should also fill out the deposit forms by herself," he added.

Doron moved inside Yariv's field of vision, obscuring Sima and grabbing his attention.

"Forget about the forms. Maybe this is the clue we need. He's one of those arrogant bastards who think they're superior to everybody. We have proof he was there. Maybe we need a little trigger, something to crack his armor so we can penetrate and break him. All I need to check is if he has a broken rib and if he has platinum there instead of calcium."

"Why did you decide to pin this on Almadon?"

"He's our only suspect. Everything points in his direction; he's our best bet. Whose DNA did you want me to match it with? All we need now is to give him an X-ray…"

"It doesn't matter if he has a broken rib or not."

"Why not?"

"No two people have exactly the same DNA. A man can't have a five thousand year-old bone in his body. You present this in court and the judge will laugh his head off."

Doron did not look amused. He found no humor in the situation. Yariv continued.

"If the bone contains Almadon's DNA, then it can't be five thousand years old. Somebody tampered with it to give such a misleading result. I don't need to know how it was done to confront him with this info. I'll just put the bone on the table. Obviously it was crucial for somebody to conceal the evidence by warping the data. That's good enough for me."

"In which case, I have something else to show you," said Doron.

"What?"

"I identified the substance covering the bone."

"What is it?"

"A compound of copper, cobalt, and hydrogen peroxide, crystallized in a monoclinic structure, with three unequal axes at right angles to each other. It's not very hard or rigid in consistency."

"Speak in simple language."

"It's a question of density and brittleness."

"Doron, give me a break."

"Never mind. This fits in with your theory that someone planted this bone or let it crystallize there, in order to hide something, or to try to wear it away. Delude us into thinking it dates back that far."

Yariv smiled. Up until now he had a pretty good hand in the poker game with Almadon, but now he had better cards to bluff with. He returned to the investigation room, only to sense a heavy silence hanging in the air, like an oppressively humid day in Tel Aviv. Barak was staring at the desk, and Mazzy was staring at Barak.

"What's going on? I leave you alone and you don't want to play?"

No one spoke. Yariv calculated his next move. He had prepared a question for Barakiel.

"Where did you go on Seder night?"

"I don't remember."

"Try."

"I guess I was at a Seder."

"With family?"

Mazzy crossed her legs. If you didn't know her, you wouldn't realize that she was very pleased with the question and concealed a smile. But Yariv knew her well.

"Yes."

"You have family?"

"People who are like family."

"Friends?"

"Yes."

"Good friends, like family."

Yariv let the answer echo in the room, to amplify how dumb it sounded.

"Cut the crap," Mazzy interrupted. "Abizu, Milka, and Professor Odem were kidnapped by the same person. We have DNA evidence. You can't argue with DNA. This guy is going to jail for a long, long time. Consecutive life sentences."

"If he's detained or barred from giving the missing women food or water, they'll die within seventy-two hours, and then it's premeditated murder. Times four," added Yariv.

"I didn't kidnap anyone, and you have no proof that I have any connection to this."

"So how did you do it? You cloned yourself? Where does the DNA come from?"

"If you can clone DNA, then you're in a league of your own and we can't nail you."

"And you don't have an identical twin out there."

Yariv picked up the box that lay at his feet, took out the bone and threw it on the desk. Barakiel recognized the smell immediately. The smell of malachite.

An ancient smell. Oh, these stupid humans! Somebody was dead. One of the Nephilim. Lilith's Daughters must have killed him, or worse. When a Naphil died, everyone paid the price. Except that he was stuck here and didn't know what the price was.

Now it wasn't just a tingle. Barakiel's stomach was in knots.

The smell that hit his nostrils was as an amalgam of all the toxic human odors that had seeped into the divine bodies of the Nephilim and polluted them: the stench of sweat and urine; blood and semen; oily secretions; decaying teeth; putrid, pus-filled lesions; excrement and vomit – all the odors that human flesh pollutes the earth with.

Barakiel rose from his seat, visibly disgusted, distancing himself from the bone. He grabbed hold of the desk to steady himself when a sudden dizziness came over him. He had to hold out only until the next abduction.

"You've got nothing on me," he spat at the detective. "You want me to help you, to pull you out of the hole you're in."

"You know the saying, God helps those who help themselves? Well, this is the time to help yourself, or else, God help you! And for someone who snatches women and threatens their lives, I wouldn't count on Him. You were so busy playing God yourself, you forgot that the real God resents such behavior. It's over, we know who you are."

Silence filled the room. The detective watched Barakiel, who was trying to hide the storm raging inside him. The fact that they knew who he was wouldn't have made any difference had he been outside. But he was inside, facing them and, again, he was the one paying the price. Could they really be on to him? Then once more he was the scapegoat. Azazel and Shamhazai wouldn't hesitate to abandon him, to humiliate him before humans, as they had done once before, with Hagar Abizu.

The Naphil and the lawyer had broken all the written and unwritten laws, and they both knew it. But at the end of the day, he was the one sent to the Athaliah to apologize, to offer contrition to a Lilith Daughter! If they didn't intend to remain here, then he was the only one liable to lose. Perhaps it was a test. A test of courage. This time he'd show Shamhazai what he was made of.

"I have no idea what you're talking about."

"We've got all we need to wrap up this case. You missed your chance. Sorry."

"So you don't need me."

"Look, nothing will get you off the hook here. So give us the location where the women are being kept. This is the only thing we're missing now. Give me the location, and we'll see what we can do."

Barakiel nodded and gave the detective a look of resignation. He waited. Yariv took out a statement form, put it in front of Barakiel and handed him a pen.

Barakiel scribbled a few words across the page.

Yariv showed the paper to Mazzy who gave Barakiel a contemptuous look.

"So you're pleading temporary insanity? You think that will get you out?"

"I said all I have to say. You read what I had to write."

He exuded an eerie calm, as if a great load had been lifted from his chest. To the two of them he looked quite sane.

"The Gate of Heaven is about to open."

THE SIXTH GATE
JUDGMENT

THE THIRTY-SIXTH DAY
FIVE WEEKS AND A DAY OF THE COUNTING OF THE OMER.

"If there arise a matter too hard for thee in judgment, between blood and blood, between plea and plea, and between stroke and stroke, being matters of controversy within thy gates: then shalt thou arise, and get thee up into the place which the Lord thy God shall choose."

DEUTERONOMY 17:8

Two days had passed since Libby saw Doula Ashtribu disappear into the clouds, carried off by the Nephilim. Since giving Doron the bone fragment, she could not sleep easy and only dozed for an hour or two at a time, her mind haunted by images of Nephilim on the horizon.

Even though Barakiel was at the police station, along with the bone and black feather, the complete picture still eluded the detectives. The primeval world which saw the dissolution of the covenant between Lilith's Daughters and the Nephilim was so distant that even the clearest signal could not apprise the sons of Adam and Eve the extent of the danger.

Dazed, Libby walked alongside the Athaliah in the

hallway, where her assistants scurried and slithered like lizards trying to shed their tails in desperation.

"You didn't see what went on there."

"I was at the ranch, or what was left of it. I saw what they're capable of; it was nothing new; we know their power. Whoever needs to know, knows. This was the reason we made the pact with them in the first place. Right now, nothing can be done about it."

Libby was about to erupt. The fact that even the Athaliah had to hark back to the distant past for an explanation almost drove her crazy. More papers were shoved into the Athaliah's hands as she passed through the hallways, more reports and intelligence assessments. No action.

"I don't intend to give them any more information; just put what they've already got in order."

"Who will you talk to?"

"Whoever will listen. Mazzy. Her team is involved. They're pretty good. More and more cases are solved thanks to them. There's information there. Perhaps they can even help us with the names."

"That's nonsense! Your job is to make sure she stays out, not to get her involved."

Libby felt an urge to grab the head of The Order and shake her. The Athaliah didn't get it because she hadn't been there. She couldn't understand the desperation, the slimy, searing feeling that grips you when you confront a cocksure Naphil who then hands you a piece of his body and mocks you. A Naphil who lets you know the real score, not how The Order prefers to interpret it.

"I know my job: to keep The Order safe."

"There is this pesky thing about secret orders: for some reason, we insist on keeping them secret."

Libby realized that if she continued to badger the head of The Order, the Athaliah would simply dismiss her. She had done all she could, and then some. It was time to let The Order act. She would operate on her own.

"Any idea when all this will end? Or when the next abduction might occur?" It sounded as if the Athaliah was thinking aloud.

Libby thought she had gotten across to the Athaliah, but now the latter's tone had changed. She reverted to her cold, peremptory tone. The young policewoman encountered a steady pair of eyes.

"All you need know is that The Order will overcome this tribulation, too. We shall renew our days as of old."

The old slogans were repeating themselves; The Order kept telling anyone who would listen that everything was all right; these were just some bumps in the road, a temporary contretemps along the way back to Kedem. For the first time in her life, Libby wondered whether calls to her office were being recorded. For political reasons. Unofficial documentation the Athaliah could use when called to the Great Chamber of Mothers.

"Yes, the Athaliah."

"Fine. Now run off. Go do your job."

With perfect timing, one of the guards opened the main door, letting in a gust of cold reality. Libby tried to hide her hurt feelings. She had to calm down. The tension was already affecting her. She was determined to talk to Mazzy, at whatever cost. If the Order didn't realize things had changed, she'd have to do what Doula Ashtribu had taught her. No single member of The Order was more important than its fate.

The Athaliah watched Libby walk away. She was aware of the despair she had sown in her; she had recognized the fear that The Order might disappear from the face of the Earth.

But the Athaliah had no time for fear and premonitions.

She knew that the timing of the great battle for the future of The Order would be decided by those who had control of events: the Nephilim.

CHAPTER TWENTY-EIGHT

Mazzy and Yariv poured over the documents and the data for the umpteenth time, trying to penetrate the warped mind of the predator they had subdued and caged. They didn't know who or what he was, but his – or his accomplices'– ability to carry out the abductions with such ease, and without leaving a trace, was awe inspiring. After going over the information yielded by the bone fragment, they had been forced to revisit the time they had spent with the apex predator, an evolutionary specimen that had ascended the ladder.

The statement he had given them was passed on to Elisha Itzkovitch, but the response he gave through the speakerphone was neither encouraging nor helpful.

"The sum of the phrase 'The Gate of Heaven is about to open' is equal to 'Pray for Heaven's mercy.' But the addition can go in more than one direction. One thousand six hundred and eighteen. Eighteen is always two-directional, ambiguous. One thousand six hundred is equal to the chain of letters in the verse, 'He that is the first in his own cause seems just, but his neighbor cometh and searcheth him.'"

"So this means that he is the just one in the story? After he abducted all those women?" Yariv interjected.

"That's why I say it could come up to one thousand six hundred and eighteen, which is equal to 'O Lord my God, in Thee do I put my trust; save me from all them that persecute me and deliver me.' Maybe this is bigger than what we can answer now. At this moment, the letters tell us to trust the Master of the Universe."

"So your advice is to pray? This is your professional advice?" Yariv couldn't mask the derision in his voice.

"At the moment? Yes."

Yariv almost ripped into Itzkovitch down the phone, but Mazzy stayed his arm. She sensed the storm had only just begun to rage in him.

"Okay, Elisha, we'll let you do your work. As soon as you come up with something, I want you over here," she said, and hung up before Yariv could add anything else.

The legal aspect of the case would be resolved in the next few weeks, but the chances of finding the missing women were fast diminishing. When they had detained Almadon, they considered the possibility they might fail in their mission. A series of skillfully executed abductions did not leave much hope for the victims' survival. Barak Almadon might be an angel of death who had sealed the fate of these women long before he entered the interrogation room.

At this stage of their careers, Mazzy and Yariv knew that such cases, those that began with a big bang, usually ended with a whimper, with nobody remembering what all the fuss had been about.

They felt they needed a break from the findings and from the confrontation with Almadon, to slow down the flow of adrenalin and restore a healthy pulse.

Mazzy conjured up divers plunging into shark-infested waters without a protective cage. She was beginning to appreciate the renewed zest for life that encounters with such primeval forces produced.

The silence in the room was becoming oppressive. Yariv was the first to break it.

"So we clinched the case for the kidnapper, but not for the victims."

"I'm sure we're missing something."

Neither of them was a great believer in God, but dealing with Death and its emissary evoked the need to find logical explanations that would prevent them from repeating their mistakes.

"Where? What have we overlooked?"

"The horizon."

"You want to look forward when we're not even clear about what happened?"

The double meaning was not lost on her, so she redirected her feelings with a practical question about data.

"What was he planning to do with them?"

"What, because we don't have the bodies?"

"We have bodies, just not those of the women. He's obviously not afraid to leave dead bodies behind. You've seen him. He's clever. Too sophisticated. He thinks he's invulnerable."

"Only because we haven't dug them up. This is a long way from becoming a cold case."

"What does he plan to do with them? Why does he need four women? What's his horizon?"

"Horizon?"

Yariv bowed his head, then lifted it toward an imaginary horizon, staring at the wall as if he were standing on the edge of a cliff overlooking vast expanses. Then he pressed Mazzy to his body in an avuncular gesture, enclosing her shoulders in his arms.

"You see, Mazzy? One day this whole case will be yours. This is the only horizon I can see."

She knew she was expected to laugh airily and diffuse the tension, but she felt a more basic desire, one she was supposed to ignore. The close contact awakened in her eddies of longing, and she put her head on his shoulder, inhaling his smell. He turned to her with unabashed yearning. Instead of putting a stop to it, she emitted a different kind of laughter, one that conveyed nervousness and capitulation.

He lowered his head and their lips touched, first lightly, then voraciously. Her incisor bruised his lower lip and her lunging tongue tasted blood, the acrid taste of living flesh. She wasn't sure why she was so repelled.

But soon the revulsion was replaced by expectation. She tried in vain to resist; Yariv was so close, his heartbeat could just as well have been hers.

Mazzy tugged at his shirt nervously, exposing his body, panting and inviting. Too much. Too fast. Too right. Too desiring.

Yariv almost lost his balance when his gun belt was released. As he cleared a space on the desk, she put her hand down his boxer shorts, cupping and steering, but the moment was fleeting and all that remained was his oppressive weight on top of her. He continued to thrust, as she lay fettered underneath. She had no idea how much time had elapsed, but with every stroke she felt more depleted. She tried to synchronize her movements with his, to hasten the end, until she heard a moaning sound at her neck and the air from his lips in a short, muffled spurt.

Mazzy patted his shoulder, as she did Noga's back after extracting a successful burp. For a long embarrassing moment, they remained coupled, until he withdrew. Mazzy gave him a critical look, unable to conceal her disappointment at the lackluster experience.

A series of urgent raps on the door made them jump. Mazzy struggled into her clothes. Yariv followed suit. The tapping on the door intensified,

"Mazzy, it's Libby! I have to talk to you!"

It was not customary to lock the doors at the precinct. The situation required a response. Mazzy motioned to Yariv to hurry. She spoke to Libby through the door.

"What is it?"

"We need to talk."

"Half a minute."

Mazzy turned to Yariv, who was still zipping his trousers. He had the look of someone wishing he was elsewhere.

"Get dressed and out of the office," she said quietly. "I'll see what she wants, and afterwards we'll try to close the case. We'll have to deal with the rest as we go along."

"I'm the one who should talk to Libby. Two days ago I asked Sima to track her down. She owes me some answers about…"

"Yariv, let me talk to her. If you still have some questions later…"

He didn't argue. Her tired, impatient tone prompted him to join her in straightening the desk. He cleared his throat and said, "This time I'm not giving up."

"What?"

"This time I'll fight for you."

"It's not war."

Mazzy breathed deeply and attempted to regain her composure. Trying to forget what had just happened with Yariv, she went off in search of Libby. But when she found her pacing near the photocopiers, Libby looked as if someone had pressed the "Fast Forward" button on the film of her life. There were dark circles around her eyes and her pupils were like two eclipsed suns. She had clearly come bearing news.

"There was another one."

"What, while we had that bastard in the interview room?"

"No, much earlier than you think. There's one you don't know about. Altogether five women were kidnapped. It's the Doula from the ranch. They took her and you don't even know about it. This is how I got the bone, the one I gave to Doron. There's no time to go into all the details and, anyway, you wouldn't understand. There's no way you can understand."

It was strange to hear Libby talk so fast about the ranch, the Doula, and the abduction. With every additional detail, Mazzy's heart sank deeper as she realized that Libby knew more than they did, and that she had not bothered to share her knowledge. Apart from the fact that there had been another abduction, the circumstances of the acquisition of the bone appeared less complicated than they had thought. After years of working in the field, and being Rachel's daughter, Mazzy recognized the feeling: Libby was telling the truth.

Lilith's Daughter then told her about The Order and about the Athaliah, about the lost names of the Nephilim and about the opening of Heaven's Gate, about the predicted battle of uncertain outcome, and about the fate that awaited the abducted women.

"There's a slim chance, but believe me, we don't have many options. I wouldn't have come to you otherwise. I'm not supposed to reveal anything to you, the head of The Order made that clear. But it's important for you to know that the names are the key. Not necessarily all of them. One or two will suffice to frighten them."

"Well, what can I do?" Mazzy asked.

"'Soothsayer,' maybe Itzkovitch, Izzy or the Russian with the cards. They're good at their job; maybe they'll find another way to approach it. I don't know what your team is capable of doing, but I know that as far as the names are concerned, you have the best chance."

Her phone vibrated. The caller ID showed Yariv. Mazzy often thought that if women were allowed to run the world, everything would be much simpler. Much more correct. Right now they were facing an ancient adversary, and here was her own private adversary, intent on explaining his sexual dysfunctions. Mazzy ignored the call.

"I'll do what I can," she said to Libby.

"The Order will watch both of us from now on."

The phone buzzed again insistently. What was wrong with him? Couldn't he control his crushed ego for a few seconds?

Mazzy was still glaring at her phone when Rachel stormed down the corridor, pushing Libby out of her way.

"For once in your life you'll listen to me!"

Her shout was still hanging in the air as an explosion tore through the hallway ceiling.

A thick cloud of dust floated into the room. Mazzy drew her gun, instinctively crouching down to make herself a smaller target. She breathed the cleaner air near the floor, cautiously straightened up and waited for the dust to clear. Her mother was nowhere to be seen, Libby had simply vanished.

Sima emerged from the hallway, gun at the ready. She kept close to the cinderblocks that were still standing. Mazzy motioned to her to cover the hallway, and Sima zigzagged to the left, creating shooting angles for Mazzy and herself. Rattles of automatic fire were heard through the smoke, then shouts and the sounds of running feet that were soon replaced by a whooshing that reminded Mazzy of whirring fans.

Silence fell for a moment, but a cacophony of screams of terror and pain soon replaced it. It barely sounded human. Mazzy and Sima held their fire.

An acrid smell of cordite was everywhere, but mixed with a faint aroma of fennel. Mazzy could see a clear, starry sky in places where the ceiling should have been. The night sky looked incongruously calm compared to the pandemonium in the precinct.

Mazzy and Sima exchanged looks. Sima, whose angle of vision included the entire hallway, motioned to her comrade in arms that the coast was clear. Mazzy came out and positioned herself outside the room, aiming her gun at the center of the hallway. On the ground lay an ancient double-barreled firearm, identical to Yariv's antique Lupara, a caliber of gun that could prove very useful in the present circumstances. As she bent down to pick it up, she noticed a blurry form with black contours hurtling toward her. The world seemed to come to a standstill.

It was clear she had nowhere to go. She had no time to be scared, though it was clear she had good reason to be. A sudden burning sensation spread through her chest, and for a moment, all she could see was a little black sun; the next moment her back hit the wall, followed by her head. Struggling to breathe, she turned onto her side and vomited.

She lay on the floor, eyes closed and fighting for breath. She felt as if her bones had turned to liquid, and the liquid spread pain as it coursed through her body. She opened her eyes a crack, and was surprised to see a few fluorescent ceiling lights still working. She could dimly discern a female figure surrounded by five identical men, who seemed to be sporting black wings. A welcome darkness enveloped her.

CHAPTER TWENTY-NINE

Yariv played possum. The excruciating pain in his shoulder prevented him from making any sharp movements. He tried to take deep breaths and relax, but his ribs were broken and each breath caused unbearable pain. His injured shoulders refused to relay orders to his arms and hands, rendering him immobile. In his mind he tried to replay the events that had brought him to this wretched position, stuck under a smashed wooden door at police headquarters.

First, part of the roof collapsed on the detectives' heads and then, like birds of prey, lithe, muscular figures descended from the sky. At first Yariv suspected the aid of hang-gliders, then he saw the black wings and thought perhaps they were wearing some type of high-tech special bulletproof vest.

They attacked from all directions. The officer standing next to him fired a burst but was knocked flat by an airborne assailant. Yariv managed to empty half a clip before something wrenched the weapon gun from his hand with a force that dislocated his shoulder. Then, with an outstretched arm, the assailant pushed Yariv against the wall, squeezing his lungs of air and dropping him to the floor like a ragdoll.

Scared and confused, Yariv stared at the fleet figures, who rushed through the hallways wreaking havoc, pummeling anyone standing in their way. Playing dead, he was able to see three of the attackers grab Libby and haul her up through the opening in the ceiling. Judging by the mayhem in the hallway, he assumed he had been out for quite a while.

The spicy smell of *shakshuka* filled his nostrils. The pain must have made him delirious. First, he saw Barak Almadon walking out of the holding cell whose door had been yanked off its hinges. Barak flashed him a victorious smile, then his shoulders sprouted two black wings, and he too disappeared through the ceiling.

Now the other figures, too, looked like angels with black wings. A solitary, noble looking woman was facing them. Yariv continued to watch the drama unfold, wondering where his feverish imagination would lead him. The woman was pointing a gun at the five angels. Yariv was slightly amused by the rich details his brain produced, until he noticed that the firearm she was holding was identical to his lucky gun, the Lupara.

The pain was making it difficult to focus his thoughts. "That must be why these five things surrounding the woman are cookie-cutter identical, and all look like Barak Almadon," he reasoned

The fact that the other assailants had soared into the sky with the captive Libby did not seem to impress the woman with the gun, who continued to aim with a steady hand. There was something disturbing in her defiance. Aiming a Lupara at a winged creature should not have inspired such equanimity, and yet neither side seemed too perturbed by it.

At this point, Yariv was no longer sure if the woman was a figment of his imagination or some faded memory that had surfaced at this strange time. It wasn't clear to him why, of all the women in the world, his brain had conjured up Rachel Simantov.

CHAPTER THIRTY

In the general maelstrom, Rachel saw her daughter smash against a wall like a crash-test dummy, then collapse feebly to the ground. Rachel rushed to her side and checked her pulse. She was breathing, but her condition looked dismal. Rachel shuddered at the implications of her sneak peek into the future.

An antique gun lay next to Mazzy's limp hand, identical to the one Libby had let roar from both barrels just before she was hoisted in the air. The time wasn't right to carry out Israel's mission, but Rachel recalled his words about the benefits of killing a Naphil. Perhaps she could use this knowledge now, not when it suited Israel.

Rachel collected the weapon and, smiling expectantly, walked straight to the center of the maelstrom. The Nephilim snarled, baring their teeth, unimpressed by the gun leveled at them. Four figures bowed to her like sumo wrestlers about to grapple.

The black angel facing her must have been their leader. He looked like he was about to ask her to dance, as if to challenge her to rise to the occasion.

Taking a few steps toward her adversaries, Rachel invoked the ancient verse of Lilith's Daughters, the Possessors of the Name. "Behold I die, but God shall be with you and bring you again unto the land of your fathers, and the land shall have rest when I am gone until the gate opens."

"You can pull the trigger. It doesn't matter. This verse no longer scares anyone."

Rachel whispered the names of the Nephilim that Israel had given her. A small spark ignited over the speaker's head, like a flicking cigarette lighter. The Naphil approached her, pulling up his shirt to expose his chest.

"God has revealed your secret to us – you do not possess the names!"

Rachel used every second of this cat and mouse game to stare deep into his companions' eyes. She went from one to the other, hoping for a stroke of luck. Again and again, she was met by her own reflection, that of a woman trying to present a firm, resolute stance before a superior foe. Then returned her gaze to the Naphil facing her and, in the whites of his eyes, saw his arrogant, self-assured image.

"Who are you trying to con? You're not even one of Lilith's Daughters."

"I am something much worse, Armaros."

The Naphil's face registered his astonishment at the pronouncement of his name. Letters flashed over his head: Aleph, Resh, Mem, Resh, Samech.

He lunged at Rachel who, without thinking, pulled the trigger. The full force of the Lupara slammed into the Naphil's chest.

At once Armaros began to glitter, and sparks, like writhing snakes, enveloped his figure. Blue lightning burst in through the hole in the ceiling, wriggling and squirming around the black angel; his feet were surrounded by yellowish-red wheels of fire. The fiery ball encircled the pair, hissing and sputtering, emitting thick pillars of smoke and blue fog. A sound of a stifled blast was heard, like a rock hitting a pond of cosmic energy sending ever widening ripples and waves to the shores of the Seven Seas. The other black-winged creatures soared toward the orange sky. The wave emanating from the shot broke in all directions, engulfing everything in its wake.

Rachel felt it pass through her. Her skin began to itch, her eyes teared up, her muscles squirmed, and an internal burning seared her being. The wave knocked down the walls of the precinct as if they were made of cardboard.

Rachel tried to take a deep breath, but the space around her seemed drained of oxygen. She hugged the lifeless body of the black-winged angel and cried bitterly.

CHAPTER THIRTY-ONE

Mazzy woke up in a green room reeking of Lysol, pleased to discover that she was still breathing. But a second later a searing pain in her head made any attempt at rising impossible.

She could hear Gaby's voice making promises to God, uttering oaths and conjurations, confessing his love to her and telling her again and again that everything would be fine. Judging by the repeated appeals to the Supreme Being, she concluded that her situation was direr than she had thought and that the burning she felt was only the beginning. Slowly, she began to recall the attack on the police station, but the order of events eluded her. For a moment, the scene with Yariv scorched her memory. Gaby's tone changed, becoming deeper and more desperate.

"You must listen to me now so you'll realize you're not going anywhere. You're not going to leave me or Noga. It's out of the question. It's not going to happen. Even if your C3 and C4 are broken and the MRI and CT show whatever they show, it doesn't matter. It's not just that I love you – I need you, and you can't walk away when someone needs you. Noga needs you and we're not giving up. If you think you are, you're wrong. I'll chase you and bring you back.

I'll get your mom and her psychos, we'll light candles and hold hands and whatever else is needed."

This was too much. Mazzy opened one eye a crack and saw Gaby was almost choking. The relief on his face when he noticed her movement only fanned her guilty feelings. The tubes and electrodes connecting her to a rack of monitors did not help either. Gaby asked her to squeeze his fingers and nod if she could hear him, then pinched her arm and leg until the sensation made her flinch.

Gaby reached for the red call button, almost breaking the cord in his repeated attempts to get the nurses' attention. The chaos that flooded the hospital after the attack had kept the staff very busy. Now that Mazzy had opened her eyes, Gaby was able to organize his thoughts.

He studied the monitors and the notes on the chart hanging at the end of his wife's bed. The data was not conclusive but where Mazzy was concerned he could brook no doubt. Gaby ran along the ward aggressively seeking the attention of one of the doctors. He was going to teach them something about triage. The security guards would have to drag him away.

A woman with black hair and charcoal eyes took advantage of the commotion by drawing the green hospital curtain and creating a private nook for her daughter and herself.

Rachel examined Mazzy carefully, squeezing herself into the space between the bed and the wall. Standing near Mazzy's head, she put her hands on her daughter's shoulders. She stared at her in silence, her eyes expressing comfort and reassurance.

"Mom?" Mazzy managed a whisper.

"I'm here."

Mazzy tried again to lift herself, but the pain made her lie back again. Rachel wrapped her arms around her; she had found her little girl, and she wouldn't allow her to get lost again. Mazzy could not hold back her tears.

"Enough, sweetie."

"It hurts so much, Mom. Deep in my bones. The pain…"

"Enough. Mommy will give you a kiss and make it go away."

Rachel kissed her daughter's brow. A wave of sweetness washed over Mazzy, filling her with a strange cloying sensation, as if she had been injected with a viscous substance, like a donut being filled with jelly.

Calmness was being restored throughout her damaged body. From her toes to the end of her hair, serenity and elation took the place of aches and pains. The dizziness and the blurred vision were gone, her neck relaxed, her spine straightened. She took the deepest breath and held it. The pain was all gone; nothing hurt.

"What did you do?"

"What nobody else had the guts to. I killed a Naphil."

Mazzy hugged her mother tightly. Rachel surrendered to the embrace, and when she finally tore herself away, she said quietly, "We have no time now. Nobody knows what happened to you or how. I must convince them that you are much tougher than you really are, or than you've been until now."

Mazzy nodded. This was not the time for mother-daughter games. They reverted to being Mazzy and Rachel.

"I have to give you something, and then go."

Something kicked Mazzy in the stomach, from the inside. She didn't hear herself ask, "Why?" but she must have blurted out the question.

"Because such things come at a price," Rachel said, stuffing a crumpled note in Mazzy's hand, and patting her clenched fist.

"Names. Six of them. I hope it's enough."

The realization that Rachel wouldn't be there for long sharpened Mazzy's attention.

"Enough for what?"

"For your 'Soothsayer'. There are very few people who can extract the other names from this little list. I'll try some of the people I know who may have a chance. It's time I cashed in some markers."

"Why can't we work together? Put our heads together?"

A slight smile creased Rachel's lips, "Because we've never been able to."

"If you know what to think and how to listen, maybe you shouldn't go. Maybe there is a way."

"This isn't the time."

"Then go! We'll manage. Even if we don't, it won't matter."

"You needn't be so dramatic."

Rachel had no patience for drama; she needed to stay focused. Black angels were descending from the sky, which may have been a good excuse to fall to pieces, but right now she couldn't afford to.

"Someone told me once that there are two kinds of people, those who run and those who fight," Mazzy persisted.

"I said this about men," Rachel corrected her.

"And what about you? It doesn't apply to you?"

"I'm a woman. I don't think only about myself."

"You're also a mother."

This barb hit right on target, and Rachel could not ignore it.

"This cannot always take precedence."

"We've heard that before."

"Don't take being a mother lightly. You must listen to your daughter. Don't be afraid to give all of yourself, no matter what the price."

This was the closest Rachel could come to parting words. It sounded as if she really cared how her last sentence came across. She knew what kind of mother her own had been, and the kind of mother Mazzy was. Right now Mazzy needed her to stay, but years of estrangement stood in the way. And a considerable amount of pride.

It was goodbye. They embraced and Mazzy, despite herself, gave her mother a kiss on the cheek. She held her for a long moment.

"When will I hear from you?"

"When I have something to say. You have enough on your plate right now without waiting for me."

Rachel kissed her one more time and then, without another word, turned and walked out of the room, her head held high.

As she watched her leave, Mazzy felt the weight lifting from her shoulders. She was alone, without a mother, without a father: an orphan. She was the responsible adult now.

Gaby was back and announcing the doctor was on her way. Mazzy wanted to jump up and hug him, seeking comfort in his arms. She rose from the bed, trying to control the dizziness that overcame her.

"What are you doing, dummy? Lie down," Gaby ordered.

Not exactly the reaction she was looking for, but understandable, given the circumstances. Still, Rachel had cured her, though it wasn't clear exactly how.

No time to think, no time to feel pain; time to go.

Lowering the metal bedside barrier, she dropped her feet to the floor. It was a short distance, but for Mazzy it was a leap, and the room began to swim. Black and white spots danced before her, her legs trembled and her knees nearly buckled. Gaby, who stood slack-jawed at the change in her condition, recovered just in time to jump to her side and catch her before she lost her balance.

Two women stepped into the curtained cubicle: one was dark-skinned and wore a surgical gown; the other was tall and imposing. The latter scrutinized Mazzy intently while the doctor, with Gaby's help, eased her back into bed.

"Ms Simantov, in your condition, you're not supposed to move," she said.

Mazzy noted the charming, lilting accent. In contrast, the tall, silent woman made her uncomfortable.

The doctor checked her quickly and expertly. She shone a thin long flashlight into her pupils and moved her head to check eye movement. She tested Mazzy's ability to wrap her fist around her index finger, then asked her to wiggle her toes, one foot at a time, which made Mazzy giggle like a little girl.

The doctor moved on to a memory test. Mazzy noticed her glancing at the tall woman, whose gaze was still fixed on Mazzy.

"Can you tell me what happened?"

"There was an earthquake. The news says the epicenter was right at the police station…"

"Doctor Aikapido," the imposing woman cut her short, "right now the emphasis should be on treatment. I will fill in Ms Simantov on details that are not related to her recovery. In the meantime, please inform Mr Simantov about further procedures and the forms he needs to complete…"

"Actually it's Doctor Simantov, and I'm…" Gaby started to correct her, but Dr Aikapido had his elbow and was ushering him out of the room.

As soon as they were alone, four shadowy figures materialized as if from nowhere, four young women who moved about like lazy, lethal felines.

"What you just heard from the doctor is what they're selling to the press. The police cannot explain what happened at your place of work. With all the mess surrounding the injuries and abduction, they don't want a slew of unanswerable questions coming their way. People tend to ignore scary phenomena they find unsettling."

"What happened to the people at the precinct?"

"There was another abduction, carried out with a lot of force. Surprisingly, nobody from your side was killed."

"Is Yariv OK?"

"Your partner? Yes, he's all right. A couple of cracked ribs, and a few new scars. They fixed his dislocated shoulders. Your mother vanished from the scene, but she was not among the injured. Libby Blackish, on the other hand, is gone, probably abducted like the others."

Was this work of the Athaliah? The woman Libby was so afraid of? Libby! Libby was gone! The last thing Libby had told her was that The Order of the Athaliah was finally confronting the Nephilim, but had been powerless to prevent a sixth abduction. Nobody, including Libby, knew the next move of the Nephilim. But perhaps the Athaliah was lying, trying to get something out of her. Mazzy kept quiet, playing for time, filing away information.

"Libby said you needed our help."

"So she managed to talk to you? Wow, Libby was young and not so tough. She could not assess the situation correctly."

"What is the situation?"

"Not good."

"She mentioned some procedure, some operation, she thought…"

"You have no idea how wrong Libby was to approach you."

"Why? Don't we have the right to know? If we're about to go to war, then…"

"No. You will remain in the dark, as usual. You can't begin to understand what roils us. We will confront them by ourselves, as the women of The Order have always done. We'll fight our war and you will sit on the sidelines."

"We have people who know about war."

"What you've had until now were not wars, just operations that got complicated. Your blood and our blood seeps only to the upper levels, while their blood seeps all the way to the bottom."

"What you're describing isn't war either."

Mazzy saw that she had succeeded in jolting the Athaliah. The head of The Order was curious enough to ask, if disdainfully, "Why?"

"Because wars end."

A ghost of a smile hovered around the Athaliah's lips.

"You really are her daughter."

Mazzy tried to rise from her bed to grab the Athaliah by the collar, imitating Rachel's methods of inquiry, but one of the guards darted from behind the curtain and positioned herself between them.

She was quite young, with an unremarkable face framed by straight, black hair. She fixed her eyes on Mazzy who was quite overwhelmed by the swiftness of her motions. The guard was about to push the rebellious policewoman back into the hospital mattress, but the Athaliah pointed a restraining finger at her, and the disappointed guardswoman retreated.

"Istahar is only doing her job. But I like you. You don't give up."

Mazzy did not respond to the taunt.

"You go places where you have no chance of coming out unscathed. You think you understand the rules, but the Nephilim will not play by the rules. So let me tell you something, gratis. When they arrive, you'll smell them. A Naphil gives off a soothing odor, evoking the most pleasurable childhood memory you have. For the most part, it is connected to a favorite childhood food. This sweet, consoling smell pacifies the person confronting them and instills confidence in them."

"When I get to them, how do I confront them? Gabriel, you're it?"

"You need to know their names. The power of the Nephilim resides in their names. In any event, you'll have to get very close to them for it to work. The state you're in now makes that prospect unlikely."

They scrutinized each other for the longest time; then Mazzy broke the silence.

"So this is how it's going to be?"

"More or less, with small variations."

Mazzy got out of bed, this time erect and sure-footed enough to walk to the door. The Athaliah and her watchwomen tensed up.

"Your recuperation is indeed astounding. Who treated you?"

"It's all in the genes. Some families just won't stay broken."

The Athaliah was quick to grasp Mazzy's meaning. For a moment she seemed to have lost her equanimity.

"She was here?"

Mazzy did not answer; she simply stepped carefully out of the room. She wondered if she should turn around and mouth off a parting shot at the Athaliah, like a movie heroine. But she decided against it, chiefly because she had nothing to say. From the corner of her eye she saw Gaby by the nurses' station, arguing with a female member of staff. As soon as he saw her, he ran over and blocked her way.

"Is this normal? You shouldn't be walking around…"

"Nothing here is normal. In fact, I must get out of here."

"You mustn't move at all, in your condition."

The last phrase was particularly galling. She had hated it for eight months, and every time he uttered it, it reminded her of her pregnancy, the nausea, and the infuriating bodily changes. She found herself now in a similar situation. Another non-verbal memory took hold. Something was taking shape inside her, something bigger and more important that was using her as a hotel, as a surrogate womb. She was experiencing the same sensations, except that now Noga was not inside to give her strength and hope, to convince her that all the suffering was worth it. For a moment she felt no love, just anger, uncontainable anger.

"First of all, you know nothing about my condition, OK? Second, things are happening right now that are more important than you or me. So, listen to me, and listen good. Rachel visited me. She did something that healed me. Don't ask me how, I have no time to explain."

"Are you in such a hurry to die?"

As Mazzy digested the question, her anger dissipated. She slapped his face, as one would a hysterical child. He held his cheek, driving back the tears. She herself was amazed at what she had done, as if she were merely a witness, not the main actor. Hugging him, she whispered sweetly in his ear, trying to explain what had happened and how, while acknowledging that all the explanations were inadequate and logically deficient. Then she broke off the embrace and withdrew into herself.

A strange serenity settled over her, a wave of natural calm, so different from the turbulent wave engendered by Rachel. Gaby hugged her again, and this time Mazzy was grateful for his love. They stood there for a long moment, united and isolated from their surroundings. But Mazzy knew their time for affection was short.

"I've got to get home."

"Stop by my mother's to see Noga…"

"That would sound like I'm saying goodbye. I can't afford to feel that way right now. I must know that I'm coming back."

Gaby's habit of clamming up at key moments was one of his most annoying traits. She'd rather he fought for his stance. But at this moment, his silence bespoke strength, proof that words were not always needed for communication.

"If you're going to die, I'll kill you."

Mazzy strode out of the ward.

At the entrance, Dr Aikapido and a patient were arguing loudly.

"You can't just walk out," the doctor was telling the man, "you have cracked ribs, and we just fixed your dislocated shoulders."

"So what will you do? Call the police?"

Yariv's sarcasm toward Dr Aikapido was underscored by his tattered, charred police uniform. The thick bandage peeking through his torn shirt was less convincing.

"You realize that this is against doctor's orders."

"I got it the first three times you explained it to me. Don't worry, Doctor, I won't sue you for malpractice. I just need to get out of here as soon as possible. Somebody just blew up my police station, and they're still at large. Being here doesn't work for me right now."

Dr Aikapido gave him a compassionate look before launching into a disquisition on patients' rights and men's resistance to women's authority.

Yariv was about to respond, but something stopped him in his tracks.

Mazzy passed quickly by him, in all her glory, looking in the pink of health. This could not be explained even by the legendary regenerative powers of the Simantov family. To Yariv's amazement, Mazzy dragged him along, ignoring Dr Aikapido's exhortations.

A moment later, the two were in a cab on their way to the ruins of the precinct.

"You look all right, considering what went on in the station," said Mazzy.

"You too. More than all right."

"It's a long story."

"Tell me anyway."

"Rachel cured me."

"Not that long."

"That's just the beginning. Do you want to hear stories, or do you want to help me nab those who put us in the hospital?"

"Any more rhetorical questions before we get there?"

"No rhetorical questions. But lots of questions in need of answers. I also need to know that we can set aside our own private stuff, at least until this business is over."

"How does 'this business' work then?"

"No change as far as I'm concerned. Soothsayer will continue to do its work. The fact that on the other side are Nephilim who have a score to settle with the women's Order which thinks it runs the world, does not concern me in the least. There are six women who nobody seems to give a damn about, and it's time somebody did."

"That sounds simple enough."

"My life is complicated enough, Biton. At least this part should be simple."

THE SEVENTH GATE
FOUNDATION

THE THIRTY-NINTH DAY
FIVE WEEKS AND FOUR DAYS OF THE COUNTING OF THE OMER.

"How much more those who live in houses of clay, whose foundations are in the dust, who are crushed more readily than a moth! Between dawn and dusk they are broken to pieces; unnoticed, they perish forever."

JOB 4:18-21

Beyond the fact that here, too, she was a rookie, Libby was first and foremost a policewoman. Her job, embedded as she was in the elaborate system of the Israeli police, was precisely defined.

All her masks and disguises were those of a daughter of Eve. But here she could drop her cover story and return to her roots.

They treated her few wounds. Despite the massive attack, her injuries were minor. The whole situation was bizarre. The last time she had been surrounded by Lilith's Daughters was when she was Doula Ashtribu's disciple, but here everyone was equal and she even addressed the Doula by her first name, Anat.

But it was not only the title that changed, or the timing. The hourglass and the counting of the Omer were drowning her under the mounting grains.

Libby discovered that the last few days had been filled with debates over self-definition and their status vis-à-vis the Nephilim. They decided to refer to themselves as POW's, not abductees. Prisoners were casualties of war, and there were traditions and standards governing their treatment and release. Whilst captive, they were still part of the war. Abductees, on the other hand, were victims, chattels to be traded or ransomed.

It was pointless to discuss the philological connotations of the agreement, but Hagar Abizu insisted on committing it to writing, if not for use in the present crisis, then for future generations. An expert in negotiations and contracts, she soon identified the weaknesses of her opponents.

Professor Odem agreed: she could not object to documentation. Milka, bothered by the possibility that she might not enjoy eternal fame, found solace in the records. Estie was not asked, because of her youth and lack of education, and Anat was dismissive of details.

Libby realized right away that Hagar had assumed the leadership role. The lawyer surprised her by being clear-headed, practical, and free of illusions. The other prisoners had been allotted tasks and missions according to their talents, and Libby felt useless.

Doula Anat Ashtribu used her time well. She gave Estie Aiello lessons she would have otherwise received at the ranch. They sat in a corner of the room, in their own bubble, far away from the quarrels and discussions of the other prisoners. This suited both sides well. In the Doula, they had a skilled babysitter who excelled at her teaching job, and the scared teenager received the means that would help her deal with her predicament.

Milka was in charge of liaison with the captors. Whenever a Naphil arrived with their food, she would harangue him their demands and engage him in long conversations to get as much information out of him as possible.

Every Naphil presented them with the same challenge. Milka assumed different personae in order to check which one of them had been there before. The duty of bringing the food was abhorrent to their captors, and the contact with Lillith's Daughters was a necessity they tried to shun. Shamhazai's horde of Nephilim drew lots to see who would meet with the inferior creatures.

Even the chance to gloat was not incentive enough for them.

Milka was successful in engaging them, and the chats that started off as strained and halting sometimes lasted several minutes. In addition, with her charisma and amiable personality, Milka persuaded the angels to get to know the women.

When Libby first arrived, Hagar bombarded her with questions and scenarios, hoping that Libby's training as a policewoman could help them make a dent in the Nephilim's armor.

The one who found fault with Hagar's plans was Professor Odem, who also furnished them with historical background and mystical sources.

This entire structure, however, collapsed two days after Libby was captured. The morning that Barakiel arrived with the food.

Milka was about to approach him when Hagar stopped her. Hagar rose from the mattress that served as her office, smoothed her wrinkled business suit, and walked over to him.

Barakiel looked discomfited, like a boy caught peeping into the girls' shower.

"I was surprised you didn't show up earlier."

"They wouldn't let me," said Barakiel.

Hagar tried to ignore the scent of warm milk and cinnamon he emitted. Perhaps she should have let Milka handle it.

"I'm glad you came," she said.

"Are you?"

"I would be happy if you had brought a cake with a saw or a razor blade in it, but just seeing you again is soothing."

Barakiel realized that he was missing something, as was the case in most of their conversations, but this time he knew he could ask.

Most references to popular culture were known to Barakiel. True, his life preceded most of them, but he was familiar with the sources from which they were taken. When you have all the time in the world and a first class home movie system, you are likely to see one or two jailbreak flicks.

"The saw is for escaping, and the razor blade? So your legs will be smooth while you run?"

"For the veins, so we can die heroic deaths. If we're victims, at least it'll be at a time of our own choosing, so as to spoil your ascent."

The idea sounded silly to him, like anything that had to do with honor or the way humans perceived heroism.

"It's not going to work. The Key won't leave you enough time to organize, once the seventh woman arrives."

"Will you tell me what might work?"

"I just came to say hello, I'm not sure why. I wasn't sure what you were going to say."

"You don't have to play games with me, Barak. You don't have to say anything, and you don't have to do anything. Not a thing."

This was a line he recognized. He also knew a thing or two about 'To Have and Have Not.' He wasn't sure if she had chosen those words intentionally, but he tried to be charming.

"I just have to whistle?"

Hagar found that reference trying. She remembered how they had gone to the Cinematheque, eaten popcorn, and seen Bogart and Bacall meet on the screen. She was amazed at what he chose to remember from that date. What happened later on that enchanted evening had meant a lot to her, and not only because a taboo had been broken. Hagar's eyes filled with tears she made no attempt to dry as they rolled down her cheeks. Barakiel had not anticipated this reaction. He had to put an end to her weeping. It was too painful.

"The first one to go down is the Key. The first one to open the Gate must pass through to ensure it stays open. I don't know any more about the Gate, and I'm not even sure this will help," Barakiel tried to mitigate the bitter truth.

Hagar wiped her tears and snuggled against him for a long moment. He knew it made no difference, but they both needed some loving-kindness and all she could give him in return for his desperate attempt to help was a hug.

CHAPTER THIRTY-TWO

It was a weird experience for Barakiel. The morning after the encounter with Hagar was marked by some strange excitement, accompanied by a sense of freedom that was even more significant than the hug he had received from his former lover.

It had been decades since he was allowed to fly over Tel Aviv in daylight. Everything was different then. In those days, Tel Aviv consisted of just a few houses in the dunes. Now they towered among cumulus clouds and smog. There was something wild and primeval in this liberating flight. He did not revolt, like Azazel, with his elegant aerodynamic forays over roofs, solar panels, and television dishes.

Over the last few years, Barakiel had been marginalized as punishment for his illicit love affair, but in recent weeks he felt part of the fold again, the family, the Nephilim. His stay at the police station was not opportune, but at the moment of truth, they came back for him, leaving poor Armaros behind.

None of the Sons of God mentioned the loss, and Barakiel was not about to break the silence. Armaros's demise forced him, as it did the other Nephilim, to consider the possibility that they were no longer immortal, that there was someone capable of harming them.

The dead Naphil's eyes looked out at him from everywhere; each of his fellows in the flying formation had those eyes, but most of all, they plagued him when he saw them in the mirror. He was the reason that Armaros had ended his eternal life but, curiously, there was something encouraging in that. He had a strong sense of belonging. Overnight he had climbed several rungs up the ladder. Now, when things were about to change and they were on their way back to Heaven, his future seemed to be assured. Azazel and Shamhazai had made it clear that his welfare and future were secure. He knew they trusted him and that he was equal to his comrades. He had an important part in the mission of returning to Heaven and opening the Gate. It was the last link in the chain, the first stage in the building of the bridge.

With the other Nephilim in the formation, he followed Karina's car from the moment she left home at 5am for rehearsals. He didn't know her schedule or how long the performance would last, but earlier observers reported that on the way back she would wave to passers-by from her car. It was his turn to watch the hall.

Barakiel surveyed the exits of the building.

The plan was clear and simple, and they had practiced it several times from a great height above the clouds.

Soon they'll circle over, and as soon as the first cars start pulling out of the parking lot, they will check the area. She'll come out, the beloved children's idol, and they will take her away. After that, it's only a matter of time, of days and for one bloody rite, until Heaven's Gate is open again.

CHAPTER THIRTY-THREE

The noise of sawing, drilling, rubble being loaded, and trucks honking finally stopped. The remains of the old station were cleared. Professionals in white plastic helmets were about to start erecting a new building while orange juggernauts and bulldozers waited outside the compound. In the meantime, Goldfinger and his headquarters insisted on maintaining, at least outwardly, a façade of calm and normality. Nobody was allowed to give interviews about the reasons for the rebuild. The official explanation was the need to make the building earthquake proof.

Large caravans had been hastily brought to the compound the night before to serve as temporary quarters. The view from the window of the caravan was dismal, as was the general atmosphere.

Mazzy had assembled the Soothsayer team the previous evening. Over many quiet hours, each member focused on their own psyche, trying to dispel the fear and foreboding that gripped them at the realization of what they were up against: rebellious uninhibited angels, hell-bent on achieving their goal.

The normally inscrutable Larissa was agitated. She mulled over the possibility that her brother had been killed by primordial forces; there was some warped logic to this explanation of the death of a minor security guard. She could thus rewrite the story of a warrior, a veteran of battles and conflicts, and not have to record him as being killed on a paltry security detail. But Larissa could find no solace in this version and was still roiled by guilt. There was no closure. The evil that bereaved her of Borislav now had a face, a face she had beheld in passing while he was being interrogated by the police. Except that she had no idea her brother's murderer was within striking distance. She could have touched him, could have reached her hand into his chest and plucked his wings.

But neither knew who the other was. It was this irony of fate that so rankled her.

Frustration mingled with revenge, humiliation with rage. She shuffled the cards furiously and laid them down. She opened a single card and the hermit showed up, reversed. The bearded wanderer with the cane and the lantern. Right side up, the card was meant to encourage introspection; it betokened wisdom, patience and acceptance, represented by the solitary guide. But when reversed: isolation, alienation, rashness, mistaken identity and bad counsel, fear of the external world, resistance to new ideas, a frustrated search for answers, despair. Larissa felt insult and derision. She knew that the card was the key to solving the riddle of her brother's death, but even now, when the answer was supposedly staring her in the face, she could not turn it into words or guidance.

Izzy, who was usually easygoing when faced with the conundrums of the universe, looked confused.

Mazzy, usually a good source of reliable information, had explained they were up against an army of godly creatures, but what shocked Izzy most was not the fact that there was an army of Nephilim, but that they were the Lord's servants. The popular Hebrew phrase "There is a God!" suddenly ceased to be something sports fans shouted in the stadium; it became a demonstrable fact.

"New Age" had not prepared her for this eventuality. God existed and His minions had declared war on the representatives of mighty womanpower, in which she trusted. Peace, brotherhood, serenity and the acceptance of the Other had not prepared her for battle. The belief in benevolent, bountiful Mother Earth did not sit well with the idea that a Supreme Being, a source of goodness, would send His servants to thwart attempts by the ancient women's Order to bring redemption to the world. Izzy wondered if she was strong and determined enough, and if her crystals could pass the test.

The first one to recover was Elisha.

He seemed to have known all along that such forces existed. His God was an avenging God that manifested Himself clearly, in unmistakable signs and wonders. Elisha was always ready for new developments and changing times. There was a time to love and a time to hate, a time to make peace and a time for war. As soon as Rachel had given them the names, he began his calculations, mumbling series, figuring out values and inferences.

It was clear to all of them that names were the key, the Achilles' heel of the ancient forces. Names were formed letters, and letters were his business.

The oppressive silence in the room was interrupted only by Elisha's pen scratching on paper, the shuffling of Larissa's cards, the rattle of Izzy's crystals when she rummaged in her bag, and the whispering of Mazzy and Yariv.

Elisha was also the first to be hit with an insight. His face lit up in the dim room. On the paper in front of him he had drawn a shape resembling a tree: its top, trunk and roots had circles around them with the words Mercy, Strength, Glory, Victory, Foundation and Sovereignty. Next to the tree he had scribbled numbers and chains of words and verses resembling an equation made of signs and ciphers. The names of the Nephilim that Mazzy had given him were written along and across the signs. Some of the words were underlined with arrows leading to the words Angel and Naphil.

"We're looking for a sequence that will allow us to confine the power of the Nephilim. The names we have are not enough, we must see them as part of a series. We have to start with a certain base if we want to find the entire series of names."

"If we can achieve this, they will become vulnerable again."

"We actually need to find out how an Angel, which is ninety-one in gematria, became a Naphil, which is a hundred and seventy. The difference is seventy-nine, which is equivalent to "he left." In order to see the difference, we have the names. Those names are remnants of ancient wisdom, wisdom somehow distilled which, by the way, also equals seventy-nine."

"Is this what led you to draw this chain? The words of the tree of Sefirot?"

"Yes, but we're still missing the name of the Naphil, if we want to harm him," said Larissa.

"I don't want to dampen your spirits," said Yariv, "but one name won't be enough. We need names, plural. We need to hit enough Nephilim for them to realize that what they're trying to do, to open the Gate, is not going to happen."

In her hands, Izzy held two smooth green stones. One was the stone Barakiel had picked, which she had been pawing and caressing over the last few weeks in an attempt to squeeze some information out of it. Its circles, stretching from the edges to the center of the stone, resembled the rings on a thousand year-old tree. The other stone looked like a transparent greenish ice drop.

Izzy turned to Elisha. "Tell me why a tree of Sefirot? Why do you call it a tree?"

"Tree in gematria is a hundred and sixty. In Genesis it says that God created man "in his image." Image in gematria is a hundred and sixty. In the Book of Illumination, which is the first book of the Kabbalah, the author, the sage Nehuniah ben HaKana, describes the seven sacred emanations of God, which are reflected in Man. As it is said, 'In the image of God created He him, male and female created He them.' These are the right and left thighs, the right and left hand, the torso and the head, that makes six, and the seventh is the wife." The last sentence he quoted in Aramaic, which prompted Yariv to ask for an explanation.

"It explains how the calculation of seven parts was reached," said Elisha. "It includes the woman, for she was created from Adam's body."

"So this tree represents Man, or God as it is manifested in man," said Izzy.

"Sort of. It's more complicated..." Elisha was interrupted.

"Because this is very similar to the chakras. There are whorls of energy in the human body called chakras, and they are located at every junction and intersection of the nervous system. There are thousands of such chakras, but seven cardinal ones located along the spinal column alone. The function of the chakras is to keep the body in a state of equilibrium vis-à-vis the universe."

"Yes, but the connection between God and Man is not based on energy," interjected Elisha, "but on prayer and Mitzvoth."

It was obvious he was trying to be as delicate as he could with the pagan who was ignorant about sacred Jewish lore.

"The chakras are also a connection with God, with the force that created the universe, the Supreme Being, or however you choose to call it. Crystals and stones help the flow of energy in the world and us to connect with it. We use crystals to make this connection. Take this prehnite, for example," Izzy said, picking up the ice pebble. "This could be our key. It operates like a transformer for a divine presence, creating a strong field of energy around us, and it can also enhance our aura."

Elisha, it seemed, was quite pleased with that connection, especially when Izzy drew some lines on his drawings. Over the tree she put a human figure in a lotus position, marking the spots of the seven chakras. Elisha then connected the tree, the words and the chakras.

The other people in the room stared at them in amazement.

"The tree of Sefirot comprises two parts: Crown, Wisdom and Understanding are the upper worlds of potential power, possibilities that may be realized. From them energies are emanated to the other Sefirot: Mercy, Strength, Glory, Victory, Majesty, Sovereignty and Foundation. If we find the spot where the change occurs, we can build the concentration that you're talking about."

Mazzy and Yariv continued to stare at him uncomprehendingly, but Izzy picked up where he left off.

"In essence, we're looking for a possible connection between the spiritual and the material, between the heavenly and the earthly. Here the malachite comes in. In principle, its lines and the way they flow indicate the direction of the energy. The stone that the Naphil held created a series of contracting circles, called Bull's Eye, which points to introspection, a connection to the Third Eye. I think the solution is here, inside us, among us; we just don't seem to see it, because this has to do with something so ancient, with such small circles. It's as if someone dropped a pebble into a lake a million years ago, and now we're trying to find the original location from the eddies reaching the shore."

"Except that here we're not dealing with a pebble in a lake but with a raging hurricane."

"In Ukraine we have a saying: the quietest place is in the eye of the storm," said Larissa.

"Not only in Ukraine. When a hurricane hits, there's usually a tract of several kilometers with only light winds," said Yariv.

"The woman who taught me how to read cards said that when there's so much noise around, we must return to the base, to the quiet in the storm," said Larissa. She shuffled the cards and picked out the Major Arcana.

"At the base you get the answers. The story of the cards has three parts: beginning, middle and end."

"Past, present and future," Mazzy echoed, as if trying to convince herself.

"You want to do it?" asked Larissa.

"No…"

"Then quiet. The first card is past."

Larissa turned over a card. The Empress. She presented it to the group.

"Past. She's the great mother. Woman. Nature. She represents the beginning of life, but also the sense of ending and death. There are pomegranates on her dress, which are like the components of an atom bomb: the tiny bits, the primary parts."

Mazzy stared at the beautiful, noble woman on a throne, scepter in hand, a stream flowing to her left, green trees behind her, and stalks of grain at her feet.

"He makes me lie down in green pastures, He leadeth me beside the still waters. He restoreth my soul; He leadeth me in the paths of righteousness for His name's sake," Elisha muttered.

"The silence, the base, the smallest circle, the beginning," said Izzy.

Larissa drew the second card: an angel with spread wings and a golden crown, pouring the fluid of life from one chalice to another, one foot standing in the water, the other on land.

"Temperance, merging. This is a woman and an angel. A chance to make peace between conflicting faiths inside us.

The mingling allows belief to turn into action and to test it against the difficulty of reality. This is the present, the middle," said Larissa, with a tinge of surprise in her voice.

"Compromise. On his breast he has a triangle inside a square: this means three and four. Again seven. And it is situated at the chakra of the heart, which is the one connecting the three superior ones with the three earthly ones..." Before she finished the sentence, Mazzy noted the change in her voice that now sounded more hopeful.

Everyone fell silent, though, when a tall man riding a winged chariot hitched to two sphinxes, black and white, appeared on the next card. Crescent moons adorned his breastplate, and on either side there were the turreted towers of a walled city.

Mazzy had seen this card, not long ago.

"Future. The Chariot is the seventh card in the Major Arcana, representing the contradictions of the physical world. The soul must maneuver in this world, even though it is spiritual. We must find our way to victory."

"God helps those who help themselves," said Yariv.

"And what about those who cannot help themselves?" asked Izzy. "Those who have given up or who are about to drown, or those who don't even realize they are in a storm?"

"If people can't help themselves, and God doesn't help them, then we're their only recourse," said Mazzy, with a look that turned her comment into a reproach.

"I think I know how to help Him help us," said Elisha. He was standing next to Larissa, speaking with confidence, his eyes sparkling as if something inside him was starting to radiate.

"So you know how to find the eye of the storm?" asked Larissa.

"Sort of. Except this is not water flowing, but more like what Izzy was talking about, a current of electricity, of energy. Perhaps a reference to Ezekiel's vision of the chariot. If I continue with Izzy's idea, then the base is a transformer of energy. Suppose we're talking about a network of electric wires. I want to turn on a bulb, bring light into the world. I won't connect the wire directly to the power station, the source; the bulb would burn and break. We need a system of transformers that will channel the energy and prevent us from burning. Each transformer has a certain capacity, just as each lens transmits a light wave of a certain length. In Kabbalah, we talk about such transformers, this electrical system, in terms of a tree. I am still talking about plus and minus…"

"The Third Eye!" Izzy interjected. She understood better than the others what he was referring to.

"I'm supposed to believe in the Third Eye?" asked Yariv.

"You don't believe in physical-spiritual duality?" asked Izzy.

"Not really, no."

"You believe in science and philosophy, don't you?"

"More. Don't take offense, Elisha, it's not personal."

Elisha wasn't going to argue. He beamed at Yariv indulgently.

"So listen a little, in the name of science. The Third Eye is located in the center of the forehead, about one centimeter above the eyebrow. Near the pineal gland. You know Descartes?"

"I think therefore I am, and stuff like that?"

"Right. So Descartes called this gland "the seat of the soul." Do you know what it produces? Melatonin. It's not a regular hormonal gland; it works as an electric transformer, mediating between the retinal nerves and the secretion of melatonin. Essentially, it explains to the body the difference between light and darkness, between sleep and waking."

"And what is this supposed to prove?" asked Yariv.

"That there are parts of our body that transmit energy, like neurotransmitters that process information and create physical manifestations. In this case, a hormone resembling adrenaline that is released into the pineal gland," said Izzy.

"But how does this connect to what Elisha said earlier?"

Elisha pounced on the piece of paper, drawing new lines between the various numbers. He was still smiling, which was starting to get on Yariv's nerves.

"Why are you smiling?"

"Because now I know exactly what we need to do to discover the names of the fallen angels. We agreed that we're looking for a link, a transformer that can distribute the energy so we can crack more than one at a time. The power is within us. Our Third Eye is a triangle. A triangle we're already familiar with. Larissa's cards help her look forward, Izzy's talent is to look at the energy in real time, and I have the ancient lore. Future, Present, Past."

"So how does this relate to the links in the chain? A triangle? Why is a geometrical shape an answer to your equation?" Mazzy tried to spur the man to explain further.

"We already know that we're facing a Naphil, which equals a hundred and seventy. But we need to find its basis. The basis of a triangle contains what Adam did when he tried to define something, to understand it. He gave it a name. So we have a Naphil, but we are missing a name. 'Missing name' in gematria is six hundred and eight. Add this to the hundred and seventy of the Naphil and you have the sum total, the whole. Seven hundred seventy-eight, which equals the most important quality we have in this struggle."

"Three times seven plus one?"

"The basis, the beginning, the thing we have in front of our eyes. Past, present, future. The value of Past is two hundred seventy-two. Present equals twenty-two, and future four hundred eighty-four. Together it is seven hundred seventy-eight, which is equal to the only advantage we have over the Nephilim – Humanity."

CHAPTER THIRTY-FOUR

Karina Klobtaza was the brightest star on the Children's Channel. Despite her weird name and thanks to her intriguing looks, she filled the theater to the rafters, and the shrieks of the children and the cheers of the adults were heard all the way up.

"Open wide."

She opened her mouth as wide as she could, and her mother's hand groped her gums, making sure the three dangling teeth were aligned before she went on stage.

She couldn't wait for her baby teeth to fall out, so she could be fitted with a bridge until her perfect smile was restored to its previous glory.

"Two minutes to go," a man with earphones and clipboard announced.

Karina sat in front of the make-up artist as he applied the eye shadow above her famous blue eyes, familiar to anyone who had ever driven along the Ayalon Freeway and encountered her memorable billboard.

The make-up artist curled her long lashes and added rouge to her cheeks and gloss to her lips. The girl looked at her mother indulgently, but the latter frowned. This was not the time for displays of affection; Karina wondered when would be the time.

"A little more hairspray, so the stylist won't be mad at us."

Karina squirmed in her seat; she hated this part, the unpleasant noises coming from the can and the cold mist spewing so close to her scalp. But the make-up artist carried on, sprinkling glitter onto her high cheekbones. The cleavage of her cowgirl outfit only heightened them, and since there was nothing protruding in the front, this was camouflage to maintain an illusion.

"You're not pressured by all these performances?" a reporter asked the star.

Knowing that her mother would answer for her, she didn't even bother to turn her head.

"Pressure? You should have come to the Hanukkah festival. The 'Little Princess' has only two performances a day: matinee and evening. Karina is big enough so that we don't have to wait for a holiday. Other stars from the Children's Channel have to wait for school holidays when parents take their kids out. With Karina, it's the children themselves who drag their parents to the show. She can fill a stadium."

"When you say 'big enough,' you mean mature?"

"Let's just say that she's very mature for her age. She has ambitions and knows what she wants. She once saw a Shirley Temple movie and knew right away what she wanted to do. So I enrolled her in a tap dancing class and the rest, as they say, is history."

Karina had never heard of Shirley Temple, but she had heard her mother tell the story so many times that she was ashamed to ask.

"Thirty seconds to show time."

She got up, put on the belt and other accessories. The brown cowgirl hat was carefully placed atop her golden curls.

She ran along the hallway and climbed the steps to the stage. Once in the public eye, she sashayed across the stage like a model on a runway. When she reached the center, she started to dance, thrashing her body, smiling triumphantly and winking at the front rows.

Karina whipped her two pistols from their holsters and shot in the air, releasing pink clouds of smoke. The music blared and the dancers around her swirled their lassos. She leaped through their loops, took her miniature whip from her belt, and cracked it. It was the high point of the show for her, before the last song and the pony ride around the stage. She always cherished the feel of the whip in one hand and the gun in the other.

Karina raised her eyes to the balcony, proudly looking at her mother, that stern looking woman who lately had become even more severe. Her mother, who had always impressed upon her that she was part of something much bigger, more ancient, a formidable female power.

Her mother, who used to tell her about the first woman and the fate that befell her, who explained why it was important that the crowds come to see her and adore her and love her, just like she herself did.

Over the last few days, her mother had taken to practicing more often, with her own belt, with the long adult whip and the weird, ancient gun whose bullets shattered anything that stood in its way.

Confetti began to pour from the ceiling, colorful ribbons and shimmering glitter, landing on people's heads. She saw the pony charging toward her and positioned herself to jump.

CHAPTER THIRTY-FIVE

High above the rooftops, Barakiel spread his wings.

Seconds earlier a close formation of three assailants had pounced on the black sedan of the Klobtaza family. They landed on the roof, clawed their fingers through the metal, peeling from the vehicle as if it were a moving tin can. Despite the mother's cries for help and the struggle of the girl's bodyguard, they extracted her from the mother's arms and flew her upwards. The mother shot at them, but the bullets just whizzed above their wings as they disappeared into the clouds. The abductions chapter was now complete; the seven year-old girl was the last.

There was a distinct, cloying sense of finality in the air, a feeling that things were about to change. During their confining earthly existence, the Nephilim had experienced no excitement. Each day and each year resembled the preceding one, an eternal prison routine.

But over the last few weeks a new wind had been ruffling the Nephilim's feathers.

Saharel flapped his wings in the air. The wind whistled through his thick plumage.

"Do you hear that sound? It's the whirr of the wings of history!"

The others emitted a hearty laugh. Barakiel laughed too, but suddenly the laughter echoed around him and he was surrounded by rows of white teeth, closing in on him like a school of sharks.

Barakiel drew his blade, but his assailants had already drawn their celestial flaming swords and were dancing their lethal dance around him. Sunrays were breaking through the clouds, lighting up the dancers' faces. As blade hit blade, sparks flew.

Excruciating pain shot through Barakiel's shoulder. Feathers flew all around as the wing detached and fell like a severed branch. He tried to ignore the pain, flapping his remaining wing, but the attempt only made his head point in the wrong direction, and he started to fall. The fear was intense. Someone could still help him. Even if he hit the ground, he wouldn't die. He'd recover. It might take hundreds of years, but he'd pull through. He was still an angel. Angels never died. A gust of wind came from above and a hand gripped his nape, stopping his fall.

Lifting his terrified eyes, he saw Azazel. The last vestige of hope was gone. A terrible epiphany hit him as he realized that the laws protecting them from humans did not apply in these circumstances. Azazel knew his name; he didn't need to use it to harm him.

With a precise and swift motion, a perfect strike, he was beheaded; his golden locks were now in the grip of Azazel's white fingers. The glorious headless, wingless body of what for millennia had been an exiled angel now spiraled downward until it hit the hood of the abducted girl's car.

An explosion and ball of fire completed the demise of the fallen angel.

CHAPTER THIRTY-SIX

The last time the Athaliah faced Mazzy, she had been surprised at the changes the detective had undergone. But now the circumstances were different, and the sense of surprise had disappeared. The Athaliah depended on the backing of The Order, but during the short ride from the crime scene, Mazzy had made it quite clear that the balance of power had changed. Knowledge is power. Mazzy had the knowledge, and the Athaliah had to back down and yield. She had no time and no answers.

There was something different about Rachel's girl. Change that had first been noticed in the emergency room, but had since grown in Mazzy.

Some primordial power, implacable, untrammeled, feral, pulsating, human.

Mazzy gazed at the murals. The eyes that looked back at her were intelligent, penetrating, resolute, warm, honest, and cruel. There were women with different hairstyles and colors, some severely braided, others blowing in the wind. Portraits of the seven Maidens of the Order examined her with a measure of justice and mercy.

Now Mazzy understood the urgency of Libby's words when she had given her the important information.

Mazzy stood next to Yariv, whose presence the Athaliah did not welcome.

"You said you'd come alone."

"I changed my mind. You should be more flexible. It's not the first time, and certainly not the last. Let's not make an issue of it. We don't have time, and right now I should be with my team planning our campaign."

"I can't let a man in here."

Yariv stood at the door like a rebuked child. He shrugged and turned to leave. Mazzy stopped him. She pointed a finger at him, fixing her gaze at Lilith's Daughter. Yariv froze in his tracks.

"So let him wait somewhere while we talk."

The Athaliah thought for a moment, then turned to her secretary.

"Judith, get someone to accompany Chief Inspector Biton to that room downstairs…"

"We just allocated it to the other gentleman…"

The Athaliah considered the options. Mazzy was getting impatient.

"What's the problem?"

"The space I was thinking about is now serving another purpose."

"What purpose?"

"The remains of the Naphil from the last abduction. It's not something you can leave in a hospital without explanation."

Mazzy would ask for the whole picture later. The two women were at a preliminary stage now, assessing each other's power, and Mazzy knew she had the upper hand.

"It's okay, Chief Inspector Biton is not unused to corpses. In fact, this could be a learning experience for him."

Yariv straightened up, as if to show the women that he was ready for action. The Athaliah motioned with her hand; Judith smiled benignly at the male visitor, and she led him down a spiral staircase. The two women were left alone.

"Would you like something to drink?"

"Something hot. Tea."

The Athaliah was about to press the button for her secretary when she remembered that the latter was busy showing their guest the way. It had been years since she had to perform any service for others. When she turned the faucet, it spouted a thick red liquid. The fluid of life. She took a deep breath, trying to control her revulsion.

"Maybe something cold," Mazzy said. "Cola?"

Her reaction threw the Athaliah even more than the blood flowing from the faucet. Mazzy's eyes looked cold, almost indifferent. It was that elusive quality, seen yet unseen, harsh yet gentle, encompassing and evaporating, the ability to reject the irrelevancies life throws your way and focus on the heart of the matter. Without calling it by name.

Mazzy took advantage of the Athaliah's confusion to knock her completely off balance. It was time to reveal another detail from her encounter with Barak, something that had become clear after her talk with Libby. Another piece of the puzzle. Mazzy asked innocently, "What happens if the Gate of Heaven opens?"

The Athaliah was not easily surprised, Mazzy knew, so she was doubly satisfied when she saw her recoil. But Lilith's Daughter quickly recovered.

"If the Gate of Heaven opens, it means we will disappear. Either the last of us will die trying to stop it or, when the Gate opens, everything we have accomplished here over hundreds of years will be obliterated. They will not tolerate our presence, a constant reminder of their failure during their period of exile. They will wipe out any trace of The Order. It's not just us here, it's everyone. Imagine a world without women in politics, education, business, or communication. An entire world of homemakers without aspirations or opportunities."

"It's not going to happen. This is the modern world. It's not something that can simply…"

"It can. Simply. Bear in mind that The Order is responsible for seventy percent of the positions of power held by women. We are not always present, but we always set a precedent, we made it legitimate, we were behind the politics, the impetus, the connections. One of our Order was always the trailblazer. In one way or another we were behind Deborah the prophetess, Madame Curie, Mary Shelley, Virginia Woolf, Golda Meir…"

"Alexandria Ocasio Cortez?" Mazzy cut in.

"No, not her. She did it herself," said the Athaliah.

"Your whole establishment will disappear if the Gate of Heaven is opened?" asked Mazzy.

"There is no connection between the superior world and Kedem. There was only one Genesis. Everything that contradicts it must disappear."

"I don't have much time, so I'll explain to you how this is going to work. You will tell me everything you know about the time and place when the Gate of Heaven will open, and I will tell you how we plan to rescue the women from the ceremony."

"I don't know what Libby told you, but we had no intention of rescuing them. We want to stop the ceremony.

These women become trivial when you look at everything that's at stake. Every war has its objectives, and we must strive to attain ours. The women know the score."

"Even Karina? And Estie?"

"A Lilith's Daughter does not choose to be one. She is born a Lilith's Daughter. It has its advantages and disadvantages. They are rank and file. Their job is to delay their death for the sake of the Order. The rest is not important; it is just an item in the archive of history."

"And their rescue won't change the picture? Don't the Nephilim need them for their ceremony?"

"They do, but they need them alive. From the Order's perspective, it makes no difference if the Gate doesn't open and the kidnapped women die, or if we manage to stop the ceremony before any of them is sacrificed."

"My only mission is to find them, preferably alive."

"So we'll do what we have to do, and you'll do what you see fit."

The Athaliah faked a conciliatory smile and invited Mazzy to her chamber. The negotiation was coming to an end.

"All the signs, observations and testimonies point to the Jabbok Crossing as the site of the opening."

Mazzy wondered if that was a place she should recognize or just a symbolic location. But there were more pressing issues.

"When?"

The Athaliah had regained the ability to surprise. "Tomorrow."

The simplicity with which the Athaliah uttered the statement shook Mazzy. This was an eventuality she was not prepared for. She was seething, though she wasn't sure if it was childish rage at the ever-changing rules that made victory almost impossible, or a reasonable, adult rage stemming from important information that had been kept from her. She opened her mouth and the question slipped from her tongue.

"I thought the ceremony was synchronized with the counting of the Omer. There are eleven days to Shavuot, when Heaven's supposed to open, so why is it tomorrow?"

"You are using the wrong calendar. You're looking in the wrong places and listening to a man, to this Elisha," the Athaliah said disdainfully. "The solar calendar has three hundred sixty-five days, and it is based on the revolution of the Earth around the Sun. It is not the calendar used in antiquity, and it certainly is not the one used by the order of the Nephilim. The lunar calendar, on the other hand, has three hundred fifty-four or five days and is based on the revolution of the Moon around the Earth. Even the men who controlled time knew that they needed to balance it. But even then, we inserted a mark unbeknownst to them, and they were obliged to add a month – seven times in every nineteen-year cycle, in order to reach the necessary balance. The fact that nineteen equals Eve according to the calculations and gematrias of men only helped us insert a little irony. Seven is always a stronger number. Our number and theirs."

This sounded almost logical. If Mazzy hadn't been so furious, she might have found it amusing. The next question shot from her mouth.

"So why didn't you bother to tell me all this before?"

The Athaliah seemed to muster all the authority and condescension still left in her enfeebled position.

"Until now you were not relevant. The fact that the information reached you surprises me, but I will get it from you. I believe it and I believe you and I don't have many options."

She really had no choice. Mazzy knew that she was holding the trump card, the method or obtaining the names. Even before entering the room, Mazzy had known what would happen. Anger and guilt made way for a new feeling. Something primordial and archaic. Revenge. She was going to fight back, to restore some control over her own fate.

"So what is this grand plan that's going to change everything?"

Mazzy went to the maps, examined them and then began to make her own plan, explaining in a confident, majestic, commanding voice. The voice was Rachel's; the hands were Mazal's.

CHAPTER THIRTY-SEVEN

The remains of Barakiel's corpse radiated somber grandeur as it lay on the shiny surface of an oak table. All that was left of his brutal majesty were broken bones, charred tissue, and black feathers hanging from a single wing like some apocalyptic foliage of an Indian summer.

Yariv scrutinized the broken figure. The shins had been shattered from the fall, or perhaps by the explosion. The pelvis was completely burned, leaving unanswered the question that led Yariv's eyes toward the groin area. Going up the torso, he examined the collarbone and the remnants of the remaining black wing.

It still had feathers stuck to it, clinging to the bone, like hair on a wig. One of the feathers appeared to have been detached a long time ago.

Yariv rummaged in his pocket. The black feather was still there in a sealed evidence bag. He took it out, absentmindedly, almost unaware.

In the general madness and confusion, he needed a fulcrum, something comprehensible. He already knew that the powers were not matched. They had never been equal. He knew his contribution was small, but he had to try. He looked at the Naphil's remains, longing for the days of yore and for the sights that a human eye could not hope to fathom.

He took the feather and tried to insert it in the wing. It fit. He realized that any of their feathers would probably fit, but he wanted this to be the one. This one would make sense, give meaning to his efforts. He was reminded of something Rozolio had said to him ages ago, when Yariv asked why he used a certain approach when examining the scene of a crime.

Rozolio had the smile of a mystic.

"Biton, one day you'll be an excellent detective. But first you have to realize that the world we live in is a little more complex than you think and not everything is logical or just. Eventually, even if you solve this particular case, tomorrow there'll be another one. You can't win alone, possibly not even with the help of others. In the final analysis, whatever we do makes no difference, and this is precisely why the only thing that does matter is what we do do. So just pick a direction and follow it."

With all the craziness that surrounded him, with Mazzy, the Nephilim, Lilith's Daughters and the Gate of Heaven, Yariv decided to go back to basics. It might not help, but it wouldn't hurt. He put the feather back in the plastic bag, covered Barakiel's cadaver and strode toward the exit.

THE EIGHTH GATE
MAJESTY

THE FORTIETH DAY
FIVE WEEKS AND FIVE DAYS OF THE COUNTING OF THE OMER

"And he was afraid and said, how dreadful is this place! This is none other but the house of God, and this is the gate of heaven."

GENESIS 28:17

A thick layer of crushed carobs covered the hill, emitting a strong stench in the air. Brown crescents kept falling from above, making a swooshing sound. Hundreds of ravens circled in the sky, and the ground bore scorch marks of two parallel lines and what were unmistakably horses' hooves.

Tiny comets of bluish flame and rings of smoke rose from those marks on the ground.

At the edge of this smoking pathway stood the chariot, Mighty Flame, resplendent in its chimera of supernatural fire. The taut reins glowed red hot and shook in the wind.

Four proud stallions stamped the ground, their muscles glimmered yellow, orange and red. Their manes shook and smoke poured from their nostrils. At their side and oblivious to the heat, stood a figure clad in black, with long flowing hair, holding a staff in one hand while the other rummaged in the pockets of his tattered cloak.

Finding what he was looking for, the figure pulled out an object dripping blood and gave it to the closest horse. The animal took it with a fiery tongue and a smell of charred flesh filled the air. The other horses neighed in protest. Elijah laughed.

His ravens flew overhead in widening circles, their shadows covered the gathering angels and Lilith's Daughters, whose camps were now facing each other.

As was his habit, Elijah hummed a song in his thick, tarry voice.

"In the country I love, the almond tree blooms. In the country I love, we are waiting for a guest. Seven maidens, seven mothers, seven brides at the gate."

Elijah twirled his almond wood staff like a drum majorette. On a nearby hill, in a semi-circle, were seven figures all bound and tethered to an improvised altar: the little girl, the judge's daughter, the actress, the lawyer, the doula, Libby and the professor. Elijah waited for her majesty the detective and his highness the chief inspector. His ageless self formed the top of the Kabbalistic tree when he hovered in his fiery chariot, twirling his staff.

Three Nephilim soared down from the hill where the seven pillars stood.

"We have walked to and fro through the Earth and behold, all the Earth sitteth still and is at rest," Shamhazai said as he stood facing him. Elijah stopped twirling his staff.

"It's about to start."

"Are you planning to stay? To take part?"

"I am a messenger, not an angel. Besides, it wouldn't be fair. They will be busy trying to survive."

Elijah pointed his staff straight at Shamhazai's face, a few centimeters from his perfect eye, halting the motion with a swoosh, like an ancient warrior.

"What seest thou?"

"I see the rod of an almond tree."

Elijah smiled and, all at once, his staff became a branch that sprouted fresh buds with pristine white crowns and pale pink seeds. The seeds soon became green almonds before all too quickly maturing into brown nuts. The smile was reciprocated. Elijah complimented his colleague.

"You have well discerned."

Darkness descended on the world and Elijah's face shone. Five pillars of light reached up from the hill opposite the mountain; the wait was over. The wanderer took out a ram's horn from his belt and began to blow. A mighty sound came from above, and the heavens opened a crack. Thunder and lightning accompanied this display until dark clouds rolled slowly toward the mountain. Elijah's horn blared louder and louder. The Earth shook and the smoke ascended from the mountain as from a furnace.

The two camps began to march toward each other and no peace was present on Earth. The curtain began to open on high. Elijah withdrew the ram's horn from his lips, but the sound carried on. He watched the unfolding scene to see what would transpire, who would prevail. One more thing was left for him to do. He returned to his chariot, cracked his whip and soared heavenward, his lips reciting the verses of the seventy-two letters of the sacred name.

"And the angel of God, which went before the camp of

Israel, removed and went behind them, and the pillar of the cloud went from before their face, and stood behind them. And it came between the camp of the Egyptians and the camp of Israel, and it was a cloud and darkness to them, but it gave light by night to these; so that the one came not near the other all the night. And Moses stretched out his hand over the sea, and the Lord caused the sea to go back by a strong east wind all that night, and made the sea dry land, and the waters were divided."

The wind suddenly became a gale, the clouds parted, and the barred, sealed Gate of Heaven was revealed. Elijah and Mighty Flame circled in the air and made toward the mountain with the seven pillars.

Two Nephilim, standing guard over the fettered Lilith's Daughters, spread their wings like cherubim, whipped out their slaughtering knives and with practiced, coordinated motion slashed their victims' femoral veins. The entire mountain blazed. Blood, fire, and pillars of smoke. From between the bars of the Gate of Heaven appeared two burnished rods, like playground slides, descending into the center of the mountain. As soon as the blazing rods touched the ground, they gave off sparks and flashes like tender buds. The buds became boughs, the boughs became branches, and tongues of fire leapt one toward the other, creating rungs and stairs leading back to Heaven. The two long rods swayed like flags in the wind, to and from the pillars of the world. An enormous conflagration seemed to consume everything in sight, casting a pall on the horrific battle about to begin at the foot of the ladder.

CHAPTER THIRTY-EIGHT

Now that they saw the blazing ladder on the horizon, the smoking bonfires, and the Nephilim flying reconnaissance missions over the valley, the detectives folded the maps with rustling dexterity.

No need for maps on a dead end street.

Without being asked, and contrary to her driving habits, Mazzy slowed the SUV. They were sliding down one hill and up another, closing the distance between themselves and the hill with the fiery ladder.

"Why here, of all places?" asked Yariv.

From the back seat, Elisha inserted his face between the shoulders of the passengers in the front seat. Larissa, at his side, silently shuffled her cards, trying to calm her nerves. She picked up a single card, a tower on a rocky crag with its battlements in the sky. The tower had been hit by lightning and was aflame. Two figures, a man and a woman, were falling from the tower, crashing into a dark abyss. Larissa didn't even bother to interpret the card for the others. No one spoke; even the motor was still, as if not to disturb the silence that pervaded the valley and the ravines.

Elisha answered the question that hung in the air.

"This must be the place. Here Jacob fought with the angel, closing a circle not just for himself but also for Adam, since the patriarch Jacob is his Tikkun, his spiritual restoration. The fallen angels, too, are seeking Tikkun."

"Aren't angels supposed to be good by definition?" asked Izzy.

"Angels are emissaries to this world. The Holy Zohar talks of good and evil as attributes of the Divine Entity. When Jacob went to meet Esau, his evil twin, he actually encountered a part of himself – a place of both good and evil. At the end of that momentous night of decision, Jacob conquered himself. He contended with people and with angels and overcame them. Only then was his name changed to Israel. Both the man and the angel were born anew. They are the good and the evil, which are both necessary in the world."

"Except that if the Gate of Heaven is opened, they won't be in the world, and the world won't be the same anymore," said Mazzy.

In an attempt to hold on to something concrete, Izzy fished out the two smooth green stones from her bag. Larissa, sitting next to the aura reader, suddenly pronounced, "The eclipse at last," in her rasping accent, rolling her tongue over the L's.

Mazzy lifted her eyes to the place where what remained of the sun was just a pale circle in the darkness: a celestial retina, reminding one and all that observant eyes were up there, watching both the good and the evil.

The day changed into night, a night different from all other nights.

A night that was no night and no day, stillness and earsplitting noise, and the surrounding hills and the mountain like sparks of light, igniting and turning off.

Mazzy gunned the engine and they sped down the hill in a cloud of white dust. When they arrived at the appointed hill, they left the car at the bottom and climbed on foot. The guards of the Order of Lilith's Daughters made way for them; only Na'ama, who was in charge of Mazzy's security, stayed with the group.

"The moment you finish and Elisha begins, we shall begin," she told Mazzy.

"It won't take long. The eclipse will soon be over."

"I'm very impressed with your strategy and with your determination," Na'ama said, "but if you're thinking only of saving rank and file members, you'll end up with more casualties."

Her face remained impassive, but her eyes shone. She came down the hill. Elisha was standing facing the mountain, at the center of a rectangle formed by Larissa, Mazzy, Yariv and Izzy.

"Listen," Mazzy said, "we're here to do our job, to prove that Soothsayer can accomplish its mission. If the world remains as it is – from my perspective, this will be an added bonus."

CHAPTER THIRTY-NINE

Rachel observed the scene unfolding on the hills encircling the riverbed. Members of Israel's Order were deployed all around, hiding in tunnels, caverns, crevices, cliffs and, burrows. Throughout this day that had become night, they lay waiting, silent and ready, watching the curtain rise over the confrontation. Rachel wondered why Israel's men did not climb the hill.

"A question of timing and destiny," Israel replied in his *basso profundo*.

"This struggle was destined to take place. It's like a released pressure valve. What's happening is clear: Lilith's Daughters know they only have a few minutes to find the crack in the Fallen Angels' armor. They'll go at it tooth and nail, throwing all they've got into the battle, regardless of casualties or the price that individual members of their Order will pay. This is their only chance. The Nephilim don't regard Lilith's Daughters as a real threat. They are trying to deceive the world. They can't be bothered with these pesky, blood-sucking mosquitoes buzzing around them. They have a ritual to perform: to open the Gate and to close the Gate."

"What exactly are we doing here?"

"We're here to make sure that nobody plays with Fate; what has been shall be. According to my scouts and observers, there's a chance that Elijah might intervene, exceeding his role as a mere emissary. From our perspective, this must not happen. No way. How this happens is no less important. The ritual. We're here to guarantee that order is maintained, not to change the course of events. But, on the other hand, we can't stand idly by when the Wanderer approaches the Gate. We mustn't be like them. There is a Judge and there is one Fate."

"That's what he thinks, too, except that in his case, he has seen the Judge. What is your excuse for justice?"

In reply, Israel removed his shirt, revealing a tattoo Rachel had not seen before.

"Very simply, we don't need an excuse, we only do what is said – 'He shutteth his eyes to devise forward things: moving his lips he bringeth evil to pass. The hoary head is a crown of glory, if it be found in the way of righteousness. He that is slow to anger is better than the mighty: and he that ruleth his spirit than he that taketh a city. The lot is cast into the lap: but the whole disposing thereof is of the Lord.'"

The words tattooed along his shoulder, arm, and forearm did not leave much room for debate. Still, Rachel intended to take him to task for the way he was leading, but at that moment, one of his acolytes came and whispered in his ear. The young man handed him a large spyglass and Israel turned around and looked through it, to a point on the horizon.

A small group of humans was hiding there, apparently trying to decide if they should put up a fight or survive for another day. Rachel, too, sensed a familiar presence, a blood relation, a cord beginning to tug.

"She's here," said Israel, concealing a smile of expectation.

He motioned to one of his men.

Rachel noticed a movement at the bottom of the hill. Members of Israel's Order emerged from the cover of the rocks and caves. They trained binoculars and telescopes skyward, searching for Mighty Flame.

In view of the circumstances and the threatening danger, Rachel was almost ashamed of her vanity. The world was on the brink of a major transformation, and all she could think about was how proud she was of her daughter.

Below her, the warring sides continued marching toward each other and the inevitable, fateful moment. The smoldering bonfires on the hills had been put out by Lilith's Daughters. Dozens of black and white pillars of smoke rose toward the gradually darkening red sky. The little encampments around the mountain, where the angels had waited, resembled the stone circles of an ancient tribe.

Ritual, sacrifice, sun, man, and his God. It always came down to this. In all languages. Everything for God, God willing, Thank God, for God's sake, God preserve us, God will avenge their blood.

"I still see some sunlight," Rachel announced to no one in particular.

"Not for long. The ceremony is about to begin," replied Israel.

The angels were standing in a circle around the seven pillars, row upon row, holding flaming swords. Their voices reverberated in the valleys and mountains. Dozens of Nephilim were performing the same sword dance, their lips pronouncing confident words that sliced through the air.

"The light of the moon shall be as the light of the Sun, and the light of the Sun shall be sevenfold as the light of seven days, in the day that the Lord bindeth up the breach of his people, and healeth the stroke of their wound. Behold the name of the Lord cometh from afar, burning with his anger, and the burden thereof is heavy: his lips are full of indignation, and his tongue as a devouring fire."

From the opposing camp of Lilith's Daughters came a murmur. They were not dancing or cavorting; they shouldered their burden, assiduously preparing for battle. Knives were sharpened, bows drawn, arrows whittled, Luparas cleaned and loaded with homemade ammunition. And through these sounds of hectic activity came a whisper that was intended to throw dust in the enemy's eyes and sow confidence in their own hearts.

"Let us swallow them alive. The Nephilim will go down to their graves. Cast thy lot among us. A wicked messenger falleth into mischief, but a faithful ambassador is health. Surely in vain the net is spread in the sight of any bird. A voice will be heard in Judea and in the Hills, 'Restrain thy voice from weeping and thine eyes from tears, for thy work shall be rewarded, saith the Lord, and your daughters shall come to their own border. Take us back to the days of Kedem.'"

Through the clouds, like a gliding falcon, emerged Mighty Flame and its charioteer, who was scanning the forces gathered below and singing lustily.

They say there is a land,
A land awash in sunlight.

Where is that land?
Where is that sunlight?
They say there is a land,
Whose pillars number seven,
And on every hilltop,
Seven stars shine brightly.

CHAPTER FORTY

Thin, wraith-like bands of fog swirled around the Soothsayer team. Elisha took a few steps toward the center of the hill. Izzy and Larissa came forward, creating a triangle with the Kabbalist, while Yariv and Mazzy remained outside. Yariv looked suspiciously at the fog.

"What now?"

"They'll try to reach the time when they knew the names. Then they'll try to connect to the present and further."

"How do we know what they're looking for? When was the time that they knew the names?"

Mazzy recounted the story Rachel had told her when she was a little girl, the tale that had prepared her for this moment on the hill. Honey was coursing through her veins now, pulsating in her heart and sweetening her lips, almost against her will. Out of the chaos emerged order and night.

"When the world was first created, there were no names, because there was no need for them. There was only sky and Earth. Man had not yet been created, and the only ones with names were the angels. Their names shone above their heads. Then God created man in His image: male and female did He create them. Adam and Lilith, the first woman and her man. They saw the angels and realized that things needed names to distinguish them from each other. Adam tried to give her a name, to define her with letters of his choosing. Lilith decided to change it, to act on her own…"

"What's going on here?"

"They're drawing a line. Larissa is running forward to the future, turning over her readings, her prognostications in her head, while Izzy is serving as an anchor to her and to Elisha; she keeps them on a continuous line between what's possible and what's already happened, the concrete present. Elisha is trying to connect with a point in time, to look back and see the past, to go further back to the time when there were no names, except those of angels. As soon as he gets to that moment and sees the names, everyone will be able to see them, as long as he holds out."

"And then what?"

"All Lilith's Daughters will run up the mountain, to the captives. The Nephilim may kill some of them, but they can't kill them all. Not when they are able to fight back."

Yariv was amazed by this simple, merciless plan. He noted the change in his lover; fate and circumstances had etched in her new, sharp, harsh lines.

"We can't kill all the Nephilim at once, can we? And what if they kill the women while they're climbing the mountain? You call this a rescue operation?"

"Whoever gets to the hill will start shooting. If we keep it at short range, they may not be able to stop the bullets and the knives. Whoever reaches the top will use her firearm. The Key will be there, the leader, the first to descend and the first to ascend. It's either fight or flight. This is our choice, and we'll have to live and die by it. In the world that I deem worth fighting for, someone has to try to rescue these women, at least some of them."

A tremor shook the hill; cracks and gullies opened up, creating a blazing path to the burning ladder. Yariv saw Mazzy raise her arm, signaling to the others to move forward.

In the middle of the human triangle, Larissa's eyes opened wide and turned pitch black, like smoky glass balls. Elisha's, on the other hand, became perfect circles of lustrous whiteness. Their heads were thrust backward at a right angle, as if their necks had snapped. Izzy, who was holding their hands, gave a loud, heartrending shriek, and her eyes betrayed an excruciating pain.

Sparks of light flashed from the corners of Elisha's eyes. Larissa, looked dazed; her pupils fluttered this way and that, trying to escape, like the wheels in a slot machine trying to find the winning combination.

Mazzy drew her Lupara and began running up the hill. Yariv followed.

THE NINTH GATE
CROWN

THE FORTIETH DAY
FIVE WEEKS AND FIVE DAYS OF THE
COUNTING OF THE OMER

"She shall give to thine head an ornament of grace: a crown of glory shall she deliver to thee."

Proverbs 4:9

Shamhazai appraised the bound women.

They were flanked by two Nephilim on each side, like guards, shielding them with their spread wings against stray bullets. Professor Abigail Odem was sprawled on the pillar, her throat slashed, oozing blood. The Nephilim on the outer flanks shifted restlessly. A few black feathers descended from above, indicating that the aerial cover, too, was getting impatient.

On the opposite hill stood the human triangle, and the pillars of light and cloud emanating from it scanned the mountain.

Shamhazai stared at the small army pushing its way up the hill, like Sisyphus, refusing to stop despite the severe casualties they suffered from the Nephilim's attack. Another second elapsed.

Doula Ashtribu collapsed under the slaughterer's knife,

writhing in agony before expiring. Moments earlier, she had smiled at Adriel, receiving the knife willingly, as if there was something ennobling and correct in the sacrifice, something divorced from the vanities of this world.

Shamhazai signaled to Adriel to proceed to Hagar, the next sacrifice to a vengeful God. There were five women left, and they had tried everything. Hagar embodied the significance of the covenant and its nullification.

Milka tried to employ her charms, Libby threatened Shamhazai, telling him she knew he was the first, the Key, and the two young girls cried and pleaded for mercy.

Adriel lifted his knife, ready to end the life of Hagar, the only Lilith Daughter who dared contaminate the Nephilim by consorting with one of them. Barakiel had already paid the price. Now it was her turn. Hagar collapsed and slid down the pillar. Now all vestiges of the execrable union between a Naphil and a pale imitation of their Queen Lilith had been expunged. The multitalented actress would be next.

Then a shaft of bright light blinded the slaughterer's eyes, and above his head, luminous and clear for all to see, appeared the fiery dancing letters: Ayin, Dalet, Resh, Aleph, Lamed. Adriel.

Shamhazai looked up at Azazel, commander of the airborne unit, and noticed that a web of glowing threads connected the Nephilim. Rays of light streamed along a fiery path from one to the other, like a giant celestial pinball machine. Whenever the rays hit a Naphil, the letters of his name appeared above his head.

A primordial sensation took hold of Shamhazai; it was like awakening from a dream, but accompanied by a muscular tremor and anxiety. Something had been lost, and something else found. Shamhazai wanted to issue a succession of orders, but he seemed to have lost the power of speech. He felt as if his mind was being scanned by radiation, searching for the past, the present and the untold future. Fog clouded the space between his lobes. He knew there were letters above his head, the same one that had shone there thousands years ago, but it was as if he was feeling them for the first time.

And he felt something else, too. Terror. Shamhazai turned and looked down the hill. The entire Order of Lilith's Daughters was climbing toward him, shooting, whipping, scratching, biting, slicing.

The hill swarmed with clanging and flares, as plumes of smoke and blue fog enveloped it like a thick cloud. An ear splitting explosion was heard from the turbulence and the world came to a standstill. The sky assumed the orange-yellow colors of sunrise.

Saharel, standing next to him, took a bullet directly in his forehead. The shockwave emanating from his wound flowed outward, sweeping up everything in its path, shoving aside the known and familiar reality.

The luminous letters of Saharel's name flew in the air. For a moment it looked as if they were trying to grab hold of the fiery ladder and climb it, but then they disintegrated and evaporated.

The remaining Nephilim sank like lead onto the wave of female force. Furiously, they tried to stem the flow of ascenders.

The women were crushed like ants, but here and there, through the fog of battle, he saw more and more Nephilim disappear. The ground and air circles were thinning fast, as their rank and file faced their death.

Blazing, twinkling Nephilim were caught in the conflagration. Blue flashes came down from the heavens, swirling around the black plumage of the fallen angels, red and yellow balls of fire snarling around their feet. It was as if someone had pulled the plug on the cosmic lake in which they had immersed themselves.

Mighty Flame and its four steeds flashed through the clouds.

Elijah, in his tattered coat, still unscathed by the fire, was hoisting his almond wood staff. Two fiery serpents leapt from the staff, pointing the way down like landing lights on a runway. Elijah and his chariot landed on the hill from where the chain of incandescent names emanated. Seconds later, the prophet reined in his horses and began surrounding the three Soothsayer members.

Elisha, Larissa and Izzy were caught in the infernal fire that trailed the chariot, reducing trees to ash and rocks to dust in its wake. Elisha fell to his knees. The glowing thread that led from the human triangle to the Nephilim, blazing their names in the sky, flickered intermittently but did not dissolve. Larissa tried to catch her breath while Izzy stood erect against the approaching chariot.

Rachel saw Israel with his arms outstretched. Members of his Order crawled out of the caverns and tunnels around the hill and scrambled toward the top. They formed seven circles around the Soothsayer trio and the landing strip of Mighty Flame.

Izzy was dazed and sure she was going to vomit, her knees buckled and she tottered and swayed. She had lost all sensation in her feet and was barely able to feel connected to the ground. For a moment it occurred to her that her study of cacti and her participation in workshops and experiments had finally paid off; she had achieved an outer-body experience, but she had no time to indulge in astral voyages. She was frantically searching her mind for the incantation against devils and evil spirits that Elisha had taught her. If it didn't help, it certainly wouldn't hurt. When she remembered the text, she was pleased with herself, but the incantation seemed impotent. The words sounding as if they were uttered by somebody else.

"Thou shalt not be afraid for the terror by night, nor for the arrow that flieth by day; nor for the pestilence that walketh in darknes; nor for the destruction that wasteth at noonday. A thousand shall fall at thy side, and ten thousand at thy right hand, but it shall not come nigh thee. Only with thine eyes shalt thou behold and see the reward of the wicked."

The voice seemed to come, not from her throat, but from somewhere deeper. When she touched her chin to her chest, she realized that her feet were not touching the ground and that, from the center of her body, a thin silvery thread spooled out, preventing her from hovering in the air.

She looked down at the scene below. At the center stood Elijah in his chariot, now surrounded by seven circles of hirsute men. Two figures were facing the fire and the smoke: Elisha and Larissa. Izzy's own body was being consumed by the fire leaping from Elijah's staff.

She watched herself shake in the paroxysm of a strange St. Vitus dance that only fed the fire. Then her body dropped to the ground, face first. Larissa rushed to her side, throwing sand and dust in a desperate attempt to choke the flames. Elisha stayed put, the luminous thread retaining its luster. Izzy felt a searing pain in her navel and touched it. Her fingers encountered the torn silvery thread. She felt as if someone was holding her by the scruff of her neck and pulling her forcefully upward.

Elijah was surrounded by dozens of people. At first they looked like regular humans, but he quickly realized that with perfect coordination, their lips were uttering an imprecation.

"Why art thou here, Elijah? Return seven times, and on the seventh I shall smite thy soul, for thou art no better than thy forefathers. The road is long, and after the fire and the malediction, a still small voice. For now, I shall make thy life as the life of one of them."

At the sound of these words, the fiery horses whinnied in fear and pranced on their hind legs; the chassis of Mighty Flame shook and took to the air. The fire scorched Elijah's feet, causing him to writhe in pain. He rolled in the dust and, to his amazement, the horses soared into the sky; the chariot flew away without its charioteer.

The human circles closed in on him. Elijah raised his staff, aiming it at his attackers. He expected flames to leap from it and consume those who had thus humiliated him, but nothing happened. The members of Israel's Order grabbed him and tied ropes around his arms and feet. They bound him to a stretcher, and his tattered cloak dropped to the ground. He struggled, scratching and cursing, but the restraining hands immobilized him. His captors carried him down the hill, and then to one of the nearby mountains.

Elisha watched Larissa as she tried to revive Izzy's burnt

body. Eventually she gave up and collapsed at her side.

"What can I do?" asked Elisha when he regained his speech.

"I don't think there's anything we can do."

Elisha looked at what remained of Izzy. In the days before the battle, he had spent long hours with the perky, graceful woman. The fact that she was a pagan witch believing in rocks and crystals didn't bother him. It was unsettling to see her lying motionless like that. Larissa fought back tears, trying to maintain her dignity.

Elisha looked deep into Izzy's eyes. They were wide open, like a doll's. Her eyebrows were singed and pieces of skin were peeling from her brow. The stench was unbearable. He looked away and his gaze fell on Elijah's cloak. He picked it up, shook off the dust, and spread it over Izzy's body, a last act of loving-kindness. Bending over her, he placed the palms of his hand over hers and whispered parting words. Then he pulled the cloth over her face and walked away.

He was about to utter the prayer for the dead when he heard a stifled sneeze from under the cloak. Followed by another, and then another.

Larissa lifted the cloak, revealing Izzy's contorted face.

She sneezed three more times and stopped.

Her chest rose and fell. Larissa put two fingers on her carotid artery, smiling in relief.

CHAPTER FORTY-TWO

The battle cries of Lilith's Daughters grew louder as they advanced up the hill. The slopes were awash with women marching resolutely toward their destiny. Every so often, one of them fell and was cast aside from the ranks, but despite the casualties, they continued to advance, either because they thirsted for Nephilim's blood or out of their blind and desperate faith.

Mazzy hoped that when they reached the top of the hill, they would not discover the corpses of the kidnapped women. She found herself praying silently to the God for whose sake the battle had been launched.

They continued to fight even after their right flank was decimated, but on the left, a few hundred meters from the front lines, some hope glimmered.

A row of Nephilim swooping from above crushed them, then took off into the air. Half a dozen warriors on her left were mowed down instantly, but the others closed ranks and continued to advance. They were a gleaming swarm, the color of blood, chanting in an ancient tongue. A battalion of Lilith's Daughters let fly with volleys of bullets, but the approaching storm was too powerful and they, too, succumbed. Their camp was in total disarray when an additional unit of Nephilim hit them.

The Nephilim crushed Lilith's Daughters and many of them were killed, shrieking as they trampled both friend and foe. Gradually it became clear that the momentum of the first assault could not be contained. They continued to bite, scratch, stab, and shoot, while behind them more waves kept coming. Some tripped over the bodies on the ground and were trampled by the next wave. The right-hand flank retreated while the Nephilim pounced from above like a deluge of death.

Mazzy saw Na'ama striking the enemy with fury and vengeance, her shrill orders drowning out the cries of the injured, until a Naphil, with the letters Aleph, Resh, Teth, Koph, Vav, Peh and Aleph shining above his head, cut her life short with one wicked slice of his flaming blade. Another Lilith's Daughter called out to Artkofa and delivered a fatal shot.

On her other side, Mazzy discerned a dark figure leaping and twirling with a long blade. It was Yariv finishing off a low flying Naphil who was bleeding from the many darts stuck in his body. Despite the blinding pain in his cracked ribs, Yariv's right hand executed a fast, barely discernible motion. He penetrated the curtain of feathers, scoring a direct hit, but the light produced by the falling Naphil threw him to the ground, where he lay in a pool of blood.

Another squadron swooped down from above. Lilith's Daughters were ready. Mazzy saw the heavy bullets hit their targets and lodge into the bodies of the Nephilim. When their wings broke, they fell into the ocean of women who gleefully butchered them.

Mazzy resumed her climb to the spot where the fiery

ladder stood, driven by her feral, fighting instincts. The slope was slippery with blood flowing in viscous rivulets, like magma seeping from a volcanic fissure.

Her shooting arm hurt from the blast of the gun; she had never witnessed such carnage.

The fighting seemed to last for eons, though only minutes had passed since the battle began. The acrid air singed her eyes and throat, filling her nostrils with the smell of gunpowder, smoke, and charred flesh. Her ears rang with the echoes of whizzing bullets, a tinnitus from the titanic collision.

Mazzy climbed the mound of cadavers that closed in on her like a human vortex, a subterranean stream pulling her down to perdition. Good God, she was in Hell!

A Naphil flew ominously overhead. Mazzy noticed a movement in the pile of corpses a few meters away. Instinctively, she swung up her gun and tracked the moving target, a bloodied head, fighting for breath.

"Yariv!" She gasped.

He didn't notice her, or the averted barrel.

"Yariv," she shouted again, and when he didn't respond, she shook him. From his reaction, she gathered that he was trying to aim his gun at her, but it was trapped underneath him.

"Mazzy," he yelled in a manner that left no doubt; his hearing had been blasted away. She gestured to him to lower his voice. He tried to whisper, but failed.

"I'm going up to finish this off. You stay here."

"I don't think so," Mazzy said, mouthing the words clearly, to accommodate his condition.

Then, the unexpected: the heavy butt of Yariv's gun

smashed into her head. Mazzy stumbled.

Extricating himself from the pile of dead and dying, Yariv leapt at her, desperate and apparently in a trance. She tried to stop him, but managed only to grab his heel. He kicked her and continued forward. Mazzy followed as he disappeared over the edge of the hill. The seconds ticked away. She had almost reached the top when that strange feeling Rachel had always warned her against awakened in her heart.

CHAPTER FORTY-THREE

Only three Nephilim remained on the summit. Three Nephilim and three bound women: Libby, Estie and Karina. The rest of the Nephilim had either escaped, fallen in battle, or were still fighting on, hoping the ceremony would be completed and the Gate opened.

Through the pain, the haze and the desperation, Yariv noticed gleaming letters over Adriel's head.

He aimed his Lupara at the Naphil approaching Karina, trying to divert his attention before he hoisted the knife.

Yariv shouted the first silly sentence that came to his head.

"Say, did it hurt when you fell?"

The black-winged Naphil turned toward him and Yariv heard him say,

"The Gate will be opened."

"We have the names now," he said aiming his double barreled Lupara. Adriel was not impressed, ignored Yariv's gun and took a few more steps toward Libby.

Yariv's first shot blasted the knife out of his hand. The slaughterer pronounced his next words very clearly.

"Now you've got only one bullet left."

Yariv assessed the situation. He was at a disadvantage,

outnumbered and facing death at the hands of three Nephilim.

"Dying is the easiest thing in life."

The Naphil's expression changed at once. Yariv was not sure if it was what he said or just a ruse, it didn't really matter. From the corner of his eye, Yariv saw something move.

It was Mazzy, with her own Lupara.

"I've got two bullets. I'll shoot whoever survives."

Shamhazai trembled. He saw a son and a daughter of Man facing him. Azazel stood nearby, ready to pounce. Adriel threw down the broken haft and turned to repel the two climbers.

Mazzy noticed Yariv's determined motion. She had seen him countless times before at the shooting range. He closed his left eye, the non-aiming one, and then everything happened blindingly fast.

She didn't hear the clicking trigger or the blast.

When the bullet hit Adriel between the eyes, he flew in the air and the hill filled with light as from a cosmic explosion. The Naphil flashed and sputtered for a long moment, then burst into flames and electricity.

Azazel and Shamhazai were faster. She could only hear their rustling movements before she was hurled to the ground. For a second, she saw Yariv's pale face. He tried to speak, but instead of words, a stream of blood gushed from his mouth. His chest cavity was torn open; his entrails were exposed and he tried to push them back with trembling fingers. Then the trembling stopped.

Frozen. Defeated. Dead.

Mazzy was on the ground, her eyes closed, trying to recover from the blow. But it wasn't the pain in her spine that prevented her from moving, nor the fear that she might be discovered. She opened her eyes a crack and vaguely discerned Azazel joining the fray, trying to help Shamhazai conclude the ceremony. Mazzy tried to get up, but was drained of strength.

All she had left was a confused jumble of sweet memories that had long been dormant: heartaches, unrelenting love and the frightful realization that he was dead.

All that was left of Yariv was a broken body and a pool of still-trickling blood.

She had been surrounded by Death all the way up the hill. Death had taken its toll of the human tide that flowed upward, peeking at her through the flying bullets and the bodies of women and angels sprawling in the blood and dust; but it had never been so close as now.

Trying to detach herself from the body, she struggled to stand upright. She tilted her head upward, toward a wind that had started to blow. The clouds had parted and the sealed and barred Gate of Heaven was open a crack. Bright white light shone from inside, and the rods of the fiery ladder began making their way toward the light.

Shamhazai approached the pillar where Libby was tied, intent on completing the sacrifice with his bare hands. Mazzy was unable to take her eyes off the opening Gate and the Naphil's back. In the dust, her fingers hit something metallic. The Lupara. Her Lupara.

Her eyes filled with tears as her fingers tightened around the short butt of the ancient gun. She was not going to die without a fight, without a last ditch effort, without hope, without the right to choose how her life would end. Some women flee, others stay and fight.

Shamhazai stared at his next victim, Libby. He wasn't going to let her leave the world without first hearing his speech. He had been preparing it for ages. He owed it to himself.

"I am God's image. Not made in God's image, not an imitation. I was the first to descend. I am the one who made the covenant. I am the one who went into exile, and now I am coming back. I am a seraph. I am an angel. I am the Key to the Gate. And you thought you could stop me? I am a primordial force. You are a cheap copy of her..."

Behind Shamhazai's shoulder Libby discerned Mazzy's slow and stealthy movements, positioning herself for a clear shot. Containing her agitation, she granted Mazzy the extra second she needed. Libby spat in Shamhazai's face as he tightened his fingers around her neck. He didn't even bother to wipe it off.

Mazzy noted the expectation in Libby's eyes, her desire to avenge, to live, to win, but she also needed another moment to fill her lungs with air and then stop her breathing. She also knew this meant another death, before she even heard the snapping of Libby's neck.

Her fingers closed on the trigger as she hollered his name, "Shamhazai!"

The Naphil turned around, recognizing the threat. The astonishment on his face turned to horror when he tried to make his way toward the fiery ladder and the Gate of Heaven. The blast from the gun sank deep inside him.

Mazzy's seed of destruction bloomed and spread to the edges of the battlefield.

A metallic thunder was heard overhead. The bright gleaming light of the Gate dimmed at once. The fiery ladder leading to the Gate vanished, its rungs dissipating with a sizzling rasp. A delicate odor of anise wafted away as Mazzy collapsed to the ground. With her remaining strength she crawled to Yariv's body, laid her hands on his chest, and hoped it would be enough.

CHAPTER FORTY-FOUR

Mazzy woke up. Darkness turned to light when she opened her eyes to find herself in a totally different place.

Black and white dots swarmed before her, forcing her to close her eyes again. Her sense of smell returned, encountering the odor of detergent and the sweet cloying smell of rubber, babies, talc and latex.

A familiar hand touched her. A gentle hand. Rachel.

The room swayed, a motion that made Mazzy heave. She turned her head to the side and emptied the contents of her stomach into a bucket. She tried to look around, but dizziness overwhelmed her.

Through partially opened eyes, she could detect a white metal roof, shelves of woollen blankets, red signs of intersecting triangles, metal hooks, sacks of fluid, and a clean smell. An ambulance. It was not the end of the world yet.

Mazzy mumbled to the figure at her side, rolling her syllables, "Rachel?"

"I'm here."

"Everything all right? Are you all right?"

"No, nothing is all right. Not with us. But the world will manage. The world is still there."

Mazzy groaned in pain. Rachel sounded confident and cold.

"What about the others?"

"Rest quietly for a bit."

Mazzy wished for one of her mother's sweet new kisses, the ones that took away the pain and made her forget her suffering. But the kiss did not come. The pain continued to course through her body.

"Take it easy, let it happen. You're awake now. Stop fighting for a moment."

It was easier than she expected. The edge was there. The abyss. Just a little push and she would tumble into the void. She let go, surrendered to the warm sweetness, the protective silence.

She filled her lungs with air and the pain was gone. Nothing hurt anymore, all the aching and throbbing had vanished. Everything was back to normal. The little lies of everyday reality. Bright light appeared in the space surrounding her. She knew who she was and where she was going. Everything was all right.

"What happened?"

"You killed an angel. The world will maintain its equilibrium. When you kill something that big, the healing will find a way to flow. It found you. Now just continue to breathe."

"What about the others?"

"Izzy is on her way to the hospital. Larissa and Elisha are with her…"

The memory assailed her. She cut her mother short.

"Yariv?"

"You can't resurrect the dead, not even with what we've

got. You'll have to learn to live with it. We are strong enough. So it would seem. I'm still alive, and so are you."

"What's going to happen?"

"Commissions of Inquiry, attempts by regular folks to understand. Harsh criticism of the rescue operation."

"Rescue operation?"

"The rescue operation involving your team. The one that cost the lives of Biton and five of the kidnapped women."

It was a mockery, an oversimplification of the action and the actors. Mazzy knew how the story would sound. History was always written by the victors, or at least by those more adept at public relations.

"So this is the story," said Mazzy.

"This is the version you will give. Our ambulance is the last in the convoy. Everybody is being briefed right now. They'll understand what they need to say, those who can provide their own version. The facts on the ground will tell the story better than a thousand witnesses," Rachel said.

"And you expect the police to believe it?"

"This nation no longer believes in miracles. The alternative is to claim that someone is running the show and this is how He chooses to do it. Not exactly a version you can live with."

"So what should we do?"

"What we've always done. We'll tell the plausible story, instead of the truth. We have a long tradition of false prophets. If they were so reprehensible, why are their words still around?"

"You sure found the perfect time to tell me."

"The timing doesn't matter. It's always the same answer to the same question. At least this time it makes sense."

"So what am I supposed to say at the investigation?"

"Tell them the best version."

"I don't know anything. I don't remember anything."

"Exactly."

"And what about us?"

"We are the Simantovs."

Before Mazzy could ask why, her mother embraced her tightly, stroking her daughter's hair in a long moment of compassion and kindness. Mazzy wasn't sure if it was the stroking, the weariness or the motion of the ambulance that put her to sleep. When she opened her eyes, her mother was gone.

EPILOGUE

It was the seventh raven to arrive since the beginning of the nightmare.

Whenever it arrived, Mazzy calmed down, knowing it was the last one and she would soon wake up with a start. It was a bit like the song of counting sheep that Noga loved so much, "The Sixteenth Sheep." She knew it was the recurring nightmare because the pillow was damp, her nightie drenched, and the sheets were tangled around her feet.

And there was the background noise. Since she had come home, the noise followed her around like a haunting. A sound like a muffled human voice mumbling syllables that fell short of adding up to words.

Noga's nights were troubled also. The child shared Mazzy's bed, ground her teeth, kicked, and 'ran' in her sleep. The first nights this happened, Mazzy had awakened her, but now it happened every night. She couldn't let her sleep all day.

Mazzy realized she had to go back to sleep if she wanted to function properly in the morning. There were things to do in the morning, Gaby needed breakfast and Noga to be washed and dressed. Morning noises drowned the racket in her head.

She considered the possibility that the noise was Yariv, calling her from the grave. He had always had a big mouth, never knew when to be quiet; and where she was concerned, he was particularly obsessive.

She was determined to ignore him, sticking to the "Whatever will be, will be," attitude she had recently adopted to face the new reality foisted on her. But this seemingly simple routine only complicated things more.

After a few weeks, she no longer had to report to the Commission of Inquiry and explain the events. It wasn't clear if the conclusions had been reached by lack of evidence, or evidence that did not add up.

The review of the Soothsayer unit after its demise stated that the hasty decision to launch a rescue operation, Izzy's injuries and the trauma they all suffered had led to the conclusion that it was impossible, both strategically and financially, to keep Soothsayer operational. Given that the failure to rescue the abducted women was a big dent on the police's reputation, disbanding the unit would stop reporters and the media from holding police top brass responsible.

Even though their failure was only partial and a few of the captives had survived, nobody was satisfied. The heavy price paid by the unit and by the chief of the investigative team, coupled with the horrendous pictures from the scene released to the public, prevented any finger pointing.

Some suggested that Yariv was the instigator, being a hotheaded trigger-happy and 'shoot first, ask later' type by nature. Even after Mazzy resigned, the rumors and wild stories persisted. Her loyalty to the dead did not earn her kudos or sympathy.

Justice Shalvi did not cooperate; he issued no statement and rebuffed all questions by investigative reporters, insisting that the incident and the dead should be left alone. Estie and Leah managed to evade even the most patient and inventive paparazzi. Bereavement trumped the public's right to know, and even the most ardent and opinionated truth seekers had to give up.

Karina's new single, "The Abduction from the Palace," was a tremendous hit. Even more successful than "The Sixteenth Sheep." Karina and her mother gave countless interviews at every mall and on every publicity tour. Somehow, by deflecting questions and supplying different answers, they were able to evade all references to her absence, abduction and rescue attempt. The interviewers and readers had to make do with generalized thanks to the authorities, family, friends and fans who enabled the star to forge ahead without looking back.

Even after the hoopla had subsided and the ink dried, Mazzy could not find a job. She found out soon enough that there was not much demand for an investigator with ties to the world of mysticism. The simplest solution in the short run was to save money by taking Noga out of her ridiculously expensive daycare. Gaby seemed very pleased with the decision.

Mazzy needed a few quiet weeks. Her mornings after the "action" were occupied with taking care of Noga, who followed her everywhere. At first this was fine.

Mazzy had survived the battlefield. But the nights were still a struggle.

Mornings began at the rehabilitation center, where she met her previous subordinates.

The quiet part of the morning belonged to Izzy. Her condition had not improved much. She was still lying there, eyes wide open, and only the monitors and instruments proved she was still among the living.

Noga accompanied her on these visits. The physical therapists who manipulated Izzy's limbs would talk baby talk to Noga, but like the patient, Noga, too, continued her wordless existence.

Mazzy would sit there with a crossword puzzle, and Noga would scribble on it. At some point, Larissa would arrive from Ashdod. Their shared experience only strengthened their connection and conversations. Only one topic was never discussed, the continuous background noise.

Elisha would visit even earlier, coming straight from early morning prayers. Mazzy watched him accept the burden with enormous love and renewed faith. He tried to put in order the piles of books he had brought into the room, but without much success, as he refused any help from his many assistants and acolytes. He took care of Izzy with the same pious dedication with which he conducted his life, except for the functions where her modesty was concerned. The medical staff would chase him away at noon every day, and his followers resented the time he spent with the speechless woman, time which they considered 'neglect of the study of the Torah' and a waste of his God-given gifts.

In the afternoon, Mazzy took Noga to the neighborhood playground, where she spread out a blanket and toys on the grass in an attempt to secure some more quiet time for herself. She tried to decipher the message she believed Yariv was trying to send her without communicating with him actively, knowing that the next nightmare couldn't be avoided.

Thus she oscillated between the dim murmurs of the day and the horrible dreams of the night. By nightfall she was always exhausted and fell into sleep that brought only terror.

Gaby woke up and caressed her cheek.

"Again?"

She nodded, exhausted.

"This time do you remember what happened?"

"No. I remember only the ravens and the smell of burnt black feathers. You were not there. I wanted you to be there. I missed you in my dream, and I felt that you were close by and I was reaching out to touch you, but I couldn't reach you, even though I knew you were supposed to be there. I was on the hill with the rest of them, and then we started to run. I was looking for you and for Noga, but you weren't there."

Mazzy raised herself to adjust the pillow behind her back. Gaby stroked her and Noga seemed to be sleeping peacefully now.

"It's as if, when I look at her, she's all right. Only when I'm asleep does she have bad dreams. It drives me crazy. Like those obsessive-compulsives who open the fridge a thousand times to check if the light is still on."

Gaby said nothing. Mazzy told him that Rachel, too, had been there and had given her fragrant warm milk to drink. It smelled like anise or licorice. She did not tell him about the murmurs and about her theory about Yariv that had taken hold in her mind.

Gaby looked at the clock. It was three, the most confusing hour. It was hard to go back to sleep when dawn was almost breaking.

"Am I going nuts? Is something happening to me?"

"Why would you think that?"

Mazzy twisted a lock of hair, then put it in her mouth. Her eyes drifted down to her crossed legs and to little Noga snuggling there, like a newborn.

"Sometimes I hear voices, unidentifiable voices."

"In your dream?"

She couldn't answer. She didn't want to lie, and she already regretted mentioning it, since any explanation would have to include Yariv, and she hadn't told Gaby the whole story.

"Sometimes I feel as if I have a generator where my heart should be. Every so often there's a power outage, and something there sends currents through my body and tries to tell me something. Maybe this is what happened to Rachel after she killed Shamhazai?"

"Mazzy, nothing happened to her. We've been through this a thousand times. These things happen, not very often, but they happen. Call it autosuggestion, self-affirmation, magical thinking, faith healing, call it what you will, but it does happen."

"Not like this. It happened suddenly, and it felt as if someone injected me with something and everything fell into place. And now it's as if somebody is grabbing me from within and trying to remind me of something. I get these twitches and flutters inside, like something is turning inside me."

"There are studies of such phenomena demonstrated by shamans in parts of Africa, with their ground herbs and grains that they soak or grill. They cure their patients without antibiotics or hospitals. Turns out, sometimes, that faith is enough. This is what's happening to you. Your mind convinced your body that everything is fine, and beyond the initial trauma, the internal damage is less severe than they thought."

"You saw my x-rays and test results."

"Yes, in the ER, and they really didn't look good, but when I examined them a few hours later, things had changed, even before Rachel arrived."

"They made the change."

"You're paranoid."

Gaby seemed annoyed. Or maybe it was just tiredness. At any rate, it was not the right time to tell him about the voice. Gaby got up to make the bed. She knew the conversation wouldn't lead anywhere, because they had had several variations of it over the last few days. Neither of them broke under interrogation or volunteered new information. Tired and alienated, she hugged her knees to her body. Fear, sorrow and misgivings suddenly surfaced, unbidden. Tears rolled from her cheeks and onto the sheet. Gaby took her hand in his and held it. With his other one, he wiped the tears from her eyes. In the past, she had resented such gestures, seeing them as attempts to deny her feelings, but now, for the first time, they made her happy, without really knowing why.

"Do you think we're doing the right thing?"

"You mean staying up?" he quipped.

"No. Taking Noga out of school and me not looking for a job."

"I don't think this is the best moment to make decisions. You need time, and we're giving you some. It'll be okay. "

"You're not just saying that because you want to go back to sleep."

"No. It's going to be okay. Even better than before, you'll see."

"Before wasn't that bad."

"Darling, the two things that drove you nuts are no longer here. That's a good thing." Gaby didn't have to offer specifics.

Without meaning to, he had brought home to her how monotonous her life had become. Mazzy was proud of her professional position, and her mother was famous enough to always be in the background; but now that both had been taken away from her, creating space for her to walk in, she didn't seem able to carve out a new path for herself.

"Unemployed and effectively orphaned, this must be the next new thing. Soon everyone will want in."

"You won't be unemployed for long."

"So you don't miss my mom much?"

'No, especially not after what you told me."

"So I'll find a new job and you'll love me, and everything will be as it was?"

"I love you now, and things will be even better."

Prolonged silence put an end to the conversation, and they each turned to their individual nightly musings.

Mazzy continued to stare at the night, but this night was different from all other nights. She wasn't sure how or why, but she felt something new stir inside of her.

Noga woke up and looked at her conspiratorially. The silence that hung like a canopy over the bed made Mazzy pay special attention to the girl's eyes. This was one of many conversations that mother and daughter conducted wordlessly with their eyes.

But tonight was different, and the background whisper, like white, static noise, began to beat in the echo chamber of her head. Mazzy realized she was fighting for her sanity, and decided she wasn't going to fade away without a struggle. She would learn to adjust and pull through; she had enough experience with things that took over your life.

Mazzy ignored all other thoughts and, for the first time, tried to listen to the voice.

Perhaps Yariv knew something. Perhaps he was seeking rest. She had to listen to him, to figure out the message he was trying to send her.

He was not going to quit; it was time to face him.

Mazzy held on to the night with all her might; she mingled with the shadows, traced specks of dust in the moonlight, checked the creases on the bed sheet, rumpled the edges of the blanket, traced its seams, watched Gaby's chest rise and fall, and stared into Noga's changing eyes.

The voice was gradually becoming clearer, piercing through the fog of mumbles and whispers. She seemed to discern a certain thread, a pattern in the repeated sounds.

It was a two-syllable word. Mazzy knew she was about to decode it.

"Ma."

Mazzy listened again, trying to understand. She shut her eyes tightly, focusing on the tone.

"Ma."

Her eyes opened wide; she could still hear the voice distinctly.

It was a voice she had never heard before and thus could not recognize. It sounded like peals of laughter.

"Mama."

This time it was loud and clear. Mazzy opened her eyes and looked down at her daughter, whose lips were sealed as she raised two expectant eyes toward her mother. Mazzy had to muster all her strength to remain calm.

"Noga?"

A soft smile of relief appeared on Noga's lips. As they reached out for each other, mother and daughter, the voice became clear as crystal, playing like music in Mazzy's head

ACKNOWLEDGEMENTS

I would like to thank all the people who made this possible; my family and friends, foreign and domestic.

To the Ashery family, the Mor family, the Alon family. Noa Manheim and Rani Graff, for being the friends they are.

To Etan Ilfeld, Eleanor Teasdale, Gemma Creffield and all the good people working in the Robot Army.

To Ziv Lewis and Imri Zertal and all the good people working in Kinneret Zmora-Bitan Dvir publishing house.

To Ilan Zahler, for managing my talent for many years.

To all my friends and colleagues through the years at The Screen-Based Arts Department, Bezalel Academy of Arts and Design.

To all the people who opened my mind and my heart to what truly defines you as a human being, your ability to choose life – every day for the rest of your life.

To Bill, may you continue to wag your tail, wherever you may roam.

ABOUT THE AUTHOR

Asaf Ashery is an author, editor, academic and screenwriter. He is also a functioning workaholic, an organic vegetable grower and a dog lover. He lives in a cooperative village in the Jerusalem Mountains with his lovely wife, Yael, and his rescue dog – Bill.

Fancy some more Israeli jan
Take a look at the first chap
The Heart of the Circle
by Keren Landsman

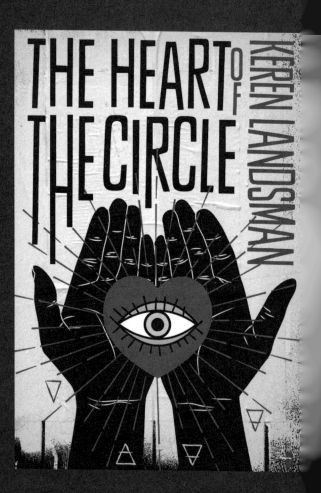

Out now from Angry Robot Boo

The day after the murder we sat in a circle at the Basement. Their food sucks, the alcohol selection leaves much to be desired, but there are books lining every inch of the walls, the smell of wood, and music you don't have to scream over to have a conversation. We were sheltered from the outside world, with only familiar faces around us. It was hot and damp, typical for mid-July, the air-conditioner powerless against a room packed with people wearing sullen pouts. We sat on the side couch, next to the shelves crammed with books, sock puppets and burned out candles. My shirt was sticking to my back; Daphne placed her head on my shoulder and I sniffed her curls. I wrapped my arm around her, letting her nestle in my embrace. They were all so sad, everyone saying, "We have to stop the next murder," but no one had any ideas. I was drained of tears.

Rhyming chants from the high schoolers' protest on the street above us infiltrated the pub between songs.

"They're going to get their asses kicked," someone behind me said.

"They have to learn to fend for themselves," came a reply. I stopped listening.

"Your curls are tickling me," I said to Daphne.

She hugged me, looked up and said, "One day your beard will tickle me."

The first murder was agonizing. Incessant tears and self-blame. It took some time to realize we couldn't have stopped it, that none of us could have changed what had happened. We have since developed a routine. Getting out of the house helps. Being around people helps even more.

I touched my chin. "Beards itch."

Letting out a sound between a laugh and a sob, she lowered her head back onto my shoulder. Her curls got into my nose again. I stroked her hair without saying a word.

This time we didn't know the murdered girl. A photo of her was placed on the bar top, next to the other photos, surrounded by little candles. The faces in the various photos began to blend together. They were all smiling at the camera, heads aslant with mischievous expressions that made them look younger than they really were, all against a slightly blurred background. Brown eyes, black eyes, blue eyes. Hair in different colors, different styles. Men. Women. When the first murder happened we cried for a week in the city square, refusing to leave until the prime minister promised she would personally investigate. After the second murder, our tears were silent. The third – we stopped crying.

There was the pathetic attempt at revenge organized by a few pyros after the first. They got caught before they reached their target. Speaking for the cameras, the spokesperson for the police Prevention of Future Crimes Unit explained theirs was a sacred duty. The bodies dangled from the gallows behind him. Daphne cursed him for a whole hour, then cried herself to sleep.

I closed my eyes. Someone switched the music to depressing peace songs. *Give Peace a Chance.*

Matthew, my brother, plopped himself on the armrest next to me. "If I hear that song one more time, I'm going to break someone's fingers."

He was wearing the same clothes I saw him in yesterday, before he left for work. A T-shirt with 'Stop the Violence' printed on it, jeans in desperate need of a wash, and sneakers.

"What are you doing here?" I whispered to him. "It's dangerous. You remember what happened last time."

"If you get stabbed, you're going to want someone around you who knows how to use a tourniquet."

I rubbed my hand where the scar still hurt. "If you get your arm broken because of me, Mom would never let me forget it."

"Don't worry, I've already landed a permanent position at the hospital. Not even a shattered arm could get me kicked off the ward." He winked, and I could feel the fear lurking inside him.

Daphne straightened her back towards him. "Hey, Matthew."

Matthew walked passed me and hugged her. "Hey, babe."

I leaned back, waiting for them to break up their hug.

Matthew unzipped his backpack. "Mom sent sandwiches. And before you say anything, I know." He handed me one. It was wrapped in a paper napkin with my name scribbled on it.

I took it from him. White bread with chocolate spread.

Matthew took out another sandwich and handed it to

Daphne. Our mom had started treating her like family from the moment she abandoned the fantasy that Daphne would magically transform from a close friend into a girlfriend. I knew Mom had expected Matthew to fill the spot I didn't want, and I knew he tried; moreover, I knew how much Daphne had hated turning him down. She said he wasn't her type, that he was like a brother to her, but I knew it was because he wasn't like us, and neither of us had the heart to tell him.

"I know," Matthew repeated, "but she's just trying to help."

I knew it was Mom's way of showing support from the first time she had sent Matthew to the pub with food for us, ignoring every social convention. She knew what kind of pasta each of us liked, and even made separate salads because I couldn't stand cucumbers and Matthew hated onions. But the announcement that another person was murdered in one of our rallies must have thrown her off balance. It wasn't like her to forget I don't eat chocolate.

I handed Matthew the sandwich. "You want one?"

His beaming smile almost made me grin. "I thought you'd never offer." He wolfed it down in three bites.

"Want me to order you something?" Daphne asked while nibbling her sandwich.

"I can't eat. I'm too, too…" I waved the idea away.

"It's the Reed Diet," Matthew said while chewing. "Stage one – go somewhere that has lots of really sad people. Stage two – be too overwhelmed with everyone's feelings to eat. Stage three – vanish into thin air."

I feigned a pout. His attempt at a joke might have worked had he himself not been overcome with fear and loss.

He poked me. "Come on, I'm just kidding."

"You forgot a crucial stage," I said, holding up a finger.

"What?"

"Be born a moody," I replied and smiled. He knew me well enough to know it wasn't a real smile. Just as I knew him well enough to read him without having to *read* him.

"I hate that term." Matthew scrunched up his napkin. "It's offensive. I don't understand how you can use it."

"It's called reappropriation," I said, wearing my pedagogical face. "You take a derogatory term and turn it into a–"

"Oh, hush already," Daphne interrupted me, slapping my knee. "I'd seriously advise hitting 'unsubscribe' to all those overbearing online groups of yours." She shot Matthew a look. "Saw anyone you like?"

Matthew grimaced. "No, but I'll take what I can get."

I looked at Daphne and sighed. "You really think this is an appropriate time for this?"

"Poor Matthew," Daphne giggled, ignoring me.

Matthew stuck the crinkled napkin in his backpack and said, "The girl behind you is cute."

I sighed again, louder this time, and turned around. Forrest and Aurora were making out on the couch behind us, his fingers running through her hair. Daphne and I met them during our college days and the four of us have been friends ever since. He was a chubby redhead and she was built like a beanstalk, almost devoid of feminine features. They had been marching close to us only seconds before the murder, Forrest making sure I was drinking enough because it was a hot day.

Matthew was probably referring to the girl wearing the

'Peace Starts Within' shirt, who was visibly ignoring all the men trying to chat her up. Next to her sat a scrawny, pasty looking guy who seemed vaguely familiar; I was busy trying to remember where I knew him from when the woman sitting on his other side looked up and our eyes met. I froze.

"Ivy," I said.

"Where?" Matthew sprang up.

She was wearing a blue shirt with a white ribbon, hair pulled back into a ponytail. She looked away and said something to the guy sitting next to her. Her brother.

"He's cute," Daphne said.

"Don't go there. He's not for you."

Daphne kept looking at them.

"He's Ivy's brother. You don't want anything to do with him."

"If I was going to judge every person by their brother..." Daphne said, cocking her head towards Matthew with a smile.

"Excuse me," someone standing above us said. It was Ivy's scrawny brother. I tried to recall his name. The last time I saw him he was about to be released from the army. Then it came to me. Oleander.

"I saw my sister was making you uneasy. I asked her to leave." Oleander smiled at Daphne, clearly ignoring my presence.

"Lovely," I blurted.

Oleander held his hands out and said, "I'm just trying to help."

"Help who?"

"I'm not my sister."

The emotions between Daphne and Oleander shot through me like an electrical current. Daphne slapped my thigh again. "Let it go. It's been years." She placed her half-eaten sandwich on my knee. "Don't eat that. You'll have the worst stomach ache tomorrow." I wanted to stop her, but she just shot me a look, got up and left. I knew that look all too well. Drop it, it said. Let me live my life. Once Daphne joined them, the conversation behind me livened up.

"I can't believe Daphne can actually find someone to hook up with in this mess," Matthew said, waving both hands in the air. "What do I have to do to find someone?"

"You think I'm the right person to answer that question?" I scooted over, letting him stretch out next to me.

Matthew fell silent, the twinkle in his eye fading. He looked down and picked at the threads coming out of the strap of his old backpack. It was standard military issue, the symbol of the medical corps printed on its side. I knew what he was about to ask, and I knew I had to let him ask it before I answered.

"Mom's asking," he said and paused. "Well, I'm asking, but also Mom."

I waited.

Matthew took a deep breath. "How close were you when it happened?"

"Close enough," I replied. That wasn't the real question.

"Because it was…" Matthew paused again, grabbed the strap of his bag and looked at me. "It was really scary this time."

It was. I knew because I was there. I saw the knife. I felt the life seeping out of the girl. I held Daphne whose knees buckled when all those futures came crashing down on her.

"We're worried. All of us. Including me. I don't... I don't know what I would have done if it had been you." He took my hand in his, like when we were children and he had to console me whenever the neighbors spat on me as we passed by them. Eventually Dad decided we had to move, and we picked up and left the north for a more centrally located city, full of all kinds of people and feelings.

"Maybe you could..." Matthew's voice cracked. "I know this is important to you and Daphne. It's important to me too. But... maybe you could..."

It was the same conversation we had had dozens of times: My parents want me to stop attending the rallies, I explain to them that without the rallies nothing will change, they don't listen, and I ignore them. But my big brother was scared, and I couldn't just shrug him off.

"I'm just really worried," he said, fixing me with his pleading eyes. "You have to be careful."

I put my other hand on his.

"Please," he begged, his voice wavering. He was supposed to ask us to stay home. Daphne had told me he would. To not attend the next rally. To sit this one out and look after ourselves, like everyone else who had stopped showing up at the rallies. There were fewer and fewer marchers each time, and more and more candlelight vigils afterwards. The police claimed they couldn't prevent the murders if we insisted on marching, but at the same time they released announcements about the arrests of potential murderers, people who none of the damuses I knew deemed dangerous.

Matthew didn't say anything but "Please." Nothing more. And left his hand in mine. I squeezed it and wondered whether we were too old to hug.

"OK," I answered the question he hadn't asked.

"Thanks." It wasn't the dialogue Daphne had predicted. She could only foresee probabilities, of course, but she saw this conversation with a certain degree of clarity: Matthew asks us to stop attending the rallies, I object, he whips out two arguments, I find a compromise, and we manage to work things out.

It would have been easier had Daphne been there with me, but she was busy flirting with Oleander. I could feel her easing up, becoming softer. It felt nice to be swept along with her. To feel her open up to another human being. I closed my eyes.

Matthew picked up the sandwich from my knee and unzipped his backpack. His fear was abating. All he needed was to see us, to know we were OK. Taking something out of his bag, he let out a small, quiet sigh, leaned back and stretched out his legs.

I opened my eyes. A weighty book with small print lay open on his knees. It was too dark to read, and he was shining a small flashlight on the pages.

I lifted the book cover. "*Approaches to Laparoscopic Knee Surgery*," I read out loud.

Matthew nodded. "And it's more complicated than you'd think."

"Good to know. I won't try it then."

Without looking up from his book, he dug into his backpack and fished out a paperback with a colorful cover and a mini clip-on book light. "I thought this might help."

It was the adventure book we used to read as kids. Five children walk into a toy closet and find a magical kingdom where it's summer all year round. I opened the book, feeling the light fragrant breeze carried from between its pages, so much more palpable than the dying breaths of air the tormented air-conditioning exhaled. This book was the reason I had decided to become a moodifier and go into the emotional design business when I grew up. I dove into the world in which children could make a difference and defeat evil all on their own.

Halfway through the book I sensed an unfamiliar consciousness. I looked up. Matthew was still immersed in his textbook. Around us people were either making out or sitting in small groups with their heads bowed. A few of the high schoolers had joined us, proudly boasting their fresh bruises and scolding the "geriatrics" for hiding in a pub instead of standing outside with them and stirring up a riot. Behind me, Forrest and Aurora were in a heated discussion, fragments of which floated my way. She, as usual, was insisting on carrying out the revolution from within the political system by infiltrating the major parties. He, as usual, supported armed resistance and forming squads to patrol the streets, ensuring our safety. They were going at it in high-pitched tones until someone mentioned the Sons of Simeon, and they both instantly turned against him.

"Excuse me?" asked a woman with short hair, standing above me wearing a floral summer dress and tightening the fabric around her thighs. "Mind if I sit here?" The tension she exuded stood in stark contrast to her bright tone.

I shrugged. "Free country."

"So they keep saying."

She was so tense I could barely feel her. I scooted over. She sat down on the ottoman next to me. "I'm Reed, and this is Matthew."

I nudged Matthew with my leg. He looked up, smiled, and went back to his book. I didn't sense a change in him. He probably won't even remember her.

"I'm Sherry." She held out her hand. A silver charm bracelet was looped around her wrist.

"I'm a moody."

Matthew muttered something under his breath. I ignored him.

"I know you don't actually need the sense of touch to do what you do," she said, looking me straight in the eye, "and I'm trusting you won't try anything. Besides…" She turned her hand palm down, fingers spread outwards. A pebble. "We have rules, right?"

We shook hands. The charms crushed against my skin. They were a nice, cool contrast to the humidity hanging in the room.

"That's a nice charm."

"My mom makes me wear it," she said and shrugged. "You know what moms are like."

I nodded. "My mom would want me to wear a hazmat suit whenever I go out."

Sherry grinned and brushed the hair off her face. Too short to tuck around her ears, it bounced right back. She looked at Matthew and asked, "Are you a moody too?"

Matthew looked up from his book and said, "No, an orthopedist. Reed takes people's pain away, and I make them feel it."

We both laughed at his stupid joke. Sherry shifted her gaze between the two of us and smiled politely. "I'm a cop."

My smile froze. "You were at the rally?"

"Every single one in the last two years, since..." she fell silent.

"Since Flint," I finished the sentence for her. At that rally, a bomb had been tossed into the middle of the crowd, detonated by an unknown pyro. It was the Sons of Simeon's first murder. Nothing was ever the same again. They saw themselves as the heirs of Simeon Ben Shetach, the Sanhedrin murderer during the reign of Alexander Jannaeus.

"I'm one of those nutcases who volunteer to actually go the rallies instead of staying at the station and getting the reports after the fact." Sherry bit her bottom lip. "I'm also involved in the surveillance of potential murderers."

"You're supposed to tell me not to worry, that this time you'll get him for sure," I said, trying not to sound bitter. I didn't mention that her volunteering didn't help us. That the police hadn't managed to prevent a single murder, and that the cops mostly stayed on the sidelines and never made any arrests.

Matthew kicked me. "Be polite."

"He's very polite," Sherry said quietly. "Most people here won't let me anywhere near them once they find out what I do for a living."

"We're nicer than most," Matthew said, smiling at her.

Before Sherry could answer, Daphne appeared above her, almost tripping over the ottoman. She crouched between us, opened Matthew's backpack and took out what was left of her sandwich. "I'm taking Oleander back to our place," she said and winked at me. "Don't come home too early."

I was torn between my desire to keep her away from him and the urge to wish her a flaccid night. "Just keep the noise down, OK?"

"Sure thing," she said, and got up.

Sherry smiled. "It's good to see that at least for some of us life goes on as usual."

Crossing his legs, Matthew said, "It's just a shame those some of us aren't into me." He sounded bitter but smiled, and we moved on to small talk, ignoring all the political debates around us, which were simmering to a boil courtesy of the late hour and the alcohol. Forrest launched into a diatribe about how 'if we don't help ourselves, no one's going to help us,' while Aurora kept countering with 'armed resistance would just set public opinion against us,' and the usual 'we have to understand their motives, we have to find common ground'.

Sherry glanced at me. "You disagree?"

I tried to show as little emotion as possible. "After the votes for Change from Within failed to reach the threshold? To get even one seat? No."

Sherry held her hand flat, palm facing upward. "We have a chance with the major parties. Flint managed to get into parliament."

"And got killed. And no one even investigated it seriously. It's been two years and not a single lead."

Matthew shifted in his seat. I looked at him and asked, "What?"

"Nothing." He shook his head.

"I'm not running for parliament."

"Good," he said, tightening his lips into a grin. "God forbid you should make a decent salary."

I tried being annoyed at him, but it was impossible. "Never mind the salary, what would I do with a car?"

Sherry looked at him, then at me, and said, "And a driver." She smiled, and for a moment she looked pretty.

"We'd never find parking. The poor guy would have to circle the neighborhood all night."

We got to talking about our apartments, and from there to even more trivial, mundane matters. Sherry had three cats, each of which had run away to a different neighbor during one of the heavy storms last winter, and she told us how she frantically knocked on every door in her apartment building late at night to try bring them home. Matthew asked whether I could have tracked them down by attuning to their feelings, which eventually led to the story of how I caught the mouse that had set up camp in one of our kitchen cupboards last year.

By the end of the evening, when Matthew gave me a ride home, I felt a little less dismal.

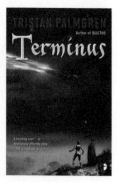

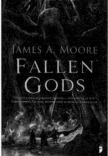
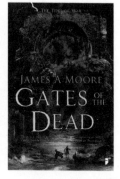

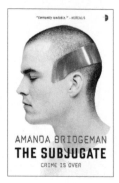

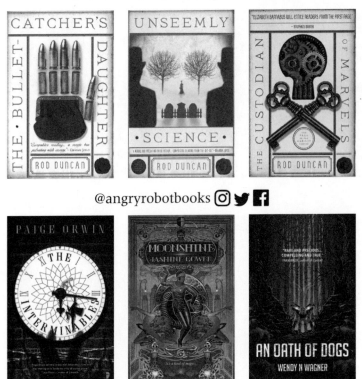

We are Angry Robot

angryrobotbooks.com

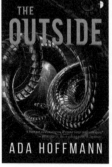